The Latest Flake of Eternity

Allan Brewer

for Sandra

Chapter 1
Safe in the Hallowed Quiets of the past.
(James Russell Lowell)

Saturday, Cheltenham, England

Betty was tossing a stir-fry in the wok when the doorbell chimed. She was not expecting anyone. She hesitated, briefly debating whether to leave the wok on the heat, risking it over-cooking; but decided to err on the side of caution, and set the wok to one side. She skittered down the stairs to the front door. MI5 had insisted she install a video entry-phone with an alert button, to the side of her door—this was their price for her being allowed to remain living in the same house after the foreign kidnap attempts. She glanced at the screen as she put a hand to the front-door latch. The face she did not recognise—but the thing she immediately noticed was that the man was wearing a clergy collar. She opened the door, keeping her finger over the alert button as she had been taught to do by the MI5 operative. However, the thought that a potential kidnapper would disguise himself as anything so glaringly comical as a clergyman brought a smile to her face as she swung the door open. Her smile, though not intended for the visitor, had the result of eliciting a responsive beam from the clergyman. Apart from the collar, he was dressed in casual clothes—surely a kidnapper in disguise would have made more effort, she considered transiently. She still suffered a small pang of anxiety and distrust when faced with strangers.

"Good afternoon, I am sorry to bother you. Are you Miss Betty Gosmore?" He sounded kind and sincere. But Betty had been simply expecting a request for a donation of some sort—why did he know her name?

"Er… yes. What can I do for you?" Betty responded quizzically, her finger still purposefully hovering over the alarm button.

"Ah, good. I'm Michael Liddington from St. Mark's, the local church on Pumphrey's Road, near the library, and I just wanted to talk to you for a moment about something strange that has happened." He paused and smiled briefly. Betty felt that he probably wanted to be invited in. It was certainly cold outside, but she wasn't about to extend the invitation.

"OK. Please go on."

"Well, this morning a rather charming old gentleman came into the church. He said he was the vicar of St. Ewold's, down in the Dorset countryside, near the coast, and that he had to speak with a Miss Betty Gosmore who lives locally, on a very important matter. He came to me looking for help as a fellow Anglican, as if he thought all the locals would be known to me as part of my congregation. To be honest, he seemed quite eccentric, a bit strange, and he obviously has no idea how to go about locating someone. So I thought I would at least humour him to see if anyone of that name did indeed live round here—I just looked in the electoral register—I hope you don't mind—and sure enough, here you are. I haven't revealed your address to him, and haven't said I was popping round to see you, so if you are not interested then we can just leave it at that. Although I suppose there is some chance he will find out your address without my help—but at least now you are forewarned."

"What on earth does he want to talk to me about?" queried Betty, genuinely puzzled.

"He wouldn't tell me any details—he just kept repeating that it was 'of the utmost importance'. He tends to use rather old-fashioned language." Liddington laughed. "Look, to be honest, he may be a crank, though he seems to be harmless enough and quite charming."

"Do you know if he is telling the truth about being the vicar of... erm..."

"St. Ewold's? No, I don't know for sure—I can check that up. Yes, I should have done that before I bothered you, shouldn't I? But he certainly seems to know all about the Anglican church—if he is an impostor then he must be a very good actor, and well researched... So it's up to you—I won't tell him your address if you don't want me to. Or perhaps you would prefer to come and meet him in the church if that would make you feel safer? Or I can just tell him I have no idea whether anyone of your name lives around here or not, and leave it at that. Though I don't think he will easily take no for an answer," Liddington chuckled. He stopped talking and looked at Betty for a response.

"Um..." Betty was rather nonplussed.

"Look, why don't I give you my phone number, then you can think about it, and let me know if you want to meet him or not?" He fished in his overcoat pocket and pulled out a business card with the church's details on it, offering it to Betty.

She took the card, glancing at the name and reading it out loud. "Reverend Michael Liddington. OK, Michael, I will give it some thought and let you know," she agreed.

"Thanks. And sorry again to have bothered you." He turned and walked back down the gravel path as Betty closed the door and watched him receding on the video screen.

Betty pondered the doorstep conversation as she ate from her plate of stir-fry. The hiatus in the cooking had definitely robbed some of the fresh crispness from the vegetables, but the taste was still satisfying enough. The invitation to meet the mysterious vicar was intriguing and therefore difficult to resist. She added some soy sauce. In normal times, she would have simply trekked along to the church to meet this fellow and find out what he had to say. But these were not normal times. Since the kidnap in Austria, she had realised that she now always needed to be extra careful about the situations that she put herself in; on the off-chance that those who had targeted her might try again. Her knowledge of hi-tech secrets was ever-present and still made her potentially vulnerable. Nevertheless, she did not want to live with perpetual anxiety restricting her choices in life. One option was simply to call in GCHQ security or MI5 to watch over her meeting this man, but then they would want to know every detail, and that in itself would feel like an intrusion if the matter, likely as not, turned out to be a personal issue and completely innocent of danger. She looked at the business card that she had placed on the table next to her plate. She could check that out for starters. Between forkfuls, she pulled out her mobile phone and googled the church's website. Yes, the phone number was the same as on the card, and there was a recognisable photo of the local vicar—so at least Michael Liddington appeared to be genuine.

There was a middle way. She phoned Alex. She had no secrets from him—well just the one about the Constanţa zap—and she fully intended to tell him about that at an opportune time. "Hi Alex, listen, I want to ask a favour." She explained the situation. "So I wondered if you would mind sitting anonymously at the back of the church to keep an eye on things whilst I talk to this chap?... Yes, I know you don't like going into churches, but just pretend to yourself that you are a tourist admiring the architecture or something?... Please?... Oh thanks, Alex, I knew I could count on you. Shall we say four o'clock?... Send me a text to say you are in place—I won't go into the church until I get the OK from you."

* * *

Alex reluctantly wandered into the church a few minutes before four o'clock, trying to look nonchalant, though feeling anything but. Churches were alien territory to him. He wasn't even sure if anyone was welcome to visit outside of a regular service. Indeed, a couple of clergy seemed to eye him as he walked in. He vaguely nodded in their direction and sat down quickly in the back row of pews, trying to look as if he were deep in thought. There was apparently no-one else in the building. Then he remembered that he was supposed to message Betty. With some embarrassment, he surreptitiously pulled out his mobile phone, keeping it low so that it would not be seen by the clergymen, and tapped a furtive and economical 'OK' to Betty.

Betty, by contrast, was not the least intimidated by the church ambience, and she sauntered in through the big wooden door a couple of minutes later, to be immediately and warmly greeted by Michael Liddington.

"Betty, I am so glad you felt able to come." He shook her hand cordially. "This is the Reverend Thomas Arbuckle, who wanted to meet with you. Reverend, this is Miss Betty Gosmore." He pursued the introductions, politely, and Arbuckle bowed slightly offering a handshake. He did indeed appear a somewhat unusual fellow. His face was adorned with a full moustache and bushy sideburns. Like Liddington he wore a clerical collar with a white shirt, but the shirt was mostly concealed by a maroon waistcoat and a regency-collared jacket that was strangely tailored—fitted in at the waist and cut away below that, revealing the lower part of his waistcoat—and with the coat tails hanging behind. As she shook his hand, her overwhelming impression was that he looked thoroughly old-fashioned—she would not have been surprised if there was a top-hat in the battered brown-leather travelling bag that was sitting on the pew behind him, though she knew it would not actually have fitted in. This first impression had now triggered the expectation in Betty that this was probably some elaborate hoax. From her involvement in amateur dramatics, she was aware that this was a set of clothes that would be acquired from theatrical costumiers for an early Victorian costume drama. Nevertheless, she was delighted by the

4

pretence and happy to play along, beginning to wonder which of her drama friends might have organised this charade.

"I am most deeply ingratiated to you for deigning to meet with me, Miss Gosmore; and I trust that our conversation will meet with some merit in your opinion." The gushing abundant style of speech brought a smile of admiration to Betty's face as she appreciated that he even had 'ye olde rural accent' off to a tee.

"Well, Reverend, I am most honoured that you would travel this long distance simply to impart information for my benefit. Pray, what subject is it you wish to discuss with me? I confess I am unduly intrigued to learn of the purpose of our encounter," Betty replied with a very slight curtsey, trying hard to echo the appropriate wordy dialect off the top of her head; with some success, she thought.

Liddington looked slightly surprised at Betty's adopted style, but seemed relieved that the two appeared to have hit it off so well. "Right, I will leave you two to talk in private," he stated. "I have some things to attend to over by the altar—I will be there if you need me," he said reassuringly to Betty.

Arbuckle shuffled along the pew toward where his bag was sitting and gestured to Betty to join him. "Do please sit down, Miss Gosmore," he entreated, waiting graciously for her to sit before he did so. "Ah, where to begin?" he sighed. "It is so uncommon a matter. You must understand that I am just a humble messenger, sent on this mission rather outside of my familiar environment."

"Then please do begin at the beginning, Reverend," suggested Betty invoking the words of 'Alice in Wonderland' which she considered might be approximately in period.

"Yes, indeed. The beginning. Then indeed I will. That would be near twenty years ago now. It was a bitterly cold winter and I had just stoked up the drawing-room fire in the rectory to provide some little comfort, when I heard a voice addressing me from the other side of the room. I lived alone, you see, so I was startled, having heard no-one enter. There stood a man, at least then I thought at first that he was a man, dressed all in white, and holding a metallic box. He raised his hand and bade me not be afraid. He spoke in a voice that was exceeding strange—an accent completely unbeknown to me," Arbuckle expounded earnestly.

"Curiouser and curiouser," interjected Betty playfully, but maintaining a serious expression.

"Ah, but such details are of no import to yourself," Arbuckle apologised, shuffling his seated position and re-focussing. "The figure told me his name was Uriel. And he explained to me at some length— and it was difficult for me to understand him for he used some strange words, and I had to keep asking him to repeat. But he explained to me at length that he was one of a group of Angels charged with the particular duty of maintaining God's will through the ages. He encouraged me to think about the extraordinary changes in factories across the land that are enabling things unheard of in previous times—the steam engine and so forth. And he encouraged me to think about how much more fantastical things might be possible in future times. He explained that, in fact, in the future, devices will be made that could even subvert the flow of God's will by changing events in the past, and he told me that the work of his group of Angels was to prevent that type of interference from happening. The use of such perverse devices is prohibited, and the appointed task of these Angels is to track down and repair any unlawful deviations from God's plan unfolding."

Up to that point, Betty had been rather relishing the bizarre conversation, but suddenly the relevance was getting too close to home. The whole story was preposterous of course, but clearly, the people behind this charade knew something about the clandestine use of the *i*-vector equipment, and that in itself was very alarming.

Alex, still sitting uneasily at the back, could not overhear any of their conversation, and so boredom was beginning to exacerbate his discomfort, to the point that he was starting to feel cross with Betty for putting him in that situation. Nevertheless, he was nothing if not a fully reliable friend and was determined to see out his duty.

"So," continued Arbuckle, "Uriel then acknowledged that it was highly unlikely that anyone would try to trifle with the course of events during the age that I lived in. However, he said that the Angels desired to appoint a few aides, men like myself, whom, if anything were to go amiss in our times, would be ready to entreat those persons who had caused the deviation from God's chosen will, to put things right again." Anxiety had wiped the cheerfulness from Betty's face.

Arbuckle lowered his voice slightly. "Although I am being non-specific, I can tell from the expression that crossed your face just then, that you perhaps know of the actions to which I refer. That is well, for I am not appraised of the specifics of the matter myself. I am just the messenger. I have only been advised by the Sentinel that I should find you, the person who is the subject of the deviation, and appeal to your better nature to find a method by which you can repair said deviation."

"The Sentinel? Who is that?" asked Betty, noting the new facet in the story.

"Ah, yes, I think I mentioned that Uriel arrived with a metallic box. That is what he called the Sentinel, and he entrusted it to me when he left. It has been silent these past twenty years. I had put the Sentinel in a drawer of my writing desk, and over time I had almost forgotten its existence. Then this morning, to my great surprise, it summoned me and told me that we—that is the Sentinel and I—have to go on a mission to a place called Cheltenham, in the future."

"And how does the Sentinel summon you?" pursued Betty.

"It plays a short musical phrase, and then repeats it until I acknowledge the summons by placing my palm on its surface. Then it speaks its instructions."

"So the Sentinel actually *speaks* to you?" echoed Betty, trying to understand the nature of the relationship.

"Yes, and I can converse with it also, though it is difficult because it speaks with the same strange dialect that Uriel used. He described the Sentinel as an embodiment of their knowledge."

"And how did you travel here, to Cheltenham, Reverend?"

"Again, the Sentinel facilitates the travel. It is the most wondrous thing." Arbuckle sat up straight as if carefully recalling his instructions. "I am required to stand, clear of any furniture, holding the Sentinel with my palm on its surface, and then with just the smallest of jolts, just a slight sense of a breeze, I am almost immediately afterward then standing, a little unsteady, in the appointed place. Still holding the Sentinel of course. So this morning I was delivered to a quiet spot in the church grounds here—presumably the nearest church to you. The only point of difficulty I find is holding my travelling bag and palming the Sentinel at the same time—it is most awkward."

"So where is the Sentinel now?" asked Betty, intrigued.

"I slipped it into my bag immediately I arrived. It looks somewhat unusual and I did not want to draw attention to myself." He glanced down at the worn leather bag sitting on the pew next to him.

Betty smiled. The Reverend Arbuckle seemed oblivious of the fact that his very person looked unusual in present-day Cheltenham.

"And have you travelled with the Sentinel to other places?" queried Betty.

"Only the once," replied Arbuckle. "Uriel accompanied me on a very brief visit to the future, so that I should become accustomed to using the Sentinel should the necessity arise, as indeed it now has."

"So where did you go, on that visit?" pressed Betty.

"Ah yes, the Sentinel took me forward 100 years to show me my own gravestone," replied Arbuckle seemingly distracted for a moment. "It was in the graveyard next to my very own church, St. Ewold's. The epitaph was most touching. And Uriel concealed the engraved date of death with his hand—most considerate."

"But," concluded Arbuckle drawing in his breath sharply, "I have said more than enough about my modest adventures. The purpose of our meeting is to discuss how you can rectify the deviation from God's plan that has come about." Arbuckle looked straight into Betty's face with a smile that attempted to convey both kindness and authority.

"Well... I am not entirely sure I understand what you are referring to, Reverend. Can you be more specific?" Betty knew she had to ask this question, to try to get closer to finding the essence in this charade or whatever it was. But she was apprehensive about what the answer would be—she did not want to hear that anyone knew anything about the *i*-vector equipment, especially about its offensive capability.

"Oh dear, I had hoped that the matter would be obvious to you," said Arbuckle, looking slightly disappointed. "But I can certainly, with pleasure, elucidate the bare details related to me by the Sentinel. It stated to me that, on January 1st most recently, God's destiny for you, Miss Gosmore, was a journey Eastward, where you would share information that ultimately has the effect of facilitating a balance of power across the factions of the world. However, some unauthorised and retrospective act prevented that journey and thus the future is compromised and rendered unbalanced. This is undesirable and contrary to God's will." He was silent for a moment. "Does that help you to understand the situation and what needs to be done to remedy it? I confess that is all I presently know, though I can consult the Sentinel further if we need more help."

Betty felt anxiety rising from the pit of her stomach—the message was frighteningly specific, but the context still very obscure. But whatever that context, the message that she should have submitted to the January kidnap was as threatening as it was bizarre, despite being wrapped up in supposed moral purpose. She stood. "No, I really have no idea what you are talking about, Reverend. Goodbye," she retorted, trying to keep her voice steady. She turned and strode off quickly down the aisle of the church and out of the door, glancing back a couple of times to ascertain whether she was being followed. She was not. Arbuckle just sat, looking pensive and perhaps slightly worried.

In her preoccupation, Betty had forgotten about Alex sitting at the back of the church and had walked straight past without looking at him. But Alex could immediately see that she was upset, and a sense of purpose now flushed away his previous feelings of self-absorbed frustration, boredom and discomfort. Who was this strange man who had upset his dearest friend? Alex continued to sit there invisibly, watching what Arbuckle would do next.

Liddington had also seen Betty depart and he now walked down from the altar to speak again with Arbuckle. "Did the meeting go well, my friend?" he queried.

"Alas, I fear not, good sir. She is, I think, not well disposed to what must be done. But God's will must ultimately prevail. I hope she will give it some consideration, and then maybe she will return," he added pensively. "But now, for myself, I am feeling most hungry, having not eaten since breakfast. Is there a restaurant nearby where I could partake of a late luncheon?"

"Yes, if you turn left out of the church, there are a couple of cafés a few hundred yards along on the other side of the road," suggested Liddington helpfully.

The two men shook hands and Arbuckle ambled out of the church carrying his leather travelling bag. Alex waited for a half a minute to avoid looking deliberate and then slipped out after him. The man was a little way down the road. Alex held back, following at a distance. After a while, the man stepped into the road, but crossing at a considerable angle. Inevitably a car came toward him from behind, the driver blaring his horn at the apparently inconsiderate pedestrian. Arbuckle was startled and half-ran quickly toward the safety of the opposite pavement, then continuing on toward the shops. Alex was beginning to become aware of Arbuckle's clothing for the first time. Here was not just a vicar, an eccentric vicar, but someone wearing very old-fashioned clothes.

Alex's phone buzzed—a text from Betty '*We need to talk.*'

He quickly texted back, '*Later. Following him.*'

Arbuckle paused in front of each of the first few shops he encountered, to look inside, and decided to enter the third—it was a delicatessen-type café. Alex decided to follow him in. Arbuckle stood curiously scanning the food on display at the counter, as a woman in front was being served. Then the girl serving turned to him. "What can I do for you, sir?"

"Could I have a meat pie, please, Miss?"

"A pork pie, sir?" she suggested.

"Yes please, that would do very well." The server put a pie on a plate with napkin, knife and fork and placed it on the counter for him.

"Anything to drink, sir?"

"Beer, if you would be so kind."

"I'm afraid we don't serve alcohol here, sir—we have tea, coffee, fruit-juices…"

"Oh, I'm so sorry. Yes, a cup of tea would be very nice." The server busied herself preparing a pot of tea as Arbuckle watched, clearly fascinated. "Here you are, sir." She placed the tea on the counter. "That will be Four Ten."

Arbuckle reached into his pocket and pulled out a bunch of coins. He selected some and handed them to the girl. She took them, but then did a double-take, her brow furrowing. "I'm sorry, sir, it's four pounds ten—I'm not sure what these coins are?"

"Four *pounds*? Uh, surely not? Umm…" Arbuckle looked bewildered.

Alex, increasingly intrigued, saw the chance to get into conversation with the man. "It's OK, let me pay for the gentleman's snack," he interjected, offering across his credit card to the server.

"I say, that's frightfully kind of you, sir. Are you sure? It seems rather… *expensive*?" He mouthed the final word to Alex out of earshot of the server.

Alex smiled reassuringly. "My pleasure. Let me help." He gathered a tray from the end of the counter, loaded Arbuckle's pie and tea onto it, and handed it to him. "And I'll have a chicken salad sandwich and an espresso please," he addressed the girl serving.

Alex collected his own snack and walked over to where Arbuckle was now sitting at a table by the window. "May I join you?"

"By all means, sir. I really am most grateful for your help. My name is Thomas Arbuckle."

"Nice to meet you, Thomas. I'm Alex… erm… *Smith*. I'm guessing you are visiting and not familiar with this area then?" Alex opened the conversation.

"Indeed, you guess correctly, sir. I arrived here only this morning and sadly I believe I am most unprepared. I felt at home in the church of course, but… These horseless carriages move so very fast, do they not?" remarked Arbuckle watching another car drive by.

Alex nodded agreement. "So how much did you think your snack was going to cost?" he asked.

"Ah, well, I thought the young lady said 'Four and Ten'—Four shillings and ten pence. Which is very expensive for a pie and tea. I never believed that… well… that she meant four *pounds*…" Arbuckle looked down rather shamefully.

"No, no, don't worry about it." Alex gestured that it was not important. "I would be very interested to see your coins though, if you wouldn't mind," Alex probed. "We do not often get to see shillings here."

"Oh, well yes. Why not?" Arbuckle pulled a handful of coins from his pocket and tipped them onto the table in front of Alex, who picked one up and turned it over in his fingers.

"What is this one?"

"That's a half-sovereign, good sir." Alex examined another, relishing the feel of the unusual coins. "And that is a threepenny piece… And that is a farthing," continued Arbuckle.

"Fascinating," beamed Alex, noting that the dates on the coins ranged from 1832 to 1850. "Thank you." He pushed the small pile of coins back over to Arbuckle.

Alex pondered in which direction to progress the conversation. The man did not seem to be hiding his vintage association, and was openly admitting his naïvety. Perhaps he was suffering some sort of personality disorder in which he identified as a Victorian.

"So what brings you to Cheltenham—do you have business here?" queried Alex.

"Yes. I am a churchman, as you can see. I have been sent here to help a woman realise that she has strayed from the destiny that God has chosen for her," Arbuckle summarised.

"I see, and will you be here long?" queried Alex.

"Ah, well, there I fear, is the crux of my problem. I had hoped, indeed I had expected, that the mission would be accomplished in one interview, and then I would be taken home. But it seems now that it may not be so easy. And I am ill-prepared for a longer stay here. Tell me. Do you know of any cheap lodging houses nearby?"

"I am sure I can help you find one." Alex was beginning to feel protective of the apparently vulnerable man, and felt that he should sort out somewhere for him to stay, until they could perhaps find out where he was normally looked after.

"You really are most kind," responded Arbuckle. "May I ask you something? I come from a place and time where everyone goes to church, everyone is God-fearing and respects God's will above all else. People all have their foibles of course but... Anyhow, so, I was expecting that all I needed to do was to remind this person of God's will. But the Reverend Liddington at the church down the road seemed to imply that not many people go to church, that it is not any longer the backbone of life. Is that true?—but you are being so kind—I am sure you are a good Christian?"

"Ah, well," replied Alex thoughtfully. "Yes, it depends on the particular country you are talking about of course, but here, church is something of a minority interest these days. However, I would gently suggest to you that kindness, or morality in general, can spring from human values; it is not essential for it to be driven by a religion." Alex suddenly felt rather hypocritical, considering that his kindness to this man was actually driven by his curiosity rather than 'human values'.

"Do you really think so?" Arbuckle nodded and was silent for a moment. "Tell me, does an establishment like this have a lavatory?"

Alex looked around, amused by the sudden change of conversation. "Yes, look, through there—there is a sign over the door."

"Then please excuse me for a minute or two." Arbuckle rose and walked across the café. Alex wondered if he should accompany the odd man to make sure he could operate the light switch and flush, but decided against it. He looked down. Arbuckle had left his worn-leather travelling bag on the floor, and Alex was very tempted to have a look inside. It would be wrong of course, and he had just been suggesting to Arbuckle that people didn't need to go to church in order to be moral. On the other hand, his strongest allegiance was to his friend Betty and her safety. He glanced over at the servery—the assistant was not looking this way. He flicked down the catch on the lock with his foot. It clicked open. He bent over and gently spread the top, giving him a glimpse of what was inside. Mostly clothes and… was that a laptop? That seemed out of character. There was a noise from the servery that caused a moment of panic in Alex, and he quickly clipped the bag shut again. It was premature as it turned out, because Arbuckle did not re-emerge for a few minutes more.

* * *

At length, both men had finished their snacks and Arbuckle said he really should try to find lodgings now, so the two set off down the road in search of a cheap hotel. It was not far. At the reception desk, Alex explained to Arbuckle that he should fill out the check-in form with his details whilst Alex, himself, again used his credit card to pay for Arbuckle's stay. It would be expensive but, for Betty's sake, at least he would know where Arbuckle was.

After a brief experiment with the offered ball-point pen, Arbuckle had laboriously written his name and address in neat copperplate-style writing. "What is 'Car Registration No'?" he enquired of Alex.

"That would be details of your horseless carriage—just leave it blank," instructed Alex, relating helpfully to the worldview that Arbuckle had consistently expressed. Alex looked at the form for a few seconds, trying to memorise the address that Arbuckle had written and noting the date of birth, before handing it to the receptionist. He hoped she would not query the absurd date. Fortunately, she filed the form away without reading it. "Good, now let me show you your room before I head off," volunteered Alex. He picked up the key-card and led Arbuckle to room number 27 on the ground floor, grateful that there was no complication of a lift to explain. He instructed Arbuckle in the use of the key-card, light-switch and taps, and amid profuse thanks from the man, left him, saying that he might drop in the next day to make sure he was getting on OK.

Outside the budget hotel, Alex took a deep breath. He quickly typed

Arbuckle's home address, as he remembered it, into his phone and headed off, at a stride, for Betty's house.

*   *   *

When Betty opened her front door to him, she seemed mildly cross. "Where have you been all this time, Alex? I needed to talk to you."

"I was finding out about your friend, Arbuckle," he defended himself. Betty put her finger to her lips and pointed to the car. Alex understood that she wanted to drive them out to somewhere completely private, away particularly from GCHQ and security ears, but he did not understand why. Alex had not yet deduced any connection between Arbuckle and the secret-classified work that he and Betty were involved in. She drove them out to 'their field', as they referred to it, in the countryside, East of Cheltenham. They sat at the top of the hill, in the late afternoon, with blankets draped around them against the cold.

"He, or the people behind him, know about the timeline change at Heiligenblut—the zap killing the would-be kidnappers," explained Betty. "In short, he says it was against God's will, and he was sent by Angels to persuade me to reverse it."

"*What?*" squeaked Alex, "that's preposterous."

"Listen for yourself then," said Betty laying her phone on the ground between them. "I recorded the whole conversation on my phone."

Alex chuckled with admiration as he heard Betty replying to Arbuckle in the same speech style that the old man used, and especially when she threw in the 'Alice in Wonderland' quotes. But then his expression became more confused and quizzical as he listened to the story and message that Arbuckle had related.

As the recorded conversation finished, Betty picked up her phone, and took a deep breath. "I'm scared, Alex. What do you make of it?"

Alex shook his head. "Well, first let me ask you—this is not one of *your* pranks is it?—Arbuckle looks like he walked straight out of one of your amateur dramatics rehearsals."

Betty looked taken aback. "No," she said emphatically. She pondered for a second. "Think about it, Alex—I definitely wouldn't have suggested to *anyone* that we maybe had the ability to retrospectively change the course of time."

"Yes, I guess that would have been unthinkably irresponsible," agreed Alex. "So is there anyone else who might have some motive to set up a charade like this?"

"I wondered about MI5 at first," mused Betty. They never got a satisfactory answer from me or Kelvin about those fortuitous zaps, so maybe they set this up to probe me and see if they could find out more?"

"But it would be a big jump in logic for MI5 to get from 'fortuitous zaps' to 'changing the timeline'—as far as we know they are not even aware that our research involves time," countered Alex.

"That's true," considered Betty. "Though it's possible that one of the senior management in GCHQ who does know, has mentioned it to them. Even so, it would seem a weird sort of strategy for MI5—it's not as if I am the kind of girl to be swayed by, or confess all to, a clergyman—and they must realise that, surely? The security services know pretty much everything about me."

"Agreed," Alex nodded. "So the other alternative is the foreign agents behind the attempted kidnaps. The message from Arbuckle is certainly consistent with that—but could *they* really believe that you would voluntarily defect just because they sent a messenger to tell you that it is God's will?"

"It hardly seems credible," concurred Betty. "But then the incongruous nature of the whole pantomime seems to argue against any of the possible explanations."

"Right," continued Alex. "And to add to that, Arbuckle seems quite naïve and vulnerable, as if he is totally in-character and unaware he is acting. While I was following him, he just ambled out across the road and got into trouble with a car. Then later, he remarked on how fast the 'horseless carriages' go. And he tried to buy food with a handful of coins from the 19th Century—he let me look at the coins—they were dated between 1832 and 1850."

"So you spoke to him then?" asked Betty, surprised.

"Yes, we had a long conversation. He even asked me about church attendance nowadays—he implied that he came from a place and time when everyone kowtowed to the church—not his words of course—and so he had expected that all he had to do was talk about God's will and you would fall in line."

"What, you talked to him about *me*?" Betty asked, amazed.

"No, not specifically. But I asked him why he was here and he said he had been sent here to help someone realise that she had deviated from God's path, and he seemed surprised, and rather bewildered, that it was not going to be that simple," Alex explained.

Betty thought for a moment. "If, like you say, he was keeping up the act after he had left the church, when he no longer needed to, then maybe Arbuckle has been hypnotised into thinking he really is a Victorian vicar, and sent on this mission?" she suggested.

"That's an interesting proposition," agreed Alex. "Up until I heard the *recording* of your conversation, I was tending toward the idea that he had a personality disorder driving him to believe his Victorian identity. I suppose that could still be true and someone is using him."

"What else did he say to you while you were chatting?"

"Let's see," said Alex raking through his hair as he thought back over the conversations. "Well, I got his home address when we were registering him at the hotel—I keyed it into my phone so I could remember it—and he filled in his Date of Birth as 1803."

Betty laughed. "The address probably doesn't help, whether its fictitious or not," she mused. "But how is he going to pay his hotel bill if he's only got ancient coins—surely the hotel asked for a credit card?"

"Oh, I booked him in on my credit card," revealed Alex. "As you say, he would have been rather lost otherwise—probably would have ended up sleeping rough in the church grounds. And the nights are really cold at the moment, especially for an older man."

"Ah, you're so kind, Alex," purred Betty genuinely.

"That's what he said, over and over again!" laughed Alex. "But of course, for me, it was more about gaining the advantage of knowing where he was. I said I would drop in tomorrow to see how he was getting on."

"I just hope he's not having an extravagant five-course meal at your expense right now, and laughing at your gullibility," proffered Betty.

"Well, if he does, I'll know tomorrow when I check the bill, and he will have blown his cover," retorted Alex. "Oh, and he said he wants to visit a particular building in Cheltenham while he's here—a training college for clergy that he said had just been built by one of his old friends. I must look that up on the map. Hey, I just remembered, I had a quick peek in his bag, and I thought I saw a laptop. But after hearing your recording I suppose that is what he described as the Sentinel."

"Oh. What did it look like?" pressed Betty enthusiastically.

"Umm… I only saw it amongst his clothes for a second—there was a noise that disturbed me and I clipped the bag up again. Something in there was grey, smooth, boxy—in that instant it was easiest to just assume it was a laptop. Maybe it was—maybe the people who are using him talk to him through a laptop, and he thinks it's something special—a Sentinel?"

Betty nodded. "You've been incredibly resourceful and helpful, Alex. I'm sorry if I was grouchy with you at first."

Alex just smiled reassuringly. "Well, I think we're agreed that we have no idea what's actually going on, so I guess we should make a plan to find out. And a plan to keep you safe—would you like to stay in our spare room tonight? I can go and see Arbuckle tomorrow morning—see if I can find out what he intends to do—presumably he will have got new instructions by then from his laptop, or Sentinel, or whatever it is."

"Yes, I think it would be wise to stay over at yours tonight. Thanks, Alex. Mmm…" Betty sounded thoughtful. "Suppose I said to him that I had thought it over and I now intend to rectify my 'ungodly' error. Do you think he would go away then?"

"That sounds a bit over-optimistic," countered Alex. "Whoever is behind him is not likely to be fooled… Do you think we should say anything to security?"

"Well, no," protested Betty. "Because that would risk bringing our 'changing-the-course-of-time' into the discussion. If we are forced to call security in at some later stage then we can always say we just thought Arbuckle was a crank so we didn't bother them about it earlier."

"True," Alex agreed. "So, how about this for a plan? I go over to the hotel tomorrow morning and offer to take him to see this training college building that he's interested in. While I am in his hotel room, I could surreptitiously jam a coin into the door-lock so that it doesn't latch shut, and then you could slip in after we leave and have a close look at his belongings to see if we can understand better what he's about?"

"Ooh, that sounds exciting… but a bit scary," considered Betty.

"It'll be easy enough," Alex reassured her. "I'll text you to let you know when he and I are well away from the hotel, and again when we are on our way back—not that you will need more than 5 minutes."

Chapter 2

Life is not measured by the number of breaths we take, but by
the moments that take our breath away.

(Maya Angelou)

Sunday, Cheltenham

The next morning, the pair of them set off from Alex's house, and Betty
decided to wait in a café some distance from the hotel until she received
Alex's all-clear text. She was just on to the last sips of her coffee when
her phone rang—but it was not Alex.

"Good morning, Betty, this is Michael Liddington from St. Mark's
church."

"Oh, hi again, Michael, how are you?"

"Fine, thanks. Listen, Betty, I owe you an apology. I finally got
round to checking up on our friend, Arbuckle, to see if he really is the
vicar from St. Ewold's, but it seems that particular church was
deconsecrated some years ago—it's now been converted into offices. For
a firm of architects, I think they said. I'm feeling very bad about it—I
should have checked up before contacting you in the first place, but he
was so very convincing. I do hope he hasn't bothered you too much or
upset you. I've no idea what he is up to."

"Ah, OK. No, don't feel bad, Michael. As you say he is very
convincing—maybe he was the vicar there before the church closed
down?"

"No, I wondered that too, but the final vicar was a woman called
Bradshaw, so he's not entitled to that excuse either. I do think it's quite
scandalous, imitating clergy. Anyway, beware. I suppose it is some sort
of scam—you haven't parted with any money I hope."

"No." Betty laughed softly. "No, I don't think he is after money.
Don't worry Michael, I have a friend trying to find out about Arbuckle."

"Ah, that's something, then. I can't keep up with what people are playing at these days. I noticed another couple of strangers in the churchyard early this morning. They asked me if I had noticed anyone unusual around. I did wonder if maybe they were asking about Arbuckle, but they were unable to give any description so I just dispensed with them as soon as I could."

"Oh!" Betty's attention was galvanised. "So what did those strangers look like?"

"Well, one was a young woman, short blond hair with a touch of purple in it. Actually, she was fairly affable and did all the talking. But the other chap was older, tall, long grey hair in a ponytail. And he was wearing a long coat—very unusual, sort of ivory colour—it looked almost plastic. Said nothing, expressionless. Honestly, fancy asking me if I'd seen anyone 'unusual' around when he looked like that!" Liddington laughed. "And they were both wearing backpacks," he added.

Betty noticed her toes curling with anxiety. Were these the people behind Arbuckle? Well, at least she knew what they looked like and could try to steer well clear of them. She glanced nervously out of the café window.

"Betty?" It was Liddington's voice on the phone. She had temporarily forgotten the call. "Well, I'll wish you a good morning and hope you have a nice day."

"Oh yes, thanks, Michael." She ended the call and decided on another coffee whilst she sorted through the possibilities in her mind and waited on Alex's message. So why had these strangers not been able to describe Arbuckle if they knew him?—That seemed incongruous...

*   *   *

Alex arrived at the hotel and got reception to show him the bill so far. Arbuckle seemed only to have added a modest snack to the overnight charge. Alex thanked the receptionist and walked through the swing doors, down the corridor and knocked on the door of room 27.

Arbuckle opened the door a little tentatively, but then his face lit up when he saw Alex. "Ah, my good friend, do come in, dear Mr Smith... I regret I have no drink to offer you in hospitality, but it is certainly a pleasure to see you again."

"And you," echoed Alex, wincing at the memory of his inept, hurriedly-invented alias. "Did you sleep well?"

"In such luxurious surroundings," Arbuckle gestured, taking in the room and the en-suite bathroom, "I most certainly did. And I have just finished my morning prayers so your visit is very timely."

"Good. I came to ask if you would like to come out to visit St Paul's Training College—I have found out where it is in Cheltenham." Arbuckle's delight was evident. "Though I hope," continued Alex, "you will not be disappointed to hear that it is no longer a church training college—it is now a residence for students of the university." Arbuckle's smile faded only very slightly.

"Still," he confirmed, "it was said to be a magnificent building, and my friend, the Reverend Close was so very proud of it. I should be most keen to see it. Is it far?"

"No, it's about 30 minutes walk, but I have brought my horseless carriage—I thought you might like to experience a ride in one?"

"Oh, indeed I would. Yes. Just excuse me for a minute whilst I button up my jacket." He disappeared into the en-suite.

Alex quickly tested a few coins from his pocket to find one that successfully jammed the door latch open, and with a twinge of guilt stepped away from the door waiting for Arbuckle to reappear.

"Now I am all ready," announced Arbuckle, reaching to pick up his leather bag.

"I should leave the bag here," said Alex. "It will be quite safe in your room."

"Oh." Arbuckle seemed to hesitate for a moment, thinking. "Yes, of course." He left the bag sitting by the bed and allowed Alex to usher him out of the room, Alex closing the door ever so gently behind them, satisfied at hearing no click.

"Perhaps," suggested Alex, as they walked to his car, "we should get some breakfast before we make the visit?"

Arbuckle looked sheepishly at him. "That would indeed be much appreciated. I do hate to impose further upon your generosity, but when I advised the Se… that is, when I informed those who sent me on this mission that I am without any financial resources here, I was simply reminded that servants of God were frequently known to fast."

Alex opened the passenger door for him, helped him to climb in and clipped the seat belt across him. "Yes, that does sound a bit harsh," agreed Alex, closing the door. He used the few seconds in walking round to the driver's side to quickly text "*Go*" to Betty, and then drove them across town, Arbuckle excited as a child by the experience.

*　　　*　　　*

Betty was dreading her illicit visit to check out Arbuckle's room in his absence, and was rather hoping that Alex's plan would not proceed for some reason. Her anxiety had been exacerbated by Liddington's news that two more strangers had arrived, and the second coffee had further fuelled her agitation. Nevertheless, as soon as Alex's '*Go*' message arrived on her phone, she immediately left the café and marched quickly round the corner toward the hotel, determined to get it over with as quickly as possible. Fondling the fine pliers in her pocket that Alex has insisted she take to remove the strategically-placed coin, she walked in the entrance and across the lobby, trying not to look furtive, through the swing-doors and down the corridor looking for room 27, which she found all too soon. Her heart was thumping now. There was no-one else in the corridor, so she surreptitiously pushed on the door of room 27, which duly swung open under the weight of her push. She put her head around the door and checked—no-one in the room. So she stepped inside and bent down to try to extract the coin jammed into the latch. Frustratingly, the coin was jammed flat against the side of the lock and she couldn't get the pliers around it. After three unsuccessful attempts, she wondered about giving up and asking Alex to find a way to do it—after all, it was *his* stupid idea. She checked the corridor again and took a deep breath to steady herself. Then she tried improvising with a fingernail to prise the coin away from the side of the lock. Finally, it worked and she could get the pliers around it and tug it out. She closed the door with relief, leaning back against it to scan the room briefly. There was not much to see.

She looked inside the en-suite. Some strange underwear hanging up drying on the radiator, an open razor, a badger shaving soap brush, a strangely long toothbrush with an ornate metal handle, a quaint little toothpaste pot, and a pillbox. Fascination calmed her nerves a little, but there was no time to waste. She left the en suite and went over to the desk. An open bible, a closed prayer book. The prayer book looked Victorian but the bible looked surprisingly modern? She flicked to the frontispiece—oh, a modern Gideon bible, of course. A hotel room staple. She turned it back to the page it was open at: Book of Revelations 14:19. '*So the angel swung his sickle on the earth, cut the grapes from the vine, and threw them into the winepress of God's furious anger. The grapes were squeezed out in the winepress outside the city, and blood came out of the winepress in a flood 300 kilometres long and nearly two metres deep.'* Betty shuddered and shook her head in bewilderment at why anyone would find such text credible, let alone instructive.

She looked around the rest of the room—there were a couple of shirts hanging in the wardrobe. And there, on the floor, was Arbuckle's leather travelling bag. She flicked the catch and opened the top gently. A few clothes and a metal rectangular box—much fatter than a laptop. This must be the Sentinel. Her heart was pounding again. From what she could see the sides were just plain metal surfaces—no visible controls. She put her hands around the top to gently lift it out. But as she lifted it, a strange gender-neutral voice emanated from it. *"Identify"*. It was too much for Betty. She squeaked rather than screamed, dropped the object back into the bag and ran for the door, trembling. But as she reached the door she realised she had not closed the bag—Alex had been insistent about leaving everything exactly as she found it. Against her better judgement, she forced a deep breath, paced back across the room to the bag and closed the catch. Then again rushed to the door, swung it open, thankful that she had removed the coin when she entered and not left it until leaving She stepped outside, panting and trembling. She pulled the door closed behind her.

She heard voices coming from the direction of the swing-doors. Still afraid, she ran on further down the corridor away from the entrance and round the next corner. There she leant against the wall, trying to steady her nerves, and hoping that whoever it was would disappear into one of the rooms before they got to her corner. Looking around, she saw that there were no more rooms in this section, just a door marked 'Cleaners' and an emergency exit. She listened intently to the oncoming voices.

"There was definitely a D-subwave pulse from one of these rooms."

"Strange. That means we are dealing with something more than just a rogue translocator. Be careful—use only the passive instruments—we have covered our tracks so far—we don't want any AI to know we are on its trail."

Betty slid her back silently down the wall to a hunched sitting position. Her breathing was fast and shallow and she was having a cold sweat, as much out of confusion as because of the events.

"There's no bio-signature in any of the rooms... except... oh..." The girl with short blond hair hurried the few paces to the corner around which her handheld-instrument indicated an individual in distress. "Hello." She slipped the instrument into a side-pocket of her backpack and knelt down in front of Betty taking her hands. "Don't worry. You're having a

panic attack. I'll look after you. My name's Gemma. Try to breathe slower. That's it. Long out-breaths. Stamp your feet a little."

The human contact was calming, and after a few moments Betty's panic passed and she burst into tears.

"Oh dear," purred Gemma, "what on earth has happened to you?" She put her arm around Betty to comfort her. They stayed like that for a minute until Betty calmed and took a deep breath. Gemma pulled some tissues from one of her pockets—she seemed to have a lot of pockets—and handed the tissues to Betty with a smile. Betty cleaned up her face and looked properly at Gemma for the first time—she had a broad face, little dimples in her cheeks and a robust smile. And a touch of purple in some tufts of her hair, just as Liddington had commented.

"Are you able to stand now? Let's go and get you a drink of water or something?"

"Yes, thanks." Betty slowly eased herself upright and took in Gemma's companion for the first time—he was exactly as Liddington had described—no smile, though he looked wise rather than threatening.

"Oh, this is Vallini, my... mentor." He nodded almost imperceptibly. "What's your name?" continued Gemma.

Betty shook her head—not willing to give anything away. Gemma didn't push it, but linked arms with Betty to keep her steady if she needed it, and led her back down the corridor, Vallini following.

"Shall we sit in the reception area and have a drink?" suggested Gemma.

"No, not here," said Betty. "I don't want to be recog... I mean, it's OK, I can make it home from here."

"I really think we should sit you down for a while," insisted Gemma. "Let's find a café nearby, then?"

"Oh, OK," concurred Betty, feeling too emotionally exhausted to argue.

*   *   *

They sat in the window-seat of a café nearby, Betty eschewing the coffee this time in favour of a mineral water.

"So do you often have panic attacks?" asked Gemma, taking her first sip of coffee and relaxing back into the chair.

23

"Umm..."

"It was not a panic attack," stated Vallini quietly but firmly. "It was an anxiety attack."

Gemma turned to him quizzically. "Why do you say that? It sounds like much the same thing to me."

"Get out the bio-signature monitor," he told her. Gemma pulled the handheld device, not much bigger than a mobile phone, from her rucksack side-pocket and put it on the table between her and Vallini. "Look, you must pay attention to the neuro-readings here. The difference is significant because panic attacks occur unpredictably, whereas an anxiety attack is always provoked by some stressful experience. So our friend here experienced something fearful *just before* we found her. And since the D-subwave pulse also occurred *just before* we found her, and in the same vicinity, it is statistically almost certain that the two events are causal."

Betty tensed visibly.

"Vallini, why don't you go back to the hotel room," Gemma castigated him. "You are being insensitive and adding to her anxiety. You can see that she is contemporary. And later we must get you some suitable clothes—even your clothes are disturbing."

Vallini rose, nodded very slightly and left the café. Betty was bemused by the relationship between the two—he seemed to be in charge over technical detail, but deferred to Gemma without protest on social matters.

"I'm sorry," apologised Gemma, "if he added to your anxiety—he doesn't yet really understand people like us. I imagine you don't trust me well enough yet to tell me what happened?"

Betty shook her head.

"Well, why don't you ask me a question first, then I'll ask you a little one, and so on. No obligation to answer, but we might be able to build some trust that way." Gemma opened her palms toward Betty inviting a question.

Betty thought for a moment and then decided this might be quite constructive. "So, where do you come from?" Betty opened.

"From Manchester. I'm a robotics post-grad worker at the uni." That sounded much more ordinary than Betty had expected, but was also reassuring—Gemma certainly had the right accent and clothes to fit that identity. "OK, my turn now," continued Gemma. "And where do *you* come from?"

"I live here in Cheltenham. I am a mathematician," volunteered Betty. Gemma smiled broadly at the answer—either she was pleased that Betty was cooperating or maybe she found some element of kinship in Betty's answer. They detoured for a few minutes of general conversation about universities and academic research that reassured Betty that Gemma seemed genuine about where she came from.

"Right," said Betty finally, claiming her formal turn to ask the next question, "what is a D-subwave pulse?"

"Ooh!" Gemma laughed. "Well, it's a pulse of communication on the D-subwave medium. That's a more advanced mode of communication than is currently in general use. But don't ask me how it works because I haven't a clue."

"But Vallini has?" continued Betty.

"Hey, it's my turn for a question! But yes, he knows how to use it, and its significance, though I don't think he's any expert on *how* it works. Anyway, my question. What is it you're afraid of?"

"Oh." Betty slumped forward.

"It's OK, you don't have to answer if that's too direct," Gemma reassured her.

Betty took a deep breath. She didn't want to reveal too much about herself, certainly not specifics like her identity. But she was intrigued and dearly wanted to keep the conversation going, if it could be done in general terms. "It's complex, but I will try to give you some sort of answer. I was… There were two attempts to kidnap me recently, one failed and the other I was rescued from. But I am afraid of yet another attempt."

"Oh, God, I'm sorry to hear that. No wonder you are anxious. What were they after—a ransom?"

"Whoa, my turn," protested Betty. "Do you know the person whose hotel room that D-subwave pulse came from?"

Gemma raised an eyebrow. "No, not yet, but we aim to find out who he or she is." She paused. "Do *you* know that person?"

"I have met him… but I wouldn't say I know him," supplied Betty. A pause. "Why do you want to find out who he is—do you want to help him?"

25

"No, we definitely don't want to help him," Gemma assured her. "He is using some very dangerous equipment without authorisation. So that's why we are here—to find out what's going on, and to stop it."

The fog of confusion in Betty's head was being gradually replaced by a little warmth of reassurance, but she was still determined to be diligently sceptical and cautious.

Gemma seemed to sense the shifting in Betty's outlook and gave her a few moments before plying her with another question. "So obviously from what I have just said, it would be very helpful to us if you could tell me what you know about this man? It's really important that we understand who is involved and what their motivations and resources are before we act."

Betty considered. She didn't want to give away information about herself, but there seemed no reason not to tell what she knew about Arbuckle, particularly since Gemma had indicated that they intended to put an end to his project, whatever it was. And that could only benefit her safety.

Betty nodded. "Well, he appears to be a Victorian vicar." Gemma looked puzzled. "Everything about him is consistent with him being… a Victorian vicar. He seems naïve and completely lost here. At first, we thought the whole thing must be an act. But my friend and I have investigated him as well as we can, and we have, as yet, found nothing to contradict his story that he came here from a church in Dorset around 1850. He says that he was sent on a mission here by God, via an angel. The angel gave him a device called a Sentinel that both gives him his instructions, and also can transport him through space and time."

Gemma did not look surprised. She just nodded thoughtfully.

"Alright," said Betty, "since I've told you about Arbuckle—that's his name by the way—the Reverend Thomas Arbuckle, I'd like you to tell me about Vallini?"

"Fair enough," agreed Gemma. "But can you hold that question for just a couple of minutes whilst I go to the toilet?" She got up and walked through the door at the side.

Betty watched her disappear, and considered her own situation. Her leg muscles had tensed as if they wanted to walk her out - to escape. This was her opportunity. She had given nothing away. She could just leave and not be involved with these people anymore. Perhaps they would deal with Arbuckle as Gemma had suggested, and the whole strange episode would be closed. But her curiosity had been piqued, she really wanted to know more, to find out about Vallini. As a scientist, her thirst for knowledge always tended to have the upper hand over dull options like caution and safety. And she had quickly developed a liking for Gemma - the woman seemed both caring and interesting. A little trust *had* developed. Surely if Gemma had any bad intentions she would not have given Betty this opportunity to leave. Gemma returned before Betty's inner debate had subsided, but the strength of curiosity had served to anchor her in the seat.

"Right," said Gemma, smiling broadly. "Where were we? Ah yes, you wanted to know about Vallini. Well, you have been very helpful and candid telling me about Arbuckle so it's only fair that I am truthful with you in response. I guess we are fully addressing the elephant in the room now." She glanced around, checking that they were not being overheard and lowered her voice slightly. "Vallini is an officer of Temporal Continuity—we call it TC. His job is to track down any use of unauthorised translocation equipment, and stop it. You see, the future is obviously very sensitive to any changes made to the past, so it's very dangerous for people to play around with translocation equipment—it is strictly prohibited—though TC still catches the occasional maverick who somehow gets his hands on equipment that has been manufactured in a clandestine factory, or even once or twice that has been stolen from TC inventory. Often, it is someone wanting to change something in the past to improve their lot in their present; sometimes it's just a traveller or explorer pursuing their dream. There are TC officers stationed at intervals throughout time—Vallini comes from the year 2243, I think it is. They have sensitive detection equipment that can pinpoint when and where translocation equipment is used. And they recruit people like me to be ready to help and advise them on local customs and currency when the need arises—which is actually very rare in these decades. I am exceptionally lucky to be involved in a real case."

Betty's jaw dropped and she shook her head, amazed. "Geez, and I thought I had a fun job!"

Gemma laughed. "It's only a very, very part-time job. In fact, most of it is really mundane. I have to occasionally make investment switches on their instructions to make sure there is always potential currency available wherever and whenever they need to visit. Money is actually the hardest part, when you translocate. Even if you've got investments, it takes days of administration to turn them into useable cash, and the financial rules and methods are always changing. I have only come from three years ago, but that means the TC card and my own credit card have both expired, so all we have is a small wad of notes that I brought with me. And the valid currency notes are often changing in design, so it's easy to come unstuck. In a decade or so things all go biometric and it gets a bit easier, so I'm told. Anyway, we're going to have to raid the betting shops this afternoon to raise some cash. Hey, why don't you come with us—it will be fun, and the more of us there are, the more money we can make quietly? Of course, we'll have to go shopping to get some contemporary clothes for Vallini first—we want to be very careful not to get noticed."

Betty sat quietly for a moment, processing all that she had been told, and assessing her relationship to it. At length, she nodded. "OK, that sounds interesting. You can count me in. But hey, Cheltenham racecourse has a *real* race meeting on this afternoon—why don't we go there, it's not far."

Gemma's face lit up. "Oh, that would be so much better—loads of bookies and some real entertainment. Beats walking around the streets between betting shops."

"Cool, I'll drive us there." offered Betty. "How about I pick you up outside here about 12—that gives you an hour or so to fix Vallini up with a new outfit first?"

"Wow, thank you… umm, I still don't know your name?"

"My name's Betty," she laughed. "And that makes it my turn to ask you the next question… but later. Right now I've got to get home. Thanks for being so supportive earlier, when I got anxious."

"It's been a pleasure meeting you, Betty," Gemma stood to shake hands. "And thanks for all the useful information. See you later."

Betty strode off back toward her house. She looked back a couple of times to be sure that she wasn't being followed—she still could not be totally confident that Gemma and Vallini had only benign intentions toward her. Though she was confident enough, and curious enough, to want to engage with them further.

*   *   *

Meanwhile, Alex had indulged Arbuckle in a gratefully-received full English breakfast, before they both set out for St Paul's training college. As they walked, Alex decided he would try to find out what instructions Arbuckle had received from his minders. "So, you were saying that your superiors told you that you could just fast, and go without food while you were here?" Alex started, choosing his words carefully because, from Arbuckle's viewpoint, Alex would still know nothing about the Sentinel.

"Yes," came the wistful reply, as Arbuckle cast his eyes down.

"They didn't make any constructive suggestions about how you could support yourself? That seems very harsh," commented Alex.

"Well, in truth, I am slightly ashamed to admit it, but, if I am honest, yes, they did suggest… that I make a wager on the result of a horse-race that takes place today. The very idea—a clergyman making wagers! Not to mention that it would be somewhat dishonest making a wager on a matter of which one already knew the result. I am sometimes surprised at the… what did you say, yes, harshness, and also the morality of what I am instructed to do."

Alex chuckled. "I suppose I could make that wager for you. I don't think I would have scruples against it," proposed Alex.

Arbuckle stopped in his tracks. "Would you?" His manner suggested that the idea had not previously occurred to him. "Then that means, in turn, I would be able to pay you back for all the financial favours you have given me. So it would ultimately result in some good," mused Arbuckle. "Let me see, they told me the name of the horse, but I was rather disturbed at the proposal hence I was distracted from committing it to memory at the time."

Alex smiled inwardly. It was the archetypal trap for someone claiming to be a time-traveller. Arbuckle would, of course, be unable to come up with an accurate prediction. He would continue with excuses about clerical impropriety or claim he had forgotten the horse's name.

"Umm…" Arbuckle had resumed walking again, tapping his forehead in frustration. Alex suppressed his smile and was silent, slightly enjoying the schadenfreude, witnessing the discomfort of the presumed act of forgetfulness.

"Umm… something to do with winter… Er… Snowball… Yes… Snowball… Cause, 'Snowball Cause'—it's a play on the phrase 'Noble Cause' you see?" exclaimed Arbuckle excitedly. It was not clear whether his wide grin was caused by his amusement at the parody, or his triumph at remembering the name.

Alex returned a sceptical smile, aware that 'Noble Cause' would be just what he expected a man with Arbuckle's moral obsession to come up with as a random name. "And where is it racing?" pressed Alex.

"Ah... that I don't know," replied Arbuckle. "They did say something about the place, but... But it was definitely to race today. Would there be more than one horse with that name?"

"Probably not," Alex had to agree. "Hang on, I'll check it out." He quickly googled 'Snowball Cause' on his phone. No results relating to horse-racing showed, just references to the causes of ice-ages. Alex shook his head, "I'm not getting any hit on that name."

Arbuckle looked puzzled rather than disappointed, as his brow furrowed. "I can't understand that."

"So what other instructions were you given last night—how was it suggested you deal with the woman that you said is slow to see that she has strayed from the destiny that God has chosen for her?"

"Uh..." Arbuckle seemed downcast. "Yes, again, as I said, I am dismayed at the moral implications of what I am instructed to do. I was told to bring the Sentinel physically close to the woman and it would transport her directly to where she should be—the journey to the East I presume. But I always understood from teachings that free will is important—that the whole point of religion is to persuade people to choose to do right of their own free will. If people are *forced* to do the right thing, then what is the point?"

Alex noted that Arbuckle had finally, perhaps inadvertently, used the term 'Sentinel' in the reply to him. But Alex was suddenly overwhelmed with concern for Betty—had he put her in danger suggesting she poke around inside Arbuckle's hotel room? Would the Sentinel be able to sense that Betty was present and do something undesirable?

"Excuse me for a moment," Alex apologised and dashed inside the shop that they were passing. He quickly pulled out his phone and called Betty, tensing as the first couple of rings elicited no reply.

"Hi Alex," she eventually answered, "How's your morning going? You'll never guess what..."

"Don't go near it, don't touch it, whatever you do..." he cut across her sentence. "Sorry, Are you OK? Don't go near the Sentinel, apparently it has instructed Arbuckle to get it in proximity with you and it will take you away to wherever it wants you to be... Always supposing such a thing were possible," added Alex, suddenly realising that he had temporarily jumped a credibility gap.

Betty was silent for a couple of seconds. "Whoa! Well, I'm OK,

30

Alex. I left Arbuckle's hotel room quite a while ago—it was pretty scary, but anyway I've just been talking with some amazing people. Look, I really need to discuss this with you at length. Can you come round to my place—have you finished visiting that building with Arbuckle yet?"

"No, not yet—I had to feed him first."

"OK, can you come round when you've finished, then, but don't be too late. I have to go to the races at 12."

"The races? What? You mean *horse*-races?"

"Yeah, I'll explain when I see you." Betty ended the call.

Alex saw Arbuckle hovering by the door, peering in, and gave him a reassuring wave. The shopkeeper shot Alex an enquiring look. It was a newsagent's. "You want a paper with today's racing in it, sir?" he suggested, clearly having overheard Alex's last comment. Helpfully, he picked out a copy of the 'Racing Post' and offered it to a somewhat bemused Alex. "Two pounds ninety, sir."

Alex decided to go with the flow and handed over the payment, then returned to Arbuckle. "Sorry, I... picked up a copy of today's racing paper," he announced to Arbuckle, trying to sound efficient, though that had in no way been his intention in darting into the shop. "So that we can check out whether your horse is racing." He watched Arbuckle's face to see whether he might be nervous about his prediction being shown to be wrong, but in fact Arbuckle looked cheered by the prospect.

Alex tucked the newspaper under his arm and continued the walk. "St. Paul's is just around the corner and along Swindon Road. Not far now." The two men strode on and were soon confronted by an impressive buttressed stone gateway, and next to it a large sign stating "Francis Close Hall."

"Oh my!" Arbuckle was clearly delighted. "Yes. My dear friend Francis Close, properly remembered and acknowledged. Though they have omitted the title of 'Reverend'—I suppose because it is no longer a Church Training College. He was the rector in Cheltenham you see. In my day it was known as an Institution for the training of masters and mistresses upon scriptural and evangelical principles in connection with the Church of England," he informed Alex proudly. "What did you say they use it for now?"

"It's part of the local university—some student accommodation and they teach social science, education and humanities here, I believe. Let's stroll round the building." He led Arbuckle in through the gate and down the entrance drive. Then they ambled round the lawns that surrounded the building.

When Arbuckle remarked on the castellated oriel of the tower, Alex had to admit to him that he had no particular understanding or knowledge about architecture. Though it was difficult for Alex *not* to be impressed by the Gothic Revival stonework building. Arched windows, an octagonal tower and chimneys were accentuated by two-tone stonework, and the walls, in places, softened by ivy. "I had a good friend George," mused Alex wistfully, as they sat on a lawn bench admiring the tower, "who was an historian and would have loved to be here and discuss the technicalities of the building with you in detail. But he unfortunately died recently."

"Oh, I am sorry," sympathised Arbuckle. "How did he die?"

"Bizarrely, he was shot during a kidnap," reflected Alex. But then he stopped suddenly, wondering if he had inadvertently given Arbuckle information that might link Alex to Betty in Arbuckle's mind. Did Arbuckle know about the kidnap? From what he had said to either of them so far, it seemed not—he had apparently not been briefed on the details.

"Shall we have a look at the interior?" suggested Alex, rising from the bench, and deliberately changing the subject. They crossed the lawn to the path and Alex was happy to find that there were no obstacles to them walking in. They encountered a few students studying or wandering the corridors but no-one paid them much attention. Soon they came across the chapel which Arbuckle explored with some relish. Finally, he said he would like to pray in there for a while, so Alex stepped back outside and went to sit on the lawn bench again.

With a few minutes now to spare, Alex leaned back on the bench, pulled the newspaper from under his arm and unfolded it, intending to scan all the racecards for that day to determine definitively if Arbuckle's punt existed or not. He ran his finger down all the listed racers at Kempton Park. Nothing remotely close. Then the Doncaster list—no match. The next page was Cheltenham which reminded him of Betty's comment—ah, so there is a meeting *here* today. He scanned down through the race-cards. And there in the third race, was the name 'Snowball Course', not 'Snowball Cause' as he had interpreted Arbuckle's words. So that was why it had not come up in his Google search. He considered the significance for a moment. Of course, that didn't prove anything—Arbuckle could easily have found out the name of a local runner. He looked at the odds, 50:1, a rank outsider. Well, that made for a bold punt if it was indeed just a guess.

After a few minutes, Arbuckle re-emerged from the entrance and Alex stood up and went to meet him. "Look, I found your horse." He pointed to the race listing.

Arbuckle peered at the paper and smiled. "Ah! 'Snowball *Course*'—so it's a homonym as well as a parody, how clever. So would you now be able to execute that wager on my behalf, good sir? I really would be most grateful as I confess I have no idea how to conduct a wager myself."

"No problem—leave it to me, Reverend. But listen, I really have to get to see someone else right now, so I'll drop you back at your hotel if that's OK. And then perhaps I'll visit you later to let you know the result of the 'Noble Cause' wager?"

*   *   *

"I've got a lot to tell you, Alex," Betty started, waving Alex to the sofa and switching on the coffee machine. "But you go first—what sort of a morning did you have?"

"Well, just two or three points, really," replied Alex. "Arbuckle seems to be having qualms of morality over what his Sentinel is apparently telling him to do. I already told you that the Sentinel proposed to just take you away directly if persuasion didn't work—and that's a problem for Arbuckle because he thinks that free will is a religious tenet. Then when he explained to the Sentinel that he didn't have any money to buy food, it apparently told him that fasting was good for his soul." Betty threw back her head and laughed. "Then it suggested a horse-race he could win money on, which didn't go down too well with him because he thinks gambling is undignified for a vicar."

Betty raised her eyebrows. "A horse? Which one?"

"Snowball Course, 14:10, Cheltenham. But the interesting aspect is that he is showing signs of a crisis of faith with his Sentinel—it sounds like the people running him don't understand a clergyman very well, or even the necessities of life."

"It may not be people," interjected Betty.

Alex's brow furrowed. "What do you mean?"

"It might be an AI," stated Betty. Alex looked surprised. "But let me go back to the beginning," she went on. "When I snooped round in

Arbuckle's hotel room, I found nothing that challenged his authenticity. In fact, I saw stuff that seemed to endorse it—his underpants for example." Alex nearly choked on his coffee. Betty laughed. "You see, if you were to hire a Victorian outfit from a costumier, you would still wear modern underwear—they don't supply ancient underwear—why would they?… no-one would ever see it. But hanging on his bathroom radiator were long Victorian underpants. Otherwise, there was a prayer-book and an open Bible on his table—he's probably the only person ever to actually read a hotel's Gideon Bible!"

Alex laughed.

"So I think he's authentic," concluded Betty.

"Authentic! Victorian? But how could that be possible?" protested Alex.

"Well, more on that later. But still in his hotel room, I found his bag, opened it up and sure enough, there is this Sentinel metal-box thing. So I started to pick it up and it croaked '*Identify*' at me. Don't you ever ask me to do something like that again, Alex, it nearly scared me to death." Betty wrapped her arms around herself, shuddering at the memory.

"What? You touched it?" said Alex, alarmed.

"Yes, but presumably it didn't know who I was, since it asked for identification."

Alex sighed. "And did you manage to get the coin out of the lock and leave the room exactly as you found it?"

"Yes."

Alex frowned. "But now I'm worrying that the Sentinel might ask Arbuckle who it was that handled it."

"But he can't know it was me," argued Betty.

"Well, think about it—even the humblest smartphone has a camera. If the Sentinel has a way of showing him pictures then we are busted."

"God, yes. I hadn't thought of that," affirmed Betty. "But even if Arbuckle found out it was me, he couldn't do anything about it, and you're not implicated."

"Well, I did encourage him to leave the bag behind—he might just put two and two together. But it's not so much him I'm worried about. If the Sentinel now knows what you look like… I'm beginning to regret suggesting that you sneak into his room."

"Anyway, there is something of a silver lining," suggested Betty eager to continue her story.

"Oh?"

"As I came out of his room I heard voices coming, so I panicked and hid round a corner..." She related the whole episode of anxiety attack, Gemma and Vallini, to an Alex who listened to her without interrupting, but looked increasingly dubious.

"So are you seriously saying that you buy into all that Time Police stuff?" Alex asked derisively when she had completed the story.

"It's Temporal Continuity," Betty corrected him.

"*Whatever!*" said Alex dismissively. "It sounds suspiciously like a more modern version of 'God's Will' as espoused by Arbuckle."

"Well, there are little bits of evidence backing up their narrative," protested Betty. "Firstly, they arrived just half a minute after I touched the Sentinel and it had reacted. Secondly, they were talking about a 'D-subwave pulse' before they even knew I was listening, so it wasn't said for my benefit. Thirdly, they found me by using some device that detected bio-signatures. And Gemma seems matter-of-fact that she can predict all the race winners this afternoon—would that convince you?"

"No, it wouldn't, because we ourselves have the ability to read from the future with the *i*-vector equipment, at least in some circumstances— had you forgotten that? Certainly, it *would* be surprising and interesting that there are others who have perfected the technology to do it, *if* these race predictions pan out. And if so, it's even *more* interesting that they have managed to find *us*—they must have some sort of detection system. And then what worries me is *why* they have come to find us. But that's all a long cry from police officers flitting through time, chasing mavericks."

"Oh." Disappointment showed on Betty's face. "OK, well, I guess some scepticism is healthy."

"What do you know about this Gemma woman?" asked Alex.

"Well, she said she worked as a robotics post-grad worker at Manchester Uni."

"Ah. I've got a friend, Dave, in the physics department there, so I can check that out," responded Alex typing a text message into his phone. "... And *why* do they want you to go with them to the racecourse this afternoon?" he then continued.

"Well, just for fun really. There's no specific purpose," considered Betty, "except I suppose we can spread out the betting more with three of us. And I suppose she wants to ask me more questions about Arbuckle."

"It's not so much that I'm sceptical, Betty, but worried for your safety. You always have been too trusting of people... though that's a very attractive part of your personality," he added, responding to the slight look of hurt on Betty's face. "Look, suppose they are all in league. Arbuckle appears first with a scary threat to you, then they appear, allegedly chasing him, so that you get sucked into allying with them, then what?..."

"The enemy of mine enemy is my friend, sort of thing," agreed Betty.

"Exactly. Or alternatively, suppose they are from a different organisation than Arbuckle, but have the same intentions—to wind back our change to the course of time that prevented you being kidnapped in the first place. It certainly sounds like an implication of their 'Continuity' message?"

"That makes sense too, Alex. But they don't seem to know who I am in that scenario, they just seem to be chasing the trail left by Arbuckle's equipment."

Alex's phone beeped. He checked the message. "Mmm... Dave says his mate in Engineering knows this Gemma girl—it seems she is well-liked and trusted," he concluded, somewhat reluctantly. They were both silent for a minute, lost in contemplating the possibilities.

"But I do feel I want to go with them this afternoon," Betty concluded. "For one thing, if I do witness them accurately predicting the winners, then it means we know we are dealing with something on a level higher than just a scam or a kidnap. I wonder—would you like to come as well? You could keep an eye on me from a distance?"

"I'm not sure Petra would be happy about me taking more time out—I spent much of yesterday chasing Arbuckle. I am supposed to look after the kids for at least some of the weekend."

"So, how about you bring Petra and the kids along to the races?—I'm sure the kids would love to see the horses close up, and there are probably funfair rides as well."

"Mmm... Well, I'll ask Petra. What time are you getting there?"

"I'm picking them up at midday, so we'll be in by half-past, ready for

36

the first race."

Chapter 3
Luck is what happens
when preparation meets opportunity.

(Seneca)

Betty saw them standing in front of the café and waved as she pulled up, at a few minutes past twelve. Vallini now looked very different. Gemma had kitted him out in casual thick cotton trousers and a black padded winter jacket so he no longer stood out as unusual. They were both still wearing their backpacks, however.

"Wow, this is a cool car," commented Gemma enthusiastically as she climbed into the front seat of the Cabriolet, having ushered Vallini into the rear.

Betty smiled a welcome. "And you look very smart now, Vallini," she said, looking over into the back seat, hoping to break the ice between them.

"Do you think so?" Vallini seemed surprised. "I must admit I do not find these primitive fibres very comfortable... or aesthetic."

"Stop complaining," Gemma scolded him playfully. Betty thought she caught the hint of a tiny smile on Vallini's face.

"Umm..." Betty was thoughtful. "I don't know what you have in those backpacks but they would get searched when we go into the Racecourse," she suggested helpfully.

Gemma snapped her fingers in realisation. "Of course, security... thanks, Betty. Can we leave them in the boot of your car?"

*   *   *

"OK, so let's discuss tactics," insisted Gemma, taking charge. "We'll make this our meeting place." She gestured to the spot they had found towards the high rear of the terraces. "It's relatively uncrowded here so we can talk without being overheard. Now, the main things are not to hit any individual bookie more than once, and not to get noticed as serial winners. It looks like there are three main areas where there are groups of independent bookies—see those guys with umbrellas and boards listing the runners, Vallini? So with seven races, we can each visit each area just twice, and choose a bookie the second time who is well separated from the one we betted with the first time. In addition, there is the tote—that's like the racecourse's own bookie system, Vallini—see the entrance with the sign over the top saying 'Unibet'? I've worked out the odds and bets so that we each win a couple of hundred pounds each race—so it shouldn't raise any eyebrows and they will be able to pay out in cash. A few thousand will be more than enough to pay for hotel and food for a few days here. Remember the procedure I explained earlier, Vallini? When you place a bet you state the number of the horse and the amount, and say 'to win.' Then the bookie will give you a ticket in exchange for the money. Keep the ticket safe, remember the exact bookie you went to. Meet back here, then as soon as the race has finished we all go back to those exact same bookies and give them the ticket to collect the winnings." Vallini was nodding to each instruction and looking confident, though Betty wondered if he understood social nuances like queuing. "Right, the first race is in a quarter of an hour so we might as well get the bets on for that." Gemma reached inside her jacket and pulled out a notebook and a small wad of notes. She handed fifty pounds to each of Betty and Vallini. "So, fifty pounds on number six to win."

"That's a bit soulless," joked Betty. "What's the poor horse's *name*?"

"Sable Camp," Gemma grinned. "Should be 'nine to two', but if you can find 'five' all the better." Vallini looked puzzled at the jargon but said nothing. "Vallini, you take that row of bookies over to the left. Betty, you take the central area, and I'll go over there to the right." They all headed off to their appointed zones.

Betty scanned the row of boards declaring the bookies' odds and chose one of only a couple that were indeed offering the better odds of 'five to one'. There was just a short queue so she was soon handing over the fifty pounds to a man in trilby hat who repeated the bet to his admin colleague before handing her a ticket. He paid Betty almost no attention, and quickly addressed the next person in the small queue that was forming behind her. Betty walked away a few metres then looked back and saw that the bookie was now adjusting the odds on his board down to nine to two. She felt a small sense of achievement in having gained the better odds, but it was tempered by the knowledge that what she was doing was fundamentally unfair, since she already knew the impending result. Since the transaction had been quick, she decided to wander over to the area where Vallini had gone, to see if he was managing OK. She spotted him walking up from the bookies' area.

"Did you get on OK, Vallini?" she asked.

"Yes, no problem," he replied, showing her the ticket.

"So, do you understand the practice of queuing?" Betty asked, trying to be helpful.

"Yes, of course," Vallini scoffed, surprised. "Even two hundred years of increasing efficiency will never eliminate groups of individuals wanting to do the same thing simultaneously."

"Oh, sorry. I was just trying to be helpful—I wasn't sure how much you understand the nuances of this society?"

"Yes. Your concern is well placed. I would be in considerable difficulty without Gemma's advice, but there are very many basics in human behaviour that do remain relatively constant. If you think back to behaviour as recorded in English history two hundred years before now, technology and conditions have changed enormously but many of the concerns of ordinary life are surprisingly similar."

"True," mused Betty, remembering how Arbuckle, for all his lack of modern knowledge, was still managing to survive here and now, without too much difficulty. And Arbuckle had clearly not been primed, whereas Vallini presumably had the advantage of training, and the benefit of Gemma as aide.

"Often the behavioural differences at one point in time between various *regions* in the world, are greater than the differences spanning two centuries in the *same* part of the world," concluded Vallini, sounding to Betty like an anthropology lecturer.

They had reached their rendezvous point, and could see Gemma, who had farther to walk, heading towards them.

"Here comes Gemma," Betty smiled at Vallini. He held her gaze with that tiny maybe-smile but said nothing. Betty wondered if he was intimidated from conversing in a more personal way with her because Gemma had castigated him during the morning for saying insensitive things whilst Betty had still been distressed. She felt an awkward silence for a minute until Gemma arrived.

"OK, you two?" Gemma asked as she arrived back and briefly examined their two tickets. "Oh, you managed to find 'five to one', Betty. Unfortunately, none of the boards were offering that by the time I got there." Betty again felt a small amount of pride as Gemma explained to Vallini that 'nine to two' or '9/2' simply meant odds of 4.5 to one, and sometimes it was possible to find better odds by scanning the offers on the boards. Vallini nodded lightly as if he had probably already deduced that. "But it's of no importance to us really—we will make sufficient cash this afternoon anyway," she finished. Betty's small bubble of pride ebbed away again.

The race started and they watched from their vantage point high on the terraces. At first, the horses were too far away to distinguish meaningfully. Gemma glanced at her notebook and informed them that the jockey riding 'Sable Camp' was in the purple and white colours. The horses began the long turn toward the final straight and Betty could see that 'Sable Camp' was running third. Excitement in the crowds was now rising as people urged their punts on, shouting encouragement. Betty felt the excitement rising in her also, contradicting her intellectual knowledge that the horse was certainly destined to win anyway. At least that was what she presumed. In the end, she decided not to suppress her emotion and started cheering encouragement to the horse with an arm waving in the air. And surely, stride by stride, 'Sable Camp' drew level to the leader halfway down the home straight and forged ahead to win by half a length. Betty punched the air and whooped, then turned to high-five Gemma who responded, despite having cracked-up laughing at Betty's logically-absurd enthusiasm. There was even a perceptible smile on Vallini's face. Betty wondered if he ever got as far as laughing.

"Right, off you two, to collect the winnings," declared Gemma. "You remember which bookie you got the ticket from, Vallini?" She received the almost imperceptible nod as he strode off.

Betty almost ran down the terrace steps. This *was* exciting, she acknowledged to herself; insight into the future did not eliminate the joy of winning. She spotted her bookie and headed over. Halfway there her emotion changed—was she effectively stealing from this man? She hesitated before approaching, but was reassured when she saw a couple of people already in front of the bookie ready to claim winnings. The man in the Trilby checked each ticket in turn and handed over the requisite cash in a very business-like manner, betraying no hint of regret at losing those particular bets. And why should he, thought Betty. He must have taken in far more than he's paying out. She handed over her ticket and received back £300 in return without him batting an eyelid. Relieved, her enthusiasm returned, and she started back up the terraces to their meeting point, carrying the small bundle of notes. She was first back, but soon spotted Gemma returning from the far side of the ring. However, just before Gemma reached her, she heard the familiar unwelcome voice of Phil Bowen behind her.

"Good afternoon, Miss Gosmore. Picked a winner, did you?" he asked rhetorically, pointing at her fistful of notes as she turned.

"Oh, hello, Phil. Umm… yes."

"Does this mean you finally got that damn machine of yours to read the future, or are you just having a lucky day?" he cackled at what he presumably thought was a great joke.

"No, neither actually, Phil," stated Betty blandly, regaining her composure as Gemma joined them. "My friend, Gemma, here, has some good inside information from the training stables. Gemma, this is Phil Bowen, one of the supervisors from work." Betty made a face to Gemma as she turned to speak to her, indicating her distaste for the man.

"Nice to meet you, Gemma." He held out his hand. "Phil Bowen, Miss Gosmore's line manager," he embellished Betty's statement. "So you know a bit about the runners, eh?"

Gemma had picked up on Betty's grimace, and a slightly wicked smile briefly flickered across her face. "Yes, I get to see some of the runners' form in the course of my veterinary work," she lied.

"Ah, so I'm fancying 'Carlovian' in the next race—he looks on good form?"

"He does, you're right, but 'Knightcap' has been showing great off-course form over longer distances and I think he has a good chance of coming through the field toward the end of the race on this surface. Particularly considering the large handicap that 'Carlovian' carries."

"'Knightcap', the outsider. Oh, that's interesting." Bowen's voice had edged a little higher as he viewed the wad in Betty's hand and valued the advice accordingly.

"So, if you'll excuse us, Phil." Betty put an arm around Gemma and led her a little way across the terrace, and Bowen strode off purposefully down toward the betting ring.

"You really shouldn't have given him the next winner, Gemma," despaired Betty when they were safely out of earshot.

"Why? Because he might really get convinced that you *'finally got that damn machine of yours to read the future'*," Gemma parodied Bowen's voice. "Yes, I overheard." But Gemma's smile faded as she saw Betty's discomfort. "Oh, don't worry. I didn't give him the winner. 'Knightcap' is a 100:1 outsider that comes in approximately last. So he almost certainly won't bother us for any more advice this afternoon." She laughed. "And we'll talk about that 'damn machine of yours' later, Miss Gosmore. Wow, I know your surname as well now—he really does give a lot away very quickly doesn't he?" Betty was still not smiling. "Stop worrying, Betty. We're on your side. Let's carry on enjoying the afternoon." It was nice to hear that Gemma thought they were on her side, but Betty was not confident that would be the outcome if they knew her whole story.

Vallini had hung back watching the short conversation with Bowen, but he now joined them again. "OK guys," Gemma took charge again, taking the handfuls of notes from Betty and Vallini and tucking them away in an inside pocket of her jacket. "This next race is a bit of a disaster odds-wise, so I think it's best if I just put on a Trifecta bet with the Tote."

"What's a Trifecta?" queried Betty, always keen to understand the intricacies and maths.

"It's a forecast of first, second and third places in the race. They're all short odds, so there's not much to be gained by betting wins or places, but when they are all lumped together in a forecast we should get a decent return. You two can take a few minutes out and chat perhaps?" And she strode off up to the indoor Tote office.

Betty was not sure that it would be easy to chat to Vallini for a few minutes, but perhaps he would now feel freer to talk after Gemma had positively suggested it. She smiled at him. "So, Vallini, do you enjoy these excursions to unfamiliar events?"

"Everything is interesting, of course," he responded. "And I realise that obtaining some currency is essential to support our presence. But I am impatient to get on with our real task here."

"So what is your task exactly?" queried Betty.

"Oh, I thought Gemma had explained to you. We are here to investigate the unauthorised use of a translocator."

"And what will you do when you have understood what is going on?" asked Betty.

"Normally we would destroy the translocator and reset any aberrations to the timeline as best we can. But we need to understand the motivations and resources behind the events so that we can best prevent any further unauthorised activities. This incident already seems a bit unusual in that the activity appears to be driven by an AI, or a remote controller, rather than the traveller who is present—this man Arbuckle. At least that is how it appears from the description you have given us thus far. We are very grateful for the information that you gave to Gemma this morning, but there are still some questions that I would like to put to you if I may?"

Betty nodded, but without enthusiasm—the questions were bound to come sooner or later.

"This morning, when we detected the D-subwave pulse, had you done something to trigger it? You told Gemma you were investigating Arbuckle—were you in that room?"

"Fair enough," conceded Betty. "Yes, I was trying to find out more about Arbuckle, so I got into his hotel room and had a good look round." Though the expressions on Vallini's face were always very slight and understated, Betty sensed that he was impressed rather than disapproving. "As I said to Gemma," she continued, "there was nothing in the room to suggest that he was not an authentic Victorian vicar. Then I opened his bag and saw the Sentinel, as he calls it. I put my hands in to pull it out for a closer look..." Betty again shuddered at the memory. "And then it spoke. It said 'Identify' in a kind of synthetic voice, and I just got terrified and left as quickly as I could—that's when you two found me."

"Ah, that explains a couple of things," Vallini responded. "It sounds as if you were bio-scanned by the machine. It's not a pleasant feeling, and if you are not accustomed to it, it can trigger a fear response. So it was not a panic attack or an anxiety attack that you experienced, it was a bio-scan reaction."

"So, what does a bio-scan mean," asked Betty, concerned. "Has it done something to me?"

"No, the machine has just established an identity pattern for you—I'm sure you would not be already recorded in any system—they are all based well into the future. So all it means is that any of those machines would recognise you as the same person if you encounter one again. The D-subwave pulse would then presumably have been that machine sharing your identity data to the others in its network."

"So, no harm done then?" suggested Betty.

"Not unless you need to hide from this Sentinel. Which brings me neatly to my next question," continued Vallini. "What is the connection between you and Arbuckle. How did you come across him—you seem very motivated to find out about him?"

"Uh," Betty nodded. "Well, that's fairly simple. He and his Sentinel came looking for *me*. He arrived just yesterday and persuaded the local vicar to help him find me. I went along to the church to meet Arbuckle because I had no idea what he wanted—and I was intrigued to find out. He told me I had deviated from God's will and encouraged me that I should submit to it. When I asked him to be more explicit, he said that God's will was that I should have gone on a journey to the East on new year's day. In fact, that was the day some foreign agents attempted to kidnap me, and presumably they would have then abducted me to the East. So Arbuckle was basically telling me I should now volunteer to be abducted to put right the failed kidnap attempt. It's bizarre, but he seemed to be under the impression that if he told me it was God's will then I would defer to that."

"Is that maybe how people would have reacted in his time?" suggested Vallini.

"Indeed," confirmed Betty, "but such obeisance to church opinion is completely anachronistic in today's world."

"Right, well whoever would benefit from your abduction must be in the present or future anyway, so it sounds like this Arbuckle man is just acting for someone else, and either they, or he, have got their historical research all wrong. If it's an AI acting without human oversight then it would perhaps not be surprising if it makes misjudgements about human social history."

"Mmm, yes, but my friend who spent the morning with Arbuckle says that the Sentinel told Arbuckle that it would transport me directly if he got it in close proximity to me. And apparently Arbuckle wasn't too happy about that—he thought it was less than moral."

"Oh!... Right, so that does sound a bit more dangerous. But don't worry, we are here to prevent anything like that happening. Though I am reluctant to destroy the Sentinel without knowing what is behind this, because they may just have further resources that they would then deploy. I'm also reluctant to communicate back to my people yet because any use of advanced communication might alert the Sentinel to *our* presence—their device obviously contains more than just a translocator."

45

"So how is it that *your* organisation detected their... umm... translocation, but *they* didn't detect you arriving?"

"That's because we deliberately arrived in exactly the same place as they did, albeit a little later, behind that church. So the Sentinel would assume that any disturbances that it detects are just afterbeats of their *own* arrival."

"Afterbeats?" queried Betty.

"Like ripples," supplied Vallini.

There was a pause in the conversation as the PA system announced the start of the next race and the sounds of enthusiasm in the crowd rose. Betty glanced over to the racetrack, but without the focus of a particular horse, she felt a lack of excitement. Vallini, standing with his back to the track, seemed disinterested.

"Another question?" Vallini seemed to be asking for permission. "Presumably you know why they want to abduct you?"

"Yes," Betty replied cryptically in a small voice.

"Are you going to explain it to me? Obviously, it would help if I understand the motive."

"They want information from me," began Betty. "I'm not free to talk about the *actual* information—my employment forbids it, but imagine that you, Vallini, were abducted—enemies might gain a lot from extracting your knowledge. Not that I am comparing my limited knowledge with your presumably advanced education..."

There were shouts of triumph and sounds of resignation from the spectators as the horses thundered past the finishing post.

"But," persisted Vallini, "what could people who clearly already have advanced knowledge—since they know how to manufacture translocation devices—what could they gain from your early 21st Century knowledge, Betty? Even if you are a bit ahead of your time? I'm not being dismissive, but it's difficult to see their motivation."

Betty shrugged. She was not sure of the answer either. She suspected it probably had something to do with the way in which that original kidnap had been foiled—by a retrospective zap. But she was not prepared to give Vallini that extra information in case it might cast her in violation of what she imagined that Temporal Continuity rules might forbid. In any case, *she* had not been directly responsible for that helpful and protective zap—she could only *surmise* what must have happened.

Gemma reappeared, walking down from the Tote office, looking pleased with herself. She glanced briefly from Vallini to Betty, as if trying to read the result of the conversation that she had set-up. "Better than expected," she stated, tapping her pocket, before the question was even asked. "Right. Third race..." She pulled out her notebook. "Ugh, favourites again, 'Beano' wins, but an outsider comes in third. So this time we bet on the outsider, number 9, 'Snowball Course', it's 50:1, so twenty pounds will be enough, and tell the bookie *'place'* instead of *'win'*—have you got that, Vallini?"

"Number 9, twenty pounds, place," he repeated succinctly.

"That's it. And we rotate the bookie areas. This time I'll go to the left, Vallini takes the middle and Betty to the right."

Betty smiled her assent and set off. She remembered that this was Arbuckle's tip to Alex but she had been under the impression that it was a winner. She pulled out her phone and called Alex to check.

"Hey, Alex, that horse that Arbuckle gave you, did he say it was a winner?"

"Yes, of course."

"And did you already bet on it?"

"Yes, I did it at the bookmakers back in town this morning."

"Well," Betty informed him, "Gemma says it comes in third—I'm just on my way to put a 'place' bet on it." Betty suddenly had a sinking feeling. She had been gaining in confidence that Vallini and Gemma were competent and protective of her. But what if the Sentinel turned out to be right and Gemma was wrong. Did that mean the Sentinel was more competent and more powerful? Did that imply that Betty was in greater danger?

"What? Wait a minute..." Alex was replaying the conversation with Arbuckle, in his mind. "I asked him where it was racing, and he said *'Ah... that, I don't know... They did say something about the place, but...'* Oh, the idiot. I think they must have told him a *place* bet and he didn't understand. The damn fool has wasted another ten pounds of mine."

Betty laughed. "Get a sense of proportion, Alex. Just put twenty or thirty pounds on a *place* bet now and you'll be quids in, even after the hotel bill. But do it on the Tote will you, so as not to crowd us?"

"Ah, OK. I will. And thanks for the warning, Betty."

Betty hoped that it *was,* in fact, Arbuckle's mistake. She briefly entertained the idea of putting an extra tenner on the horse to *win*, just in case Arbuckle was the one who was right. But she knew the extra money would not come anywhere near to soothing her consequent loss of confidence in Gemma and Vallini.

The betting ring on the right-hand side was the farthest away, so this time Betty was the last one back to their meeting place. She assumed that Vallini would have been briefing Gemma on what he had learned from Betty's answers to his questions, and probably Gemma had told him what she had learned from Bowen's brief interaction. Gemma's greeting was as cordial as ever.

"So," asked Betty, following her own line of thought. "Is it even remotely possible that any of your race forecasts today could be wrong, Gemma?"

Gemma looked surprised. "Well, it's very unlikely. It would mean that either we had been very clumsy and done something that had changed the future after I had checked the race results, or more likely someone else, like your Arbuckle and the Sentinel, had *deliberately* done something to change the future. Why do you ask?"

"Just idle curiosity really," Betty replied. "In fact, Arbuckle recommended to my friend to bet on 'Snowball Course' but didn't make it at all clear to him whether it was to win or place. We concluded that Arbuckle was confused and probably didn't understand the difference."

Gemma laughed. "That sounds consistent with the picture you are painting of him."

Vallini intervened. "It would actually be extremely difficult to change the future so that a particular horse won the race—you would have to get access to all the other horses that came in front and do something to them to compromise their performance. And still that wouldn't guarantee your result because the race might play out in a different format. Conversely, there are, occasionally, outcomes of events that are on a knife-edge, that can be determined by the inadvertent flap of a butterfly's wings, as the saying goes. It's that type of event that we are most wary of when we inevitably intervene during a mission like this, though mostly the course of time is fairly robust. Just occasionally we need to do a bit of repair work afterwards." Betty felt appreciative that Vallini was now going to the trouble of explaining his craft. Mostly the reasoning seemed fairly obvious after it had been explained, but this was clearly Vallini's area of expertise, and a subject in which Betty was more

48

than a little interested.

"I am a bit concerned," started Gemma quietly, "that we are being observed." She was leaning back against one of the sets of terrace railings as she talked to the others. "Don't turn round suddenly—it will give the game away, but up behind us to the left. Tallish man with dark hair. I don't understand it because we have only collected two sets of winnings so far, so surely no-one has noticed that as unusual—I just hope it's nothing to do with the Sentinel crew."

Betty moved over to Gemma's side, feigning a look at her notebook, so that she could casually get a look in the indicated direction. "Oh," she laughed after a second, "that's just my friend Alex—he's keeping an eye on me for my safety. But he's not a very subtle spy!" Betty felt a pang of regret that her safety-net had been compromised but decided to just go with the flow. "Come and meet him." She waved to him and the three of them walked back up the terraces to where Alex was standing, with his wife Petra and the two children.

Betty introduced them all. She had felt a bit guilty dragging Petra and the kids out too, so was relieved to hear that the kids were hugely enjoying themselves having been on a roundabout and down to the paddock to see the horses parade close up. Gemma was quickly down on her haunches talking to the children. "Hey, shall we take them down to the railings at the edge of the track so they can see the horses race past really close and fast?" she suggested. "The race is in about 5 minutes time." They all hurried down to the trackside.

"Daddy's got a favourite horse in the race—it's called Snowball."

Gemma laughed. "Has he? I've got a favourite racing as well—he's called 'Beano', but he needs a lot of encouragement—will you help me cheer him on? You can tell which horse he is because the lady riding him is dressed in green."

"What colour is Snowball?"

Gemma looked at her racing card. "Well, snowballs are usually white, but this horse is brown, and the jockey is dressed in red and white stripes."

"What's a jockey?"

"The jockey is the person riding the horse."

"Mummy, she's got purple in her hair. Can I have purple in *my* hair?"

49

It was decided in the end that Mia would help Gemma cheering on 'Beano' because he had a lady rider, and Charlie would help Betty cheer on Daddy's favourite 'Snowball'. Meanwhile, Vallini had struck up a conversation with Petra after finding out that she was an artist.

The loud enthusiasm of the crowd was even greater at the perimeter fence. Charlie screamed with joy as the ground beneath them shook from the pounding of hooves while the horses thundered past. Mia was ecstatic that 'Beano' won, and Charlie, initially disappointed, was mollified when it was explained to him that 'Snowball' was a very young horse and had done extremely well to finish in third place.

Alex took his family home after the next race via a final visit to the children's roundabout. Betty had noticed that although Vallini had not presumed to interact directly with the children, he had watched their antics with affection and the first definite smile that Betty had seen on his face.

"So do you have a family where you come from?" she asked him as they were waiting for the fourth race to begin.

"No, I have not had children, but I do now have a young cousin that I have a duty to look after. Actually, this mission came at an inopportune time—I really should have visited her this week."

"How old is she?"

"Biologically, she is about 18 years old, though she has also spent several years in hibernation en route back from another star system, so her recorded age is greater. My father's brother emigrated to a colony planet and she was born there. But after some years there, her parents foresaw that the colony was becoming likely to fail, and they shipped her back to Earth as soon as she was old enough for the journey; so that she could have a more fulfilling life. She had just arrived and she will know no-one—she has not even met me yet." Vallini looked wistful.

"Wow, that's amazing," Betty commented, trying to get her head around the idea.

"But surely, when you have finished here you can simply travel back to the day she arrived, in order to welcome her?"

"I could not," stated Vallini. "As an officer in Temporal Continuity, such an action would be hypocritical. Although such a translocation would in all probability result in an insignificant change to the future, we have a very strict code of ethics. We always return to the day that we left, plus the duration we have been away."

Chapter 4

Time is a fickle traveller, A wicked unraveler. A sickened babbler. For a nickel he'll bang his gavel there, And sell you to the lowest bidder.

(Jeff W. Watson)

After Alex had settled the children at home, he decided he would go to visit Arbuckle to share with him the good news of the wager, but when Arbuckle answered the knock on his hotel room door, it was immediately clear that Arbuckle was not in good humour.

"Oh my friend, come in, I have had the most terrible day. Not, I hasten to add, the morning, when you kindly took me round Francis Close Hall. That was most agreeable, a delightful visit. But it was when I returned here, to my room, I discovered that the woman, of whom I have told you, who is the subject of my mission here, had somehow got into my room and, like a common thief, had rifled through my belongings. I was shocked. I had begun to maybe feel some sympathy toward her, that perhaps she had chosen a different path, that she maybe had a right to do so. But now I realise she is a minx, not to be trusted at all, and deserving of all God's punishment." Arbuckle had been pacing the room, backwards and forwards, as he unleashed his tirade. "Such temerity. Such a brazen…"

"But how did you know it had been that specific woman," protested Alex, though he already suspected what the answer would be.

"Ha, she picked up the Sentinel, not knowing that it had powers. So after I returned, the Sentinel summoned me, described the intrusion and showed me a picture of her face. There was no doubt. But that's not the end of my troubles. There is more. I knew that I needed to speak with her again, so I went back to St. Mark's church, where yesterday the vicar had been so helpful in finding her and asking her to come and meet me. I assumed that he would be kind enough to give me assistance again. But when I approached him he was extraordinarily rude. He accused me of

52

being an impostor, a charlatan. He said that he had checked and that I was not the vicar of St. Ewold's, that I had deceived him and tricked him into finding Miss Gosmore. I tried to explain to him that there was simply an issue of time, that he was mistaken. But he would have none of it and threatened to call the police if I ever visited his church again. I was never so embarrassed. A man of the cloth haranguing me in such a way. I left in a hurry and came back here. But my heart has been pounding ever since—I feel so distraught."

Alex observed that Arbuckle's face was an unhealthy crimson colour—the man was clearly emotionally agitated. He needed calming down. He needed his mind taken off those unpleasant encounters. Now was probably not the right time to try to mollify him with the relative triviality of the result of his wager. "I think we should go and have a meal—perhaps you will feel better if you explain all about these difficulties over some food?" suggested Alex. For a second, Alex thought that he might refuse. Arbuckle made some sort of gesture with his arms. But the offer of food always seemed to find Arbuckle vulnerable. He seemed to shift down into humble mode.

"Oh, but I, I… You have already been so generous, I couldn't possibly…"

"But this time you will be the benefactor—you can buy a meal for both of us with some of the money from your wager."

Arbuckle finally stopped pacing. He seemed stunned for a moment; this obviously *did* make a difference for him. "Oh. Oh, my dear friend… Then yes. That would be splendid. Let us go and eat."

"There is a pub next door called 'The Red Lion' which serves good food—let's eat there." Alex had quickly calculated that the hotel bar itself would be an incautious place to eat, aware of the possibility that Betty might just come back into the hotel with the others after the races. Arbuckle picked up his travelling bag, following Alex out of the hotel room, and Alex was relieved when they got inside the doors of the 'Red Lion' without any unfortunate encounter. They found a table towards the rear, behind the bar. Arbuckle studied the menu with interest, not asking for any interpretation, and chose the 'Duck a La Mode'.

"OK, I'll go to the bar and order. Would you like a drink while we wait?" asked Alex.

"Ah yes… I'd very much like a glass of port. Would they have that here?"

"I'm sure they do," Alex replied, noting that a smile had already returned to Arbuckle's face.

Alex reappeared with a beer for himself and a glass of Special Reserve Port. He still felt some satisfaction in pampering this old man, and was chuffed when, after a sip, Arbuckle remarked that it was decidedly the best port he had ever tasted.

"You know," Arbuckle continued, "there is distinctly a sense of luxury in these times. The beds are soft, the rooms are warm with running hot and cold water..." He took another sip or two from his glass. "And the port is simply magnificent... So, my friend, what sum did we win on that wager?"

"Well, after last night's hotel bill, there is a little over 400 pounds left."

"What! Good grief—that is as much as my entire year's stipend!"

"But you can't take it back with you."

"Why not, my friend?"

"Because the banknotes will not be legal tender in your times."

"Ah, yes of course... But what if I bought gold and took it back?"

Alex laughed at the man's naïvety. "The amount of gold you could buy here with 400 pounds is very small. You have to remember that although money is relatively easily had in these times, on the other hand, things are also very expensive. That amount of money will only cover your food and hotel bill for a few days."

"Nevertheless," countered Arbuckle, "I will not resist feeling well-endowed for this evening. A poor man is entitled to celebrate a financial success—even though it be fleeting. And I will have another glass of port to acknowledge that—can I get you another drink?"

"I'm OK for the moment, thanks." Alex had delved into his pocket and pulled out the small wad of notes that were the remainder of Arbuckle's winnings and handed them over to him. "Make sure you keep them safe."

"One note will be sufficient for the drinks?" asked Arbuckle.

"More than enough for the drinks and the meals," smiled Alex, observing that the man was brandishing a fifty-pound note. Arbuckle slipped the rest of the stash into his travelling bag and went over to the bar carrying the bag. He was clearly taking no chances after finding out about Betty's foray earlier. Alex smiled again—it was always entertaining being with Arbuckle, and he was also enjoying the role of helper and adviser. About half an hour ago, Arbuckle had been quite disturbed emotionally, yet now, there he was, jubilant and confident enough to approach a bar nearly two hundred years in his future. Alex wondered if he, himself, would have the nerve to do the same if the roles were reversed; or if he had to visit Vallini's era. The thought brought unease back into Alex's mind. Alex was an accomplished physicist. Everything he knew informed him that translocation in time was not possible, at least for a human. He himself had devised a method of translocating a certain type of simple particle… but *people*? And yet it was difficult to dispute the evidence in front of him that today, bizarrely, he had been consorting both with a person from the past and a person from the future.

Arbuckle seemed to have managed the transaction with the bartender without any problem, and he returned with his glass re-filled. Probably, to his advantage, his eccentric-looking attire reduced the expectation of normality in conversation and manners, pondered Alex. And he was always overly polite and amiable which can only help when dealing with people.

By the time the food arrived, Arbuckle was on his third glass and chattering away about the parishioners in his village. Alex, for the second time that day, remembered and regretted that George was not around to listen to the anecdotes. The historian would have been entranced, and eagerly asking questions. Alex himself was not following everything that Arbuckle was relating, since the old man was rambling somewhat, although he did slow down, to a degree, as they ate their meals. However, when he finished eating, his glass was empty, and he trotted up to the bar again. Alex was cognisant that he needed to keep an eye on how much Arbuckle was drinking as there was no sign of restraint on his part, but he thought maybe a fill of alcohol was just what the man needed after his emotionally difficult encounter that afternoon, so he did not begrudge the man his solace.

*　　　*　　　*

The final three races had gotten progressively more dull for Betty. The initial excitement and thrill of winning had given way to routine, and Alex had taken the kids home. She did manage some interesting conversation with Vallini, though he always refused to elucidate on any technical details that she asked about. He was clearly wary of the danger of prematurely introducing technological ideas into the present time that might be prejudicial to the natural continuity of the unfolding future. But with Gemma, who held back nothing, as far as Betty could tell, she felt increasingly comfortable.

"So," suggested Betty, as Gemma collected up the winnings from the last race into one of her bulging inside pockets. "I think such a successful afternoon calls for champagne all round?"

"Yes, good idea," agreed Gemma as they joined the crowd heading for the exits. "Have you ever tasted champagne, Vallini?"

"Often," affirmed Vallini. "It is a drink that has stood the test of time well."

"OK," said Betty. "Well, I'll drive us back to your hotel—I can easily walk home from there after drinks, and collect the car tomorrow morning."

But when they arrived, Betty hesitated by the car. "Actually, I don't want to sit in the hotel bar in case I might run into Arbuckle, so let's drink in the pub next door." She pointed to the 'Red Lion'.

"Good point," agreed Gemma. They walked in through the door and found a comfortable, fairly private alcove at the front with a sofa and two chairs. Betty sank into one end of the sofa and Vallini took a chair whilst Gemma went off to the bar to get a bottle of champagne and three glasses.

"So, Vallini," asked Betty. "What's your next move, now that the money problem is solved for the time being?"

"Well," Vallini considered. "One approach is the direct one—if I contrive to meet Arbuckle and see if I can get him to explain to me what he is doing."

"I don't think you'll get any further than what I have already told you. He thinks he is on a mission to send me somewhere, and he is simply taking his orders from the Sentinel."

"Yes," agreed Vallini, "though he might be able to explain to me more about the Sentinel, where it came from and who is behind it."

"I doubt it," dissented Betty. "I don't think he knows. I already explained to Gemma that he thinks an angel came and entrusted the device to him."

"An angel?" Vallini looked puzzled.

"Oh, an angel is supposedly a supernatural being in his religion, a sort of benevolent intermediary between God and humans who carries out certain tasks on behalf of God. They are often depicted with wings and halos and glow with light."

Vallini looked surprised. "I definitely need to learn more about the role of religion in early times."

"The point is," continued Betty, "that he has totally bought into a con that someone has perpetrated on him. Arbuckle is just following orders, thinks he is doing God's will, and knows nothing about the origins of the technology or the people behind it. Though to be fair, Alex said he was beginning to question the morality of what he was being told to do."

Vallini nodded. "Well then, it might be possible to drive a wedge between him and those behind the Sentinel. But it doesn't sound as if he would have much information to help us, even if he turned against them. The other approach to analysing the situation is by trying to understand the motive. It seems that you are the intended victim of their proposed translocation. You have already told us that this has echoes of the kidnap attempt on you that failed, and that the kidnappers wanted information. Then Gemma apparently overheard that work supervisor of yours, earlier this afternoon, suggesting that maybe you finally got that 'damn machine of yours to read the future'—I think that was the phraseology he used? I accept that you are not allowed to talk about this valuable information that you have, but it seems as if you have developed some sort of temporal device. And that is the information they are after. Am I right?"

Betty's head dropped. "I am not allowed to discuss the subject, but your logic is sound."

"Well, I am surprised, and impressed, that you may have discovered some temporal science at this early date. But it still doesn't make sense to me, because owners of temporal devices already have advanced knowledge of temporal science. They wouldn't need your knowledge. There must be something else to this. Is there something you are not telling us?"

At this point, Gemma returned with the bottle of champagne in an ice-bucket giving Betty pause to consider Vallini's question. Gemma laughed as she tried to fill the glasses with the rapidly bubbling liquid. The three clinked their glasses together. "To a job well done," toasted Gemma.

"Though it wasn't that hard, to be honest," added Betty. She downed the glass thoughtfully, enjoying the sensation, and leaned forward for Gemma to refill her glass.

"OK, Vallini," Betty sounded decisive. "I will tell you the last piece of the jigsaw that I know. I didn't want to, because your stated purpose is to maintain Temporal Continuity, and I suspect we, my colleagues and I, may have broken that continuity. You see, that kidnap attempt on me was foiled, as far as I understand, by a retrospective zap sent back in time, to kill the kidnappers. The past was changed to save me from kidnap and torture. So as I stated, the motive for the original kidnap was to extract information, temporal science, from me, for the benefit of other regimes in the present. But, the motive of the *Sentinel*, I guess, is probably more to do with setting the past back to how it was, or should have been, or how they would like it?"

Vallini looked initially puzzled. "But the past has not been changed. It is as it should be. The future is intact and as it should be." He took a long sip from his glass, still looking pensive. "Unless…"

Arbuckle stood. "I must visit the toilet, my friend. Have you noticed where it is in this establishment?"

"Through to the front, on the right," replied Alex.

Arbuckle picked up his bag and followed Alex's indications. As he stepped through to the front of the pub, he suddenly saw Betty sitting on the sofa in the alcove. He stopped abruptly, the encounter being quite unexpected. Then he recalled the indignation he felt at what she had done. He marched toward their table. "Miss Gosmore," he called rather loudly. "I am deeply displeased that you entered my room earlier today and rifled through my belongings. It is the height of discourtesy." He stumbled over the last word, the alcohol slurring his speech slightly.

Betty looked up, surprised and alarmed. "Oh, hello Reverend. Umm…"

The sound of a ringtone intervened in the exchange. "Ah, excuse me," Arbuckle seemed flustered. He flipped open his travelling-bag and pulled out the Sentinel that evidently was producing the sound. Alex had heard the encounter and was rushing up behind Arbuckle to defuse the confrontation. He noticed Vallini reach into one of his pockets and draw out some device that was concealed within his palm. But it was too late. The Sentinel had disappeared from Arbuckle's hand and reappeared a half a second later on Betty's lap. She jolted back in fear letting out a short scream, but within another half-second, she, the Sentinel, and a large part of the sofa that she had been sitting on, disappeared. The rest of the sofa, detached from its legs on one end, toppled. Gemma jumped up in alarm.

"No!" exclaimed Alex putting his hand on Arbuckle's shoulder.

"Oh, I... I...," stammered Arbuckle turning to him.

Then, as Alex and Gemma watched, the image of Vallini gradually faded from the chair on which he had been sitting.

Gemma replaced her glass on the table and pushed past Arbuckle, whispering in Alex's ear as she passed: "Room 113." She walked out of the pub.

"What have I done?" remarked Arbuckle looking troubled.

"I think you had better go back to your room now," replied Alex noncommittally, looking round to see if the events had garnered any unwanted attention, "before the pub landlord notices the damage. I will walk with you."

They walked back into the hotel in a shocked silence. "But how will I get home?" wondered Arbuckle out loud as he reached his hotel door.

"You had just better pray that the Sentinel returns for you," replied Alex, torn between contradictory feelings of anger and compassion. He left Arbuckle and went in search of Gemma's room 113 on the next floor up. He knocked.

Gemma let him in. She appeared to be packing her things into her rucksack.

"What? You're not just leaving?" protested Alex raking through his thick hair.

"No, no. On the contrary... Look, the first thing is I want to get away from here quickly, in case the Sentinel or its accomplices come back here snooping around. You know this town—can you help me find another hotel? Then we need to talk." She closed the top of the rucksack and headed for the door.

"Ah, OK, sure. I'll drive you across town—there's a small hotel near where I live." They made their way quickly down to Alex's car.

"Look, I'm really worried," continued Alex as he pulled out of the parking space. "Where is Betty now? And where has Vallini gone? Has

59

he followed?"

"Mmm… Well, I don't yet know where Betty is, but my equipment will have recorded fairly accurate coordinates of the jump since we were so close to it. So I will be able to tell you that, once I get established in a new hotel room. As for Vallini—the news is worse. He didn't follow. He just faded out of existence. Whatever the exact details of that seizure of Betty are, they have somehow changed the future so that Vallini no longer exists." Gemma's voice cracked as she spoke the final sentence, and she was silent for a minute.

They pulled up outside a Travelodge and signed Gemma in at reception for a couple of nights. Once inside her new room, Gemma pulled several pieces of equipment from her rucksack and laid them on the bed. Alex watched intently and silently but could discern little of their functionality from the way they looked—mostly grey flat boxes, one black. She unfolded one out so that it became a screen, and another a keyboard.

"I have to follow protocol, Alex," she stated, "so I must first *try* to report what has happened to TC control." Alex nodded and wondered why she had used the word 'try'. He leaned in so he could read the screen. She tapped some characters on the keyboard. After a few seconds, a message appeared on the screen 'No connection available'. She typed some more. "I'm trying the alternative backup service." Again the screen returned 'No connection available', this time with the appendage 'DD273'. Gemma buried her head in her hands and rocked forward on the bed.

Finally, Alex broke the silence. "So what does all this mean, Gemma?"

Gemma recovered her composure. "It means that the whole of TC has ceased to exist, Alex. The change to the future made by Betty's abduction has been so radical that TC never developed, it never came into existence." She looked pale and grim. "It is an eventuality that TC considered and planned for, of course. It's the doomsday scenario that people like me were trained to react to. I have protocols in my data store that I must read up now, but basically, it's up to me to try to recover Betty which, in turn, would restore the legitimate future. I'm going to need your help, Alex?"

Alex nodded, thinking. Gemma tapped some more keys on her keyboard and a mass of text appeared on the screen that she started to read.

"Wait a minute," interrupted Alex. "If TC now never existed, how come you have some of their equipment—it should all have vanished along with Vallini."

"You're right, Alex," Gemma glanced up from the screen only briefly. "But TC anticipated that problem, so they set up a modest fabrication plant in the deep past and made a small batch of equipment there. That's the stuff that is issued to people like me, so that TC still has a handle, a bootstrap, to re-establish itself if the future organisation disappears. Stuff made in the past is still with us now, stuff made in the future has ceased to be?" She glanced up again, looking at Alex's face. Then the grave expression that had been veiling her usually-affable nature lifted for a moment, giving way to a smile. "I remember our trainer telling us hilarious tales about how difficult it was setting up a fabrication plant in the past. They had to keep it all hidden of course. They had to make their own power supply and try to source from the indigenous population the essential minerals, or in some cases even mine them." She laughed briefly. "Look, I need to finish reading these few pages of instructions. Would you be a dear and make us both a cup of coffee?" She pointed to the kettle and ingredients on the desk at the side. "I only had one glass of champagne, but I feel the need to sharpen up a bit."

Alex did as she had requested, his mind lost in questions that wouldn't quite form. But he knew that Gemma was Betty's only real hope, so he was happy to be guided by her and not interrupt. However, he was already tempted by ideas of retrospectively zapping that damned Sentinel. Though he realised that was just an unsophisticated approach— better to listen to Gemma's TC expertise. Indeed the original Heiligenblut zap on Betty's behalf had apparently not solved the problem—there was more than one player.

Alex sat in one of the chairs, watching Gemma sipping her coffee and working her way through her briefing. At length, she sat up straight and drew a deep breath. "OK."

"Can we find out where Betty is now?" Alex asked, concerned to remind Gemma and promote the issue up her agenda.

"First, I have to put out a call to find out what other operatives might be available to help."

"I thought you said the whole organisation had winked out of existence?"

"No, only that part of the organisation that exists in the future. But there are maybe a few other operatives like myself in various places at various time points who might be able to help us—the ones with equipment that was deliberately manufactured in the past. And I need to put a call out to alert them to what has happened and let them know that we, here, are coordinating, as we have detailed knowledge of the actual temporal violation. She again spent time on the keyboard and Alex found himself waiting. He finished his coffee.

"And I needed to do that now whilst we know the Sentinel is not close by to detect any outgoing communication. We will know for sure when and if it returns because my equipment will alert me if any translocative jump disturbance is recorded. Our greatest advantage at the moment is that the Sentinel probably has no idea we are here, monitoring everything. So it probably wouldn't return on our account, but it might return to pick up Arbuckle, I suppose." Alex remembered that Arbuckle must be sitting back in his hotel room feeling bewildered and lost, worried whether the Sentinel would return for him, or whether he might be stranded forever in the here and now.

"Right, so now I'll query what the translocation exit coordinates are for Betty." More typing on the keypad. The screen changed to a world map. Gemma looked at it carefully and zoomed in. "So the temporal exit is back at the first of January this year, and the exit location is on the Black Sea Coast, the city of Constanţa in Romania." She looked over at Alex to see if he recognised the significance. He did.

"Oh God, this is a nightmare." Alex was distraught. "I wish I'd never discovered that damn *i*-vector. It's now the third time that Betty has been kidnapped, and my other colleague, George, got killed." He slumped forward with his head in his hands. Gemma gave him a second or two, and then came over and put her arm around him.

"Alex, we can fix this. We can fix it once and for all. We have good capabilities and the advantage of surprise. But you will need to explain to me the circumstances of those kidnaps—so that we know what we are up against. Betty told us, or at least implied, that you guys were working on some aspect of temporal science, and that the kidnap attempt was presumably aimed at extracting that information from her. But she didn't say that there had been more than one attempt. Can you explain the details to me please?"

Alex drew a deep breath and sat up, raking his hair back into place. Gemma sat on the bed opposite him. "OK, yes," he began. "So we had discovered, as you put it, some temporal science. It was intended to be

62

used as a surveillance device, picturing chosen sites at present or in the past, and we also accidentally discovered that if we overloaded the energy of the projection then we could cause a small explosion at the specified time and place—we called it a zap. And that we kept secret to ourselves. Somehow malign agents got wind that something important was happening in our building and they managed to hack a couple of peoples' phones—Betty's was one. So then, when she went on holiday to Austria, they knew her moves and attempted the kidnaps. The first kidnap was foiled retrospectively by sending a zap back in time to kill the kidnappers en route. At least that's what we assume—it would have been sent from a different timeline of course. But then there were other agents around who tried the following day. First, they erroneously abducted a woman driving the car that Betty had previously hired, but later they successfully snatched Betty from a hospital, that's when George was shot and killed. Fortunately, MI6 were on to it and they rescued Betty some hours later. Then a couple of days after that, one of the other workers, Kelvin, in our buildings was snatched and taken to a yacht in Constanţa. It just so happened that Betty learned the telephone number of the Russian agent on the yacht, and used the location of the phone to send a zap that killed him, enabling Kelvin to escape. She never actually explained to me that she did it—I just deduced it afterwards when I was looking at the log of coordinates used on our equipment. I thought she probably didn't want to talk about it, so I didn't ask."

"Hang on, so when exactly was the Constanţa agent killed by Betty's zap?" asked Gemma.

"Oh, that was a few days after Betty's kidnap. It was the Thursday I think, that would be the fifth of January."

"Ah, so too late to help us, then," remarked Gemma. "That timeline will have changed anyway. So are you still able to send those explosions, those zaps as you called them?"

"Yes, and surveillance. We can get pretty good pictures of anywhere."

"And are there any other team members apart from yourself and Betty?"

"Um, well, there's Harriet—she's an expert on surveillance pictures, but she's part of the military and doesn't know our whole story, so I wouldn't want to involve her too deeply".

"So basically we are up against both the Sentinel *and* Russian secret agents?" concluded Gemma.

Alex nodded resignedly. "I suppose I could notify MI6—they might help, though the explanations would be excruciatingly difficult."

"It's too late," argued Gemma. "The boat will have sailed by now, literally. Remember Betty was taken back to the first of January, that's weeks ago."

"True. Unless you send the MI6 agents back in time?"

Gemma blew through her teeth. "No, I think we'd better try fixing it by stealth and intellect before we resort to anything as blunt as that, thank you very much." They both managed a wry smile.

Chapter 5
Where there is much light, the shadows are deepest.
(Goethe)

Sunday 1st January, Constanța

Kuznetsov was poring over his maps in the cabin of his motor yacht. He had originally hoped to set off at first light the next morning, assuming the Romanian hirelings had done their job, and driven all the way from Austria to deliver the Englishwoman before then. That way he could cover the 200 km sea journey from Constanța to Yalta during daylight, and be on Russian soil at dusk. But they had fouled up. His agents in Vienna would now have to drive down to Villach the next morning before making the abduction, so at best he reckoned they would not arrive until well into the morning after. That meant delaying yet another day, unless he attempted the Black Sea crossing during darkness. He wondered about Sebastopol instead—it would take two hours off the journey time, but was busy with heavy shipping. He considered himself an experienced seaman but was still debating between destinations and the competing ills of darkness and delay when it happened.

A dull thud broke his contemplation as something landed on the polished teak floor near the corner of the cabin behind Kuznetsov. Startled, he wheeled around, his hand instinctively grabbing the pistol from his pocket. He sprung up, initially confused at seeing the woman sprawled on top of the piece of sofa, holding an empty champagne flute awkwardly. Following the instant of confusion, he then recognised her. It was his target—the Englishwoman—the face from the photos. His spirits lifted. But how was she here, what had just happened? How had he missed her arriving? Had he dozed off? The Romanians had succeeded after all? Where were they? He bounded to the door, flung it open, looked out and shouted for Dmitry.

Betty, as she fought to regain balance from being flipped backward and to the side on the broken sofa, cursed the fill of champagne that had tipped down her front. She thrust away the Sentinel that was still lying in her lap, surprised to see it tumble away, just as if it were any ordinary light metal box. She blinked as she tried to take in the new surroundings. The first impressions were of wood panelling and brass trim and strangely shaped windows, but her attention rapidly came to focus on the man standing with a gun in his hand swearing—in a foreign language. Russian, it sounded like, as memories crashed across her consciousness—that was the voice she had heard when she unleashed the killing zap. The voice of the boss agent as Kelvin had described him. And then the memory of being in the van, and the associated imperative feeling of needing to escape. And then the memory that she had a weapon—her phone. The man had run to the door, opened it and was calling. Here was a chance. Without taking time to get to her feet, she reached into her pocket for her phone, tapped on the killer app. The man turned in the door, facing her again. The chance would only last a second. She glanced at the screen—devastatingly, the indicator was only orange, not green. No matter, she just had to hope there was enough energy in the equipment to constitute a zap. He advanced a pace, the distance was right. She pressed the button... Nothing...

He ran across to her. "No, no, you can't phone your friends for help now." He grabbed the phone out of her hand. "Why the hell didn't Dmitri take that from you—the damn fool. Will they never learn?" He turned the phone off unceremoniously and slammed it on the table, all the while pointing the gun at her, as Betty struggled to her feet. "Now listen, Miss Gosmore. I am very pleased you are here." He grinned maliciously. "If you are sensible and cooperate, then you will not get hurt." He glanced at the Sentinel that Betty had tossed away. "What the hell is this?" He bent down and picked it up curiously, then reeled slightly at the sensation of the bio-scan, dropping it again.

Betty sensed his moment of vulnerability and rammed the empty champagne flute at his face as hard as she could. He half-dodged, but she caught him on the cheek and the glass broke, gashing his cheek. He fell backwards, swearing angrily. Betty bolted for the door. But he was up again, and on her before she could get through it. She had neither the strength nor the skills to deal physically with an experienced agent.

Angry now, he roughly pinned her against the wall and put a tie round her wrists, then round her ankles, and retrieved a syringe from one of the drawers. Betty took a small amount of satisfaction from the abundant blood flowing from his cheek that was now messing his clothing, parts of the floor, and her own clothes. But she wouldn't remember that. The memory would never form. The sedative took effect…

Kuznetsov tended to the wound in his cheek and cleared up the broken glass and blood, before carrying her limp body down to a bunk below decks. The brief action had largely displaced any curiosity that he had about the strangeness of her arrival. He took a hammer to her phone, then ditched it over the side of the boat. He contemplated doing the same to the Sentinel, but decided on caution, and pushed it with a broom out of the door and over the side into the sea. He was now back on track for departure at first light. Satisfied, he sat down at the charts with another whisky to make a final decision about the route.

*   *   *

Sunday evening, Cheltenham, Gemma's hotel room

"So these jump coordinates that the equipment has monitored are only accurate to within about 50 metres. This indicates the marina at Constanța, but we need to know more precisely. Didn't you say that your work colleague—Kevin was it?—that he was taken to a yacht—presumably the same one? So perhaps he knows the name of it?"

"Kelvin, yes. Though I'm not sure if he would know the name of the yacht. But I haven't got a phone number for him. I can ask him tomorrow at work—I am sure he wouldn't be in today, on a Sunday evening."

"OK, well, let's get it done then. I'll jump us into tomorrow morning."

Alex opened his mouth to say something, then closed it again.

"No need to be afraid of it, Alex. The jump is simplicity itself." Gemma packed her instruments back into the rucksack and started keying into her handheld controller.

"But what if I'm already *there* tomorrow morning?"

"You already know now, not to go into work tomorrow morning."

"And what if someone sees me materialise out of thin air?"

Gemma laughed. "No, we'll jump in time to tomorrow morning, but stay in this hotel room. That way no-one will see anything."

"What if the cleaner or someone is in this room?"

"That's part of the validation and checking process that the

67

translocation equipment makes in the split second before transporting us—that there's no-one in the line of sight, and no objects in the way. Come on. Stand over here, away from the bed and chairs, and get as close to me as you can. Put an arm around me."

Alex sighed heavily and shuffled over to where Gemma was now standing.

She grabbed him around the waist and pulled him close. "Right, now just bend your knees very slightly—it makes the landing easier." She poised her finger over the control. "Ready?"

"No, no." Alex pushed himself away.

"It's OK Alex, really just…"

"No, I mean I've just remembered. We don't need to ask Kelvin. When Betty initiated that zap that killed the agent, he was on the boat. So the exact coordinates will still be stored on our computer at work. I can just go in there now and look them up."

"Oh… OK. Can you get in there on a Sunday evening?"

It seemed to Alex that Gemma was still keen to project them into tomorrow. "Yes, that's no problem. Security are on the door 24/7. Harriet might be in—she works nights on the equipment."

"Ah, OK then. How long will you be? I'll go get a pizza or something and do some more thinking."

"About half an hour, there and back," guessed Alex.

Alex set off in the direction of GCHQ, whilst Gemma walked down the road the other way to where she remembered seeing a pizzeria when they were driving to the hotel.

*   *   *

"Evening, Fred. Is Harriet in?"

"Yes, she came in a while back, sir. Poor girl—having to work all these nights."

"Like you, you mean?" joshed Alex.

"Ah, I'm only on till two o'clock tonight, thank goodness."

Alex walked on briskly down the corridor and into the lab.

"Oh, hi Alex. Didn't expect to see you in?" Harriet greeted him.

"It's OK, I won't disturb you. I just wanted to look up some information. Can I use this computer for a few minutes?" The lab always looked different when Harriet was on shift—she had satellite surveillance photos on each of the computer screens with notepads neatly positioned in front of them.

Alex retrieved a list of the machine executions and searched back to early January to find Betty's Constanța zap—January 5th—that was it, and the further picture she had actioned two days later when she checked the scene. He jotted down the coordinate information carefully and double-checked it. He was just about to close the computer window when he noticed that the previous entry looked remarkably similar in coordinates. And… he was sure that the entry had not been there when he had looked a couple of weeks before—when he had been curious to check if his suspicion was correct that Betty had initiated that fortuitous zap that had killed the agent and freed Kelvin. He looked at the action date on that previous entry. It was on January 1st. It was impossible for an entry to appear retrospectively… unless… Had Betty managed a zap with her phone to free herself from this latest misadventure? He noted down the coordinates of the new entry and then called up the full information on that execution to examine it. No, it was not a zap, it was just a picture. And the data showed that the picture had never been processed. Intrigued, Alex checked whether Harriet was using the supercomputer. No, she was still charging the main device, so he set this newly discovered picture to process. It meant small-talking with Harriet for 15 minutes whilst the graphics supercomputer assembled the picture. Normally he would enjoy conversation with Harriet, but this evening his mind was full of Betty's problem and he dared not explain to Harriet what had happened. She was too close to GCHQ management and not party to the full capabilities of the device that she routinely used for surveillance pictures. Fortunately, as it happened, she was busy most of the time fielding phone calls from her satellite team.

Finally, the processed picture scrolled up onto the screen. The top showed a man's face, very close up, with a door behind and an unusually-shaped window. Ah, a marine window, realised Alex. Parts of the bottom of the picture were obscured, presumably by parts of the man's body, reasoned Alex, deducing that Betty had probably intended a zap, but the equipment had not been sufficiently charged, and so had delivered a normal picture instead. He felt a pang of sympathy for Betty who must have been bitterly disappointed at that outcome. So what had happened next?…

He snapped his attention back to the present, considering what to do. "Harriet, would it be possible for you to do me a favour and run two or three pictures for me tonight?" he pleaded.

"Sure Alex, if it's important. Who's that?" asked Harriet, leaning over and looking at the image on the screen.

"Not certain, but I think it's the foreign agent who organised the kidnap of Betty and Kelvin last month—we think we've got a lead on him. He's on a boat, and I wondered if you could run a couple of pictures so we could see the layout of the boat?" suggested Alex.

"The bastard. Sure I will, Alex. Those are the coordinates of the original picture are they?" she asked, copying the numbers from Alex's piece of paper. "Would you like me to run a facial recognition check on him as well?"

"Can you do that?" asked Alex surprised.

"No problem."

"But not if it will raise questions," protested Alex. "We need to keep all this completely under wraps at the moment."

"OK. I'll do it all quietly—completely routine. A facial only takes about three minutes," stated Harriet, cropping the face from the picture and entering some commands. "*If* he's in the database at all, that is," she added realistically. Alex printed off a copy of the picture while he waited, folded it and stuck it in his jacket pocket with the note containing the coordinates.

Harriet's screen pinged. "Bingo. There he is," she reported triumphantly. "Maxim Kuznetsov, Russian intelligence officer," she read. "I'd better not let you copy the dossier though." She skimmed through the text on her screen. "Bit of a drinker apparently... Anyway, when I've done the pictures of the boat I'll leave them in a file on your desk, so you can look at them in the morning." Her phone rang again.

"Thanks so much, Harriet," affirmed Alex, as he left to get back to the hotel and Gemma.

*   *   *

"Where the hell have you been?" barked Gemma, as she opened the hotel room door to him. "You said half an hour. It's been 55 minutes. I was worried sick that you'd got scared of the translocator and weren't coming back. Worried you were going to leave me to try to rescue your friend all by myself."

Alex noted the presence of the word 'try' and felt a bit disconcerted—so was Gemma not that confident of succeeding in a rescue? "I'm sorry," apologised Alex briskly, "but I had the chance to get some extra information. Look." He showed her the photo, explained the scenario and the promised pictures of the yacht's layout to come.

"In that case, I forgive you," said Gemma with mock generosity, taking the picture and trying to smooth out the fold creases. She placed it face down on the piece of equipment that usually served as a screen and made some keystrokes.

"What are you doing?" queried Alex.

"Well, scanning it in to let the TC equipment know that this is one of our targets. Some things might be easier to do with autonomous equipment. It's not only the Sentinel that can play that game."

Alex became aware of the smell of pizza in the room, and glanced over at the closed carton lying on the side table. Gemma noticed him looking. "Yes, there's a couple of slices left for you if you want them. But they are cold because you took so long," she warned.

"No problem," replied Alex and he picked up the carton and headed for the door.

"Hang on, where are you going," protested Gemma, still obviously concerned that Alex might abscond.

"There's a microwave for babies' food at the end of the corridor," explained Alex as he left the room. He returned a couple of minutes later with hot pizza, and sat at the side table to eat.

"So, listen," Gemma started. "I was having a good look on Google Maps while you went to your lab to get the exact coordinates. It's quite an extensive marina, but the coordinates point to yachts grouped near the end of a long concrete breakwater. Actually, it's wide enough to drive a vehicle down. That should make it easier for us to get near the boat than if it was moored on a floating pontoon—*they* tend to have locked-gates at the access end. Anyway, now we've got the exact coordinates, I think it would be a good idea to do a quick sortie just to see which actual boat it is and how the land lies."

"That sounds a bit dangerous," cautioned Alex, between mouthfuls. "There might be guards, or we might get noticed?"

"Indeed," Gemma nodded, "So that's why I suggest we go back to the night *before* January 1st—*before* Betty gets delivered there. I'll land us on the breakwater and we can just stroll along it like an ordinary couple out for a walk on New Year's Eve, and then jump back here. It will take 10 minutes tops."

"Look Gemma, no offence, but how much practice have you had in using this equipment?"

Gemma looked a bit defensive. "I've had six weeks of training."

"So how many times have you actually translocated yourself?" pushed Alex.

"Well, six. Seven, counting coming here."

"So that's not an awful lot of experience is it?"

"No, but managing the controls is mostly learnt in the weeks studying the tutorials, just like any technical knowledge. Actually pressing the button is not such a big deal. Besides, the equipment does an awful lot of checking around safety issues before it commits the translocation process. What is it you're worried about Alex?"

Alex sighed. "Well, I have a family, Gemma; a wife and two children. They are my prime responsibility. I owe it to them not to do anything dangerous."

Gemma didn't answer straight away. She nodded her understanding.

"For example," continued Alex. "I know you're proposing to land on the concrete breakwater tonight, not the boat itself. But suppose you did want to land on the boat. Have you considered whether it's low tide or high tide—the elevation coordinate could be radically different? If you didn't take that into account you could meet with a nasty accident."

Gemma took a deep breath and pulled her feet up under her. "I confess I hadn't thought of that Alex. However, in an instance like that, the translocator would mitigate the problem. If I had keyed in an elevation that was much higher than deck level, then it would not action the jump because it protects against falls greater than a few centimetres. Nor would it land me in collision with any object, wall or ceiling. And nor would it land me in water—though I think there is an override for that if it's needed in exceptional circumstances. But that's exactly the reason I need you to work with me—you can see technical issues that I hadn't thought of. And you've already delivered a picture and a name with your own technology that I couldn't do—although to be fair I suppose you can do all that without actually *travelling* with me." Gemma's voice betrayed some disappointment with her own conclusion. She started keying into her device again.

Alex raked through his hair with both hands, as he tried to work out the best thing to do.

"Ah," Gemma exclaimed, looking up. "Of course. The Black Sea is landlocked, so there is not much tidal variation at Constanţa—just a few centimetres between low and high tide… Sorry, Alex, I wasn't trying to rubbish what you said. I just wanted to check."

Alex nodded.

"One other thing I should explain. Before I jump I always program in the return jump so that it's ready to execute with a single button press. I could give you a duplicate controller if you like, so you can get yourself back by pressing the button even without me?" Gemma pulled out a handheld controller from a pocket in her rucksack, as if to offer it to Alex, but then she hesitated. "Oh, I'm sorry Alex, it's really not fair for me to try to persuade you. I understand your responsibilities. Look, I'll do that quick sortie to the Constanţa marina now, on my own. I'll return back here in a few minutes time. Will you wait for me so we can discuss what I see, please?" She grabbed her coat that was lying on the bed and put it on. "It's going to be cold there," she said by way of explanation, as she keyed into her controller, and stepped into an empty space in the room, away from the bed.

Finally, intrigue, curiosity and excitement overcame Alex's caution as the window of opportunity threatened to close. "No. Hang on, I'll get *my* coat," he quipped, jumping up and retrieving it from the chair he had tossed it across. He stepped over to where Gemma was standing. She grinned broadly, evidently buoyed by his decision. He held out his hand, palm upward. "The duplicate controller?"

Gemma pulled it out of the pocket she had stored it in and pressed a few buttons. A couple of synchronising bleeps issued from it and her own controller. She handed it to Alex and pointed at the recessed controls. "So you just press that main button and it will return you to here a short time after we left. OK?"

Alex took a deep breath, slipped the controller into his pocket and stood close by Gemma as she had instructed earlier. She put an arm around his waist. Alex assumed that the tightness of the hug reflected her gladness in his companionship, rather than being necessary for the process. "Bend your knees slightly." With her free hand, she pressed a button on her controller.

Alex felt a slight puff of breeze. Despite having been warned, he staggered slightly at the unexpected drop on landing, albeit only a couple of centimetres. Gemma steadied him with the strong arm around his waist. She laughed gently. "That always happens the first time. You quickly get used to it."

A metre or so away, facing them, was a high concrete wall topped by stones, and the cold air and slight drizzle struck them abruptly after the warmth of the hotel room.

"Damn," said Gemma, frustrated. "Sorry, I forgot to check the orientation again. It doesn't really matter; though it's nice to land facing the right way." She turned a dumbstruck Alex through ninety degrees and half-towed him into a walk alongside the wall, now on their right-hand side. "Stroll! We're just an ordinary couple out for a walk, remember."

It was dark and deserted. To their left now the odd boat was moored alongside, and across the water they could see a large number of yachts lined up against long pontoons, beyond which the city lights sparkled in the crisp winter drizzle. They both shivered and pulled their coats tighter around them, Alex putting his collar up. Ahead, the flat concrete of the breakwater stretched in a straight line for a couple of hundred metres before ending abruptly.

"We walk up to the end and back," stated Gemma, slipping the controller into her pocket and pulling out a handheld screen very similar to a mobile phone. "This will point us to the exact coordinates that you deduced, I keyed them in back at the hotel." A simple green arrow showed on the screen. They diverted a bit closer to the water's edge to get round a boat that had been raised onto the breakwater for repair. One of the boats they passed had interior lights on and they could hear what might have been a TV, but otherwise, there was no sign of life. Finally, toward the end of the breakwater, the green arrow was turning from roughly ahead, in toward the boats, until it pointed straight off at one of the motor yachts.

"So that's the one then," remarked Gemma, slowing slightly, but carrying on walking. "Can you read the name? It's in Cyrillic characters."

"Don't worry, it will be on Harriet's pictures tomorrow morning I'm sure—she's very thorough." The yacht looked similar to many others and there seemed to be no-one at home.

"It's almost tempting to try the door and have a look inside," remarked Gemma. "But there's no real purpose so it's not worth the risk."

"True," agreed Alex. "Even though the lights are out, there could be someone sleeping below decks." Suddenly a flash reflecting in the water grabbed Alex's attention. There was a loud bang. He startled and stiffened, his heart racing.

"It's OK," Gemma reassured him, laughing gently. "Fireworks. It's New Year's Eve here, remember?"

Alex drew a deep breath and looked over in the direction Gemma was pointing—onshore behind them. A couple more rockets fed flower-bursts into the sky terminating with bangs, delayed by the distance.

As they approached the end of the breakwater, marked by a triangular sign on a post and a pile of rocks, the wind, no longer held at bay by the high wall, whipped the rain across into their faces.

"Right, that's far enough," decided Gemma, and she guided Alex into a turn so that they headed back the way they had come, getting another look at the yacht as they re-passed it. Gemma had put the handheld device back in a pocket and retrieved something grey, no bigger than an ice-cube, which she tossed up to land amongst the stones on the top of the wall as they passed the boat.

"So what's that for?" enquired Alex.

"It's a miniaturised surveillance device," explained Gemma, "completely passive unless, or until, I send it a command. So it won't be detected. Just nice to have something in place in case we should need it."

They walked on. "We'll jump back from the same spot we landed on," stated Gemma. "That way we minimise any disturbance tracks. I'm thinking that we are close enough to the arrival point of the Sentinel tomorrow that our tracks would be assumed to just be echoes of their own. But we don't know how meticulously they scan for tracks, or if they'd bother to scan this area before they arrive, so I'll use another of the miniature devices to confound our track immediately after we leave."

They reached the approximate spot where they had arrived and stopped walking. Gemma retrieved another miniature device from a pocket. Alex took her hand gently so that he could look at the device. It resembled an irregular pebble, clearly having been designed non-geometrically, presumably to conceal its relevance. She keyed into her controller holding it against the 'pebble' that, in turn, bleeped its acknowledgement. Then she placed the pebble on the ground. "OK, ready to return, Alex?"

He nodded, actually quite wistful that the adventure was ending.

Again the puff of wind and the pair found themselves back in the hotel room, but facing a different direction than when they had left. This time Alex wobbled on landing but did not stumble, already beginning to anticipate the tiny fall on landing.

"So how was that for you?" asked Gemma.

"Extraordinary," replied Alex, swinging off his coat.

Gemma laughed. "Yes, that's a fairly accurate word for it, I guess."

"I've got a few questions though," he added sitting heavily down in a chair.

"Fire away." She resumed her cross-legged position on the bed.

"Well, firstly, what's that puff of air I felt each time?"

"OK, well, the translocator also takes along the bubble of air surrounding us, so, as we land, the air then immediately has to equilibrate with the ambient air there—it might be a different pressure or temperature so there's always a little disturbance."

"And the little fall when we jump—why doesn't it just place us neatly on the ground?"

"That's to do with the boundaries of the bubble. Whilst it's fairly easy for the translocator software to establish the actual boundary between the bottom of your shoes and the carpet here when you translocate out, it would be much more difficult for it to *predict* how your shoes would lie on an uneven surface—say we were landing on gravel or stones or grass. And the result of getting it wrong would be dire—the soles of your shoes welded into stones or whatever. So the designers decided to go the easy, safe route and just drop the traveller the final centimetre or so. The same goes for landing on a carpet—if it landed you on the top of the pile of the carpet then you would still sink slightly into the carpet, and until your weight is resting on your shoes, it would be a nightmare to try to calculate exactly how the individual strands of material would compress. So, given the risk of fusing shoe with carpet, it is just safer to stay with the standard drop. In fact, if you remember when Betty was snatched, she was sitting on a sofa, which must be non-standard for the Sentinel too, and the boundary was not clear. So the translocator ripped out the part of the sofa surrounding her and took that too."

"Ah, yes. I remember Arbuckle saying he was supposed to stand clear of the furniture!" Alex chuckled, although the humour was tempered by concern, as he recalled seeing Betty disappear. "And then

76

that pebble thing that you left behind on the ground when we returned—what was that supposed to do?"

"Right, yes. That was to cover our tracks. A fraction of a second after we left, the pebble would also translocate to some arbitrary place and then keep jumping a few more times, leaving a false trail so that we could not be traced back to here and now. It would normally end by jumping to a TC safe Way-Station, but because the Way-Stations no longer exist in this timeline, the pebble will just end up in an arbitrary place. I suppose I might be able to recall it later, after we fix the problem—I'm not sure." Gemma adjusted her position on the bed drawing her feet up under her.

"So what are you proposing to do next?" asked Alex after there was a short silence.

"Actually, I'm not sure," Gemma admitted. "I think I need to do a lot more studying of the TC guidelines drawn up for situations like this—there's plenty of information and advice accessible through this device." She gestured to the screen. "I think I'll spend a few hours reading and then sleep on it. Will you come back in the morning, when you've picked up the pictures that your colleague Harriet is doing, so we can discuss a plan?"

"Yes, sure. But I'd better get back home now. I'll return about 9:30 tomorrow morning if that's OK." Alex swung on his coat and headed out the door.

Now alone, Gemma allowed herself a moment of weakness and buried her face in her hands, humbled at the weight of responsibility she felt. Up until today, her association with TC had provided only fun and fascination. Now it had suddenly turned deadly serious with expectations on her, way exceeding what she felt qualified to deliver. The moment of payback had arrived for all the pleasure and excitement. There was no way she could retreat from her duty to rescue Betty—let alone her duty to the organisation that had trusted her with so much. She straightened up, took a deep breath and started studying the information and instruction that had been carefully compiled by TC on how to deal with a situation like this… But a situation that they could only theorise about and speculate on; the exact details of their possible demise they could never predict.

Whilst Gemma sat into the early hours studying, Alex by contrast, was fitfully tossing and turning in bed unable to get to sleep. Gradually, he sorted out that his worries were of two different kinds. The most straightforward concern was for Betty—his mind would keep flitting back to that boat and worrying about what she was being subjected to; and more diffusely what he could do about it, hopefully with Gemma's help. And there was an additional concern about Gemma's confidence in executing this—he had noticed her using the word 'try' on two occasions, rather than expressing confidence. The other strand that was repeatedly causing disturbance in his thoughts was the sudden challenge to his scientific knowledge. Today, he had witnessed things that challenged the very bedrock of his scientific understanding; and that understanding was broad and deep. He was having to try to accept, as fact, things which, two days ago, he would have dismissed as impossible, and scoffed at any suggestion of their plausibility. Such acceptance, without due explanation, comes only with emotional difficulty to the educated and scientifically gifted. At length one of the children cried out for some comfort after a bad dream, and it was the straightforward act of giving that comfort that brought his frenetic thinking to some sort of equilibrium. So that after a brandy, he was eventually able to get a few hours sleep.

Monday morning, Cheltenham

But the alarm went off far too soon and he felt wrecked as he sleepwalked through the routines of breakfast and getting ready to go to work, with the worries resuming their trampling through his mind. He could explain none of it to Petra, his wife, when she questioned his state. She was, of course, used to him not being able to discuss the secret aspects of his work, so did not press him, but she was clearly aware and concerned that something was seriously wrong. She cautioned him to take care of himself as he set off for the lab, knowing something of what had befallen Betty a few weeks before.

Alex was hoping to just pick up the file of photos that Harriet had promised to process for him, and then get over to Gemma at the hotel. But he found one of the MI5 officers, Clements, waiting in the lab office for him to arrive. He wondered immediately if Harriet had said something inopportune about Kuznetsov and the boat. He disliked Clements, remembering him as asking endless questions after Betty had been kidnapped, in a very officious way.

"Good morning, sir, how are you?"

There was no point pretending to these security people, so Alex admitted he was dog-tired, citing the half-truth that he had been up in the night attending to one of his children.

"Ah, sorry to hear that, sir. The reason I wanted to talk to you is that we are concerned about the whereabouts of your colleague, Betty Gosmore. She suddenly dropped off our radar last night. Do you know where she is?"

"Your radar?" queried Alex, trying to ascertain how much they knew before committing to an answer.

"Her phone went off the network yesterday evening at the 'Red Lion' pub and hasn't come back on. And we visited her home last night to check on her but she was not there."

"You mean you're tracking her phone?" Alex retorted, feigning a little outrage.

"Yes, sir. You know she had some troubles a few weeks ago, so tracking her is part of our strategy to keep her safe. Do you know where she is, sir?"

"No, I don't." Alex knew he couldn't avoid the direct question any longer. "Perhaps she has gone to visit friends where there is no phone signal?" he proposed, suggesting naïvety in such matters.

"But you were with her last night, in the 'Red Lion', were you not, sir?"

A pause. "So you are tracking *my* phone too?" again the feigned outrage, to buy a little thinking time.

"Yes, sir." Clements sounded as if he thought Alex was being very tedious. "We aim to keep *you* safe from hostile agents, as well, sir. I thought you would be pleased that we expend the effort, unless you have something to hide? Now, do you know where she went when she left the pub? Who was she with?"

"Well, no, I wasn't actually *with* her in the pub. I did say hello to her there briefly—she was with some friends from elsewhere. I was having a drink with someone else."

"Did you see her leave, sir?"

"Erm… No." Alex found his inner self briefly debating whether 'leaving' meant walking out of the door—in which case he was being honest.

"And do you know who these 'friends from elsewhere'—who they are, sir?"

"I'm afraid not—they seemed very nice," proffered Alex, wondering whether his lying was transparent to Clements.

"But she must have introduced them to you, if you said hello?"

Alex felt himself being backed into a corner with little room for manoeuvre. As if the situation wasn't complicated enough without MI5 wanting to know what was going on. And they would be no help in this. At that moment the door swung open and Phil Bowen walked in.

"Good morning Alex; ah… and… Clements isn't it? I heard you had come in—I hope there's no problem?" He offered a handshake.

"Ah, good morning, Mr Bowen. Yes, we have lost track of Miss Gosmore and I was just asking Mr Zakarian here, if he knows where she is."

"Ah, you should have asked me," Bowen whined in his managerial tone. "Of course I know where she is. She told me on Friday she had to go to the John Radcliffe Hospital in Oxford for another treatment appointment." He lowered his voice. "She has a serious genetic disease you know." He resumed the managerial tone. "I always ask my staff to let me know when they are going to be away."

"Ah, good." Clements seemed to perk up now that he had some concrete information. "That should be easy enough to check up on. John Radcliffe Hospital, you said?" he repeated the name, writing it into his notebook.

"Alex," Bowen continued, "I urgently need to check some details on that equipment order for the military with you."

"Sure," replied Alex, taking the opportunity to follow Bowen back into his office, assuming and hoping that Clements would be satisfied for the moment.

Bowen, as ever, seemed completely obsessed with the details he wanted Alex to check, and was unaware of the smile on Alex's face reflecting the serendipitous nature of his intervention. However, Alex's relief was tempered by the knowledge that MI5 would be back on his case soon and were likely to be an unwelcome complication. As he scanned the details that Bowen was fussing over, the back of his mind was already thinking about ways to throw MI5 off the track.

A couple of minutes later he was back in his own office hoping to pause only briefly for a coffee as he looked through the photos of the boat in the folder that Harriet had left for him. The five photos were thorough, as he had expected, showing the outside and inside layout of the boat, both above and below deck. However, Harriet had also left a note asking Alex to ring her as soon as he collected the file. He rang her number.

"Oh, hi Alex," she began. "You got the photos OK?"

"Yes, thanks a lot, Harriet, They're very helpful."

"Good. But there's one thing I don't understand, and that's bothering me, Alex. I actioned all the pictures with the same timestamp you gave me—on the 1st January. But the last photo in the main cabin has got Betty actually in it, sitting in the corner holding up a glass like she wants a refill. And there are two incongruous aspects to that. Firstly, why would she be socialising with this Kuznetsov guy? And secondly, I distinctly remember Betty, when she explained the events of the kidnap to me, saying that she was in Villach that particular evening with George—that's over a thousand kilometres away. What's going on, Alex? I can hardly believe it, but do you think Betty has been deceiving us about the kidnap and giving information to the enemy?"

Alex slumped forward at this new line of complication from Harriet.

"Alex? Are you still there?"

"Yes, yes, of course, Harriet. I was just a bit nonplussed by what you said, and thinking about how to explain things to you. So, firstly, no, Betty is definitely not deceiving us. There's lots of evidence from the Austrian police and MI5 that proves Betty was in Villach on January 1st, exactly as she said."

"So how do you explain her being in that picture then?"

Alex was thinking fast. "Well, maybe it's a double, that Kuznetsov was setting up?"

There was a brief silence.

"But in the picture, she was wearing Betty's exact clothes. Wait, come to think of it, that outfit in the photo—Betty only bought it last week. I remember her showing it to me out of her bag, with the label still on it, after she'd been shopping that afternoon. It must have been Monday or Tuesday. But that's impossible. How could she be wearing clothes in January that she bought weeks later? Have you been messing with the dates in the equipment Alex? What's going on?"

"Ugghhh..." Alex sighed deeply. "Look Harriet, I'm just going to have to ask you to trust us. You know we deal with some strange and clandestine science, which I am not allowed to explain to you. Right now

I have a difficult issue to deal with, and you have helped me by doing these photos. I just need some space to sort this problem."

A short pause. "Well, OK. But you sound wrecked Alex; are you OK? If you need any more help with anything, you will ask?"

"Yes, thanks, I will, Harriet. I didn't get much sleep last night. And if I need any more help I will definitely ask you again. I'm really sorry I can't explain things to you."

Alex ended the call and looked again at the photo with Betty in it. She had her phone in one hand—it was the instant she was trying to action a zap; and the raised champagne flute in the other. He could see Harriet's interpretation, but knowing what was actually happening at that instant, he could see that her expression was actually a rictus smile. He slipped the folder of photos inside his coat and turned to head out. Hesitating for a moment, he decided to leave his phone on the desk. He didn't want MI5 tracking him to Gemma's hotel. To MI5, if they even noticed, forgetting his phone would maybe seem credible and forgivable; but he was getting past worrying what might happen later on, and focussing more on ensuring the next few hours with Gemma were uninterrupted—hopefully, she had a plan. He crossed the road and headed down toward the street where Gemma's hotel was. The coffee had woken him a little but, despite the cold day, the sun was bright and his eyes felt jittery—he wished he had worn sunglasses. As he approached the roundabout he thought he saw Betty's car drive across. It was an instinctive assumption which, when he thought about it, he had to immediately dismiss as impossible, even though he would rarely ever see another midnight-blue cabriolet in Cheltenham. He rubbed his eyes and walked on to the hotel entrance.

*   *   *

"Uh. Why are you always so late?" Gemma was again stressed, worrying that Alex would not turn up. "You said 9:30."

Alex held up his hand to stop her. "Complications," he stated. "Big complications. Firstly, turn off your phone. MI5 noticed that Betty's phone went off-network last night so they are looking for her. They noticed that I was in the pub too, by tracking my phone, so they have been pestering me, and it's only a matter of time before they collect all the mobile phone data for that pub location and start tracing everyone. We may need to move you to a new hotel because both our phone signals would have registered together here yesterday evening, and that would connect you to me and the pub; then they'll start asking you awkward questions." Gemma obediently nodded and turned her phone off.

"And... unfortunately Harriet saw Betty in those pictures she did for me and has tried to put two and two together, getting impossible results. I think she will back off for the moment; I asked her to just trust me and give me some space. But to make things worse, I didn't get much sleep last night," he finished, slumping into a chair. "I think I'm almost hallucinating—on the way here I thought I saw Betty's car driving past."

"Uh, lack of sleep—me too," concurred Gemma. "I was studying, how about you?"

"I was worrying. And trying to square in my mind you guys trashing all the scientific understanding that I rely on for peace of mind..."

Gemma smiled some sympathy. "Yes, I found it disturbing for a couple of days when TC first enlisted me, but of course I didn't have a crisis to deal with at the same time, so I understand it must be perplexing for you."

"It certainly is. Anyway, how did the studying go? Have you worked out a plan to get Betty back?" Alex shuffled down wearily into the seat of the chair, desperately hoping for a simple positive answer.

Gemma squatted on the bed opposite him. "Well, there is a large amount of advice in the TC manual, but the bulk of it is about how to counter particular technical threats. And since TC was completely unaware of the existence of the Sentinel, or whatever organisation the Sentinel is part of, we have no way of knowing what specific technology might be used to defend their position. But we have to assume that there might be some defence, even though I still hope they have no idea we are on their case. So far the Sentinel has not revisited to pick up Arbuckle by the way—I have detected no more local translocations. So I imagine that device is still with Betty, perhaps guarding her against any attempt at a rescue?"

Alex nodded.

"Then there is the problem of getting past the Russian agent, or agents—there might be more of them. Oh, I've had contact from a couple of other TC operatives. One of them is actually a Russian woman. She offered to go with me and speak to him, distract him in some way, but I think that's just too dangerous and ill-defined. I also have to consider whether her loyalty to TC trumps her loyalty to her country, so I declined that suggestion."

"Who was the other operative, then?" asked Alex.

"Oh, a Korean scientist." Alex noticed Gemma look uneasy. "But I don't think he'll be much use either," finished Gemma.

"Why's that?"

"Oh, he just sees the situation rather differently from me. So I think," Gemma carried on, not giving Alex time to question that further, "that trying to do it in person is not a good idea—better to use the equipment to do it autonomously." Alex nodded his agreement—he had thought all along that trying to outwit a gun-toting foreign agent was foolishness.

"So what I propose we do," said Gemma firmly, shifting her legs to one side on the bed, "is to send six of these coordinated miniature devices together, as a swarm, from that spot in St. Mark's churchyard. Using that spot again helps to confound any tracking back by the Sentinel devices as much as possible. I'll program two of the devices to act as guards for the other four that will contact Betty, and translocate her back to the churchyard. So we will need to wait by the churchyard with the car so we can whisk her away quickly. There's a very good chance that she may be pursued by a sentinel device, so we want to be clear of the area as soon as possible."

"So what do you mean by the devices 'contacting' Betty?" asked Alex.

"Well the devices have to jump to somewhere near the ship, then locate her and make actual physical contact to be able to activate her translocation."

"But surely we know exactly where she is in the photograph—can't they just translocate in to those coordinates?"

"No, it's not quite that easy, Alex. There's an uncertainty principle connecting the time and place of the jump exit. You can get the time fairly accurate but be kilometres away, or you can get the position fairly accurate but be hours out. When we did our jump to the marina yesterday, I had programmed it to be positionally accurate to within 3 metres—that meant the time of our arrival was plus or minus about two hours, which didn't really matter—it was the place that mattered. And when Vallini and I jumped here, we again wanted to land fairly close to that spot in the churchyard where Arbuckle and the Sentinel had landed, to confound any tracking by them, so we couldn't specify the time of our arrival very accurately."

Alex had perked up and straightened himself up in the chair. "That's really interesting..." He looked lost in thought for a moment.

"So," asked Gemma, "is it the same for your... what did you call them... zaps?" asked Gemma.

"No, that's what is interesting. Our zaps are absolutely precise in time and position, so we must be using an entirely different physical principle than your translocators are using. But anyway, yes, let's get on and get Betty back. What do you want me to do?"

"OK, well, I've got the devices programmed," she patted one of her many pockets, "Can you drive us down to the St. Mark's graveyard?"

"Umm, yes. But I haven't got the car with me. I tell you what. There's another hotel about a few hundred metres along the road. You check out of here and into that other hotel, then we know, with your phone turned off, that you're lost to MI5's prying. Meanwhile, I'll walk home, get the car and pick you up from there."

Chapter 6
Time cuts down all, Both great and small.
(New England Primer of 1683)

Perpetuity Palace—Year 2792

"Grand Commander, I apologise for the intrusion, but I have to report that there has been a perpetuity outage."

"Yes, I am aware, I sensed a jolt. What duration was the outage?"

"The repair occupied 17 transpired units, sir. The discontinuity occurred early in the 21st Century. Only a few of our ancient Sentinel units were still available. The historical divergence was identified quickly enough, but examining the then-current records to establish the exact causal event was a difficult process; you will appreciate that ancient records were not always easily accessible online, or in great detail. However, our units eventually established that a communication of knowledge about early temporal science had not been completed as it should have been in our legitimate history. It is not understood exactly what caused that discontinuity, but one of the Sentinel units has rectified the situation by translocating the purveyor of that information directly into the hands of the intended recipients."

"Good. But we must have some idea of what caused the discontinuity?"

"Our working assumption is that some early temporal science was used intentionally, or accidentally, causing the discontinuity. We have detected no use of translocation equipment around the events, so there is no evidence to suggest that there was any organised attempt to disrupt our perpetuity. But, as a precaution, we have assigned multiple guard units at the site of the persons concerned, to protect against any possible attempt to further interfere with the course of the knowledge purveyance. Discreetly of course."

"This event is disturbing. I am minded to order the installation of more Sentinel units in ancient times."

"Indeed, Commander. But the difficulty is that the analysis capability of those units is hampered by the piecemeal nature of ancient records. In this case, the unit had

to coerce primitive human help to find the subject person."

"Such vulnerability is not acceptable. We must review our protection policy for early history. Please instigate such a review and report the proposals back to me."

*   *   *

Monday, late morning, Cheltenham

Gemma and Alex headed off in the car toward the graveyard to attempt the swarm-rescue of Betty from the yacht. The route back to St. Mark's would take them past Arbuckle's hotel and the 'Red Lion' next door. "I suppose I should drop in and see Arbuckle at some point," mused Alex, as he anticipated the landmarks.

"He'll be no use to us now," commented Gemma coldly.

"No, but he'll be frantically worried if the Sentinel has not returned for him, poor guy. Imagine being stranded 200 years in the future," Alex rebuked her.

"Oh, I didn't realise you had a soft spot for him?"

"Yes, I do," confirmed Alex. "It's not his fault what happened. He's lost and alone. And conned."

"We'll translocate him back to his home when we have sorted things out," suggested Gemma more warmly.

"Thanks. Yes. I'll tell him we can arrange that—I'm sure it will cheer him up."

As they drove past the hotel and 'Red Lion', Gemma looked out, replaying the events of the previous evening in her mind. "That's odd," she said, craning round and looking back at the road in front of the hotel.

"What is?"

"Well, Betty parked her car right outside the hotel last night—she said she would come back for it in the morning since we were all drinking. Though obviously she got snatched away so she couldn't have… But the car's not there."

"What?" Alex rubbed his eyes, remembering he thought he had seen that car crossing a street in front of him earlier. "God, I hope it hasn't

87

been stolen, Betty loves that car… Though I guess that's the least of her worries at the… moment." The slight hesitation betrayed Alex's difficulty in finding a word to express 'moment' for someone who was 'presently' in the past. He rubbed his eye again and snapped back to thinking logically. "Do you remember if she locked it?"

"I've no idea," responded Gemma. "But you don't think she might have got back somehow?"

"What? No, she would have phoned me… Damn!" Alex remembered that he had deliberately left his phone at work. They had now reached St. Mark's. He pulled over to the other side of the road close to the church and turned off the engine. He thought for a moment. "No, she can't have gotten back. It's not possible. Even if she managed to escape from the boat, she would have had no way of getting back to the here and now without a translocator, which she doesn't know how to use anyway…"

"… And I would have caught a translocation event on my detector, which I didn't," added Gemma.

"But do you think we should check my phone first, just in case?" questioned Alex.

"No, I think we should carry on," concluded Gemma.

"What would happen if the swarm try to rescue her from the boat and she's not there?" asked Alex.

"They would just return if they can't locate her—it's not a problem," Gemma reassured him.

"OK then. So I wonder if I should report the car as stolen, to the police?" suggested Alex.

"Then they would ask where the owner is—it would just add more complication. Like you said, it's the least of Betty's problems at the moment."

"Right, let's get on with it then. So what do you need me to do?" offered Alex.

"Well, come with me into the churchyard—we don't know what condition Betty will be in when she returns—it might need both of us to support her getting back to the car. But leave the doors unlocked and be ready for a quick getaway. We want to be some distance from here before any possible pursuing device arrives," warned Gemma.

"Let's go in by the side gate to make sure we're not seen by the vicar," Alex proposed. "Betty said he was getting a bit tetchy about strange people around, after Arbuckle, and then you and Vallini."

Gemma laughed. "He seemed quite polite to me. But, yes." They pushed open the ageing wrought-iron gate which made an unhelpful loud grating noise, then stepped through mildly overgrown creepers to a spot near the centre. Gemma knelt down and laid out her swarm of six pebble-shaped devices in a pattern on a grave there.

An unwelcome recognition occurred to Alex that it resembled a magic ritual scene out of a horror movie, albeit in broad daylight. He glanced over toward the church again, hoping, more so, that the vicar would not spot them. "So why are two of the devices a bit larger than the others?" queried Alex.

"Oh, they're the armed ones," explained Gemma. "They contain weapon functionality as well as the translocation capability."

"And what you were explaining yesterday about the linked uncertainty of time and place..." queried Alex. "Does that mean we may have to wait a while before Betty is brought back?"

"Yes. The fact that previous jumps have occurred through this place helps the localisation to be a bit more exact, and I've already programmed the devices to return within only a broad 50-metre radius, so the time uncertainty is not too great. Also, return trips are always more time-precise. They should reappear with Betty inside of 20 to 30 minutes. We'll wait over there under the yew tree where we'll be out of sight." Gemma pulled out her handheld controller and pressed a button. The devices bleeped synchronously and data showed on the small screen in her hand. "All good. OK. Here goes." She pressed another button and the tiny devices disappeared without ceremony. Gemma took a couple of paces toward the yew tree, but then stopped dead as her device made an uncharacteristic sound. She looked at the messages on the screen and stiffened. "We need to get out of here, Alex, quick..." She half-ran with difficulty through the creepers, round the graves.

Alex, alarmed, followed close behind. "Why? What's happened," he called.

"I'll explain in a minute. Just get us out of here, quickly," she responded, reaching the car and jumping into her seat, slamming the door behind her.

Alex did his best at making a fast getaway. Gemma was craning her neck back watching the graveyard intently, and glancing at her handheld monitor. "Back to the hotel?" asked Alex.

"Yes, but take the first corner and do a few extra turns just to be sure our route is not obvious."

Alex obediently took a cryptic route back to Gemma's new hotel. Neither of them spoke further during the rest of the journey, until they reached the relative perceived safety of Gemma's room.

"So?" plied Alex nervously, slumping wearily down into one of the armchairs.

Gemma took a deep breath. "I lost contact almost immediately with all of the devices in the swarm. Our quick exit was just to make sure that if any adversary came looking—we weren't there to be seen. I don't know yet what happened to the swarm but I can find out. You remember that miniature device I left on the top of the wall in front of the boat when we visited the marina last night? Well, it has been covertly monitoring and recording whatever happens in that area, so hopefully I can get it to transmit back to us. A bleep from her handheld controller startled Gemma. "Oh, an alien translocation—that is, I mean not one of our TC devices—has just been detected, presumably a Sentinel device. Probably into the graveyard investigating. But they are too late; we're long gone." She managed a grin.

"But couldn't it just keep hopping back a minute at a time until it finds us there?" Alex's throat was tightening.

"Theoretically, it could. Backwards surveillance is one of the tactics I read about last night in the TC information. But the time uncertainty between jumps makes that a difficult survey to achieve. And it would be making the Sentinel a sitting-duck as it performs the backward jumps. It doesn't know whether it's up against multiple enemy resources, so it probably won't want to chance a confrontation. But if it does try that, I'll have no choice but to quickly go back to the graveyard with an offensive weapon. A different blip sounded on the detector. "Ah, a D-subwave pulse. It's probably reporting back."

Alex took a modicum of reassurance that Gemma seemed to be able to monitor all the activity, though he felt sick with worry. He decided to visit the bathroom. When he returned, Gemma had unpacked the rest of the equipment from her backpack, and was studying data displayed on the large unfolded screen.

"So, Alex, the detector data confirms that the recent Sentinel translocation arrival was indeed somewhere in the graveyard, and the D-subwave pulse also originated there. Then while you were in the bathroom, there was another translocation event out of the graveyard. So it has either gone home, or will reappear, starting its backwards minute-by-minute survey of the graveyard, as you feared. We should know within a few minutes, because the time uncertainty for such a short jump is not big."

"So are you going to find out, from that monitoring device you left near the boat, what happened to our swarm of devices?" asked Alex.

"Yes, I will… eventually. But I dare not send a D-subwave request to our monitoring device at the marina until I'm sure the Sentinel device has gone from Cheltenham; because if not, we could reveal our position to it. We have to wait a few minutes to be sure…"

The few minutes seemed like an interminably long time as they waited, dreading another bleep confirming the re-arrival of the Sentinel. Alex decided to busy himself making a coffee for them both—his tiredness through lack of sleep again demanding some attention.

Another bleep sounded and they both tensed visibly. "Gemma read the information on the screen. "*Shit…* it *has* returned; about two minutes earlier. It must be starting a backward survey. We have to return to the graveyard, Alex, and send back an offensive device to lie in wait for it. Otherwise, when it does eventually work its way back in time and comes across us planting our devices in the graveyard, completely unaware of the danger, it will likely kill us; in the past—but we'll still be dead." Gemma hurriedly grabbed a couple of devices, threw them into her backpack, and urged Alex out to his car.

Alex was shivering slightly, but he did his best to drive them quickly to St. Mark's again. "So how confident are you that your offensive device will be able to eliminate the Sentinel device?" croaked Alex, as they got held up at yet another traffic light.

Gemma had been keying instructions into her controller. "Mmm… well our device will have a few milliseconds advantage since it will be continuously monitoring the area. Whereas the Sentinel device has to switch modes from translocating to detecting, when it arrives. I'll try to put ours in an advantageous position for monitoring, maybe on top of a gravestone so it has a view of the whole place. Though I suppose that might be a bit obvious—I'll think of something."

Alex did not feel reassured. "And is that our final hope? What if it fails?"

"No, that's not our final hope. If that fails, then we have to go back in time to yesterday evening and warn ourselves not to attempt that swarm rescue of Betty. Change the whole sequence of events. But that's an absolute last resort because TC warns that the time-loops created by meeting and advising oneself can get very complicated and ragged. At the moment it's a bit like a chess game, but we do have the advantage that *we* initiated the sequence of moves, and we actually have the nuclear option to *retract* that sequence of moves, by pre-warning ourselves. Whereas, *they* can only react to what we do."

Alex finally turned into the road leading to the church. "I don't understand why meeting our younger selves to warn them would get complicated, though—surely that's the easiest option?"

Gemma drew in air through her teeth. "As soon as we start to tell our younger selves not to attempt the rescue, then the future from which we came is completely different—we would no longer have had the need to go back and warn them, so we wouldn't be there with them. If our younger selves didn't then go ahead and attempt the swarm rescue, it creates a paradox that we were ever there to advise them so."

Alex palmed his forehead. "Of course! I think I may have already been through something like that once: I presume that I heard about Betty's first kidnap at Heiligenblut, and engineered a zap to save her, which seems to have succeeded. But, of course, I remember nothing about doing it because that action changed the past, making the kidnap not happen and my zap as a reaction, unnecessary."

"That's… interesting!" she replied with widened eyes. "You can explain it to me later though; right now I have to focus on this." She finished keying instructions to the controller. "So I have programmed our offensive device to translocate back to just after we visited the graveyard, placing the swarm. It is programmed to then wait, scanning for the appearance of a non-TC translocator which it should then attempt to destroy. Now, where should I place it?"

"How about in the yew tree?" suggested Alex.

"No, that is high. But because the standing gravestones are at right angles to the line of sight from the tree, there's a lot of hidden area behind them. Maybe on top of that tomb-thing to the side?" considered Gemma.

"Like you said before; that's a bit obvious. Hey, how about on the window sill of one of the church-windows; the middle one is high and has quite a good angle of view over the whole grounds," Alex suggested.

"Yes, perfect. OK. You wait here and I'll go and place it." Gemma jumped out of the car. Alex watched as she made her way in via the gate over to the church on the other side. She reached up, but couldn't get high enough to access the window sill. She waved at Alex to come over and help. He, in turn, worked his way round the stones and creepers to the church wall but, despite being tall, he also couldn't quite reach. Ultimately, he helped Gemma climb onto his shoulders so she could place the offensive device where she wanted on the sill, hoping that the vicar would not discover them and ask what on earth they were doing. It was the first time that the two of them had had any strong physical contact, despite working together for some hours, and the action caused them both to feel more bonded—though Alex could not help but become aware of Gemma's shapely muscle-toned legs, usually hidden by baggy cargo-pants with their numerous pockets. She jumped back down and checked her handheld controller again. "OK, off you go to protect us," she murmured, pressing a button. The assault device, rather larger than the others, though still irregularly shaped like a small stone, did not disappear.

Gemma made to leave. "Hang on," said Alex. "The device didn't go?"

"It did," Gemma contradicted him, glancing at her handheld controller to check. "I sent it back an hour, but of course it's still here an hour later. Come on." Alex palmed his forehead again.

*   *   *

"So, shouldn't be long to wait now," said Gemma as they arrived back in her room. "The Sentinel has done three more hops back whilst we were returning to the hotel—that makes ten in total, so I estimate the confrontation should be within the next 10 minutes or so. But if our armed device doesn't stop the Sentinel, then I will quickly translocate myself back to talk to ourselves in here yesterday evening, and warn us not to try the swarm rescue."

"So, explain to me again why that is problematic," asked Alex, furrowing his brow.

"Well, imagine it… I arrive… They, or rather, *we*… are surprised, of course. But that's beside the point. As soon as I say 'Don't try a swarm rescue…' that would probably be enough to dissuade them from doing it. So that this, my future from which I go back to warn them, no longer exists; and therefore I am no longer there with them anymore. I can only gabble out a few words before my future is eliminated, I disappear and they are left to figure out what future to pursue. There is no time to pass on detailed information, because as soon as I speak a word that *changes* the future, I, from the future, am gone."

Alex nodded thoughtfully. "So would we, then, no longer exist anymore?"

"Are we separate or different from them?" replied Gemma rhetorically. "The spotlight of time, which is where our consciousness resides, is now. But when our 'now' no longer exists, the spotlight reverts to 'then', I guess. I don't know, I have never tried it out. Vallini could probably explain it better. But I know TC are discouraging about doing such things except as a very last resort."

"Ah," said Alex enthusiastically, "I remember we once did an experiment in our lab where we created two parallel presents; there were two of me, two of Betty and two of George. And I found it was possible to switch between the awareness of one or the other of myself at will."

"Wow," Gemma enthused, "you must discuss that in detail with Vallini and myself sometime. You have certainly broken some interesting ground with your—what did Vallini call it—*primitive* temporal science."

"I think we were following a very different path from TC technology—your science is based on an uncertainty relationship of time and location whereas ours is precise. But *you* can translocate actual objects and people, whereas we could only do it to a small uniform cloud of particles..."

"Anyway," continued Alex, "why did you say *you* would go back to warn us yesterday? Could I not go too?"

"Oh, no reason. No purpose, either. Why? does it bother you?"

"Yes... I don't feel I would like to be alone when I cease to exist," suggested Alex

There was a pause of a second or so whilst their brains tried to assemble reason out of the koan-like statement. Then they both laughed.

"OK," purred Gemma. "You can come too. We'll cease to exist together—I'm sure that will be more romantic." Unfortunately, that word crashed Alex out of the enjoyment he was getting from discussing deep issues; as his thoughts jolted back to Petra and his children, and his mood reverted to anxiety about Betty, tiredness, and the safety of all of them..."

Gemma noticed his sudden shift of mood and posture, and regretted that she had maybe carried the fun, a word too far. She was about to apologise when a double-beep sounded on the detector. Gemma quickly rolled from her semi-recumbent posture to look at her screen.

"Yeess!" she announced. "Our weapon on the church window sill destroyed the Sentinel device the first time it saw it reappear. Right. Now I'm confident to send a request to our surveillance device back at the yacht without giving our location away. Of course, as soon as our surveillance device there starts transmitting, it will reveal its own position. I anticipate it may well then come under attack from Sentinels guarding the boat, so we may not get a very long stream of surveillance data. I'll instruct it to start sending the view as it was a couple of seconds before the arrival of our swarm." She spent a while assembling a set of commands on the screen, double-checked them and then with a small flourish of her index finger sent the request.

A couple of seconds later there was the characteristic beep, followed about a second after that by an unusual beep sound that Alex remembered from the graveyard, when something had gone wrong with the swarm. Alex moved from his chair over to the bed where the screen was laid out anticipating that there would be something to watch.

"OK, so here's the view from our miniature device on top of the wall just before our swarm arrives." It was dusk in the marina; the boat was visible below, with a light on in the cabin. Otherwise, it looked very much as they had seen it during their brief visit to the marina, except that there was a bag sitting on the breakwater above the boat. There was no obvious sign of any Sentinels. "Right, now I'll run the video," said Gemma, pressing a button. For a second or so, nothing changed. Then there was a brief confusion of flashes and loud cracks—Alex was surprised that there was sound on the recording—and some pieces of debris appeared to fall on the boat and into the harbour beside it. Gemma breathed in sharply. "Well, I suppose that was about what I expected," she commented.

"Can you replay it in slow-motion?" asked Alex. "So we can see more clearly what happened."

"Yes. Oh, wait." The video had continued—the scene quieting to how it had been before the swarm arrived. But then a man emerged from the cabin door. Cagily at first, gun in hand. Scanning round about.

"Ha. That woke him up," remarked Gemma coldly. "Presumably

he's got no idea what's going on. He doesn't know he's being protected." Then the picture cut out abruptly. "As expected, they must have destroyed our reconnaissance device as soon as it revealed itself by starting to transmit... Anyway, I'll play the whole thing back in slow motion now."

In extreme slow-motion, it looked like a scene out of Star Wars. Lines of tracer extending from various points on the ground into the space above and around the boat, mostly ending in broad flashes. Two tracer lines from above the boat toward the ground ending in flashes on the ground. It was all over in half a second. Gemma read the data that had been transmitted with the video. "Wow, our reconnaissance logged 37 alien devices around the boat. Our swarm never stood a chance, though it looked like they took out a couple of the Sentinel devices in the melee."

"So, what type of offensive weapons are they?" asked Alex. "Some sort of laser?"

"Oh Alex, you know I don't understand the TC science—I just *operate* the equipment. Vallini wouldn't explain it even if we asked. My guess is it's some sort of focussed emf pulse."

Alex nodded disappointment.

"So," continued Gemma. "The big question is what to do next. We know that they have big resources, but they don't know what little we have, although they do know we can do them damage. So I expect they will prefer to keep their resources defending the boat rather than try to assault us here. I will have to call in the other TC operatives, though—I am almost out of devices apart from my personal translocator. But I think I will ask them to arrive somewhere other than that churchyard— we have overused that. Is there a suitable park or something nearby?"

"Umm, yes. There's a massive grassy area called 'Fiddler's Green' not far from here. Gemma looked at the map of Cheltenham on her screen. "Ah, yes, perfect. The bigger it is the more uncertainty we can allow in location and the smaller the time-arrival window. I'll ask them to arrive around dusk today, and I'll meet them and book them into this hotel. Why don't you go and get a couple of hours sleep, and we'll meet again this evening?... Oh, but can we just pop by St. Mark's graveyard one more time—I ought to collect the debris from the destroyed Sentinel. I don't want to leave any suspicious or dangerous stuff lying around."

Ten minutes later they were again opening the wrought iron gate and trudging through the undergrowth. "Do we need to search the whole graveyard?" asked Alex wearily.

"Not at all. I know where it is from the data and the mapping on the detector," Gemma replied, heading purposefully to an area near the back, away from the church. She pointed. "It should be somewhere near that gravestone with the Celtic cross on top." They walked round the area and sure enough soon came across an apparently metallic book-shaped object, smaller than the Sentinel as Alex remembered it, lying incongruously across a bunch of wilting flowers.

"Hang on," Gemma put her hand on Alex's arm to stop him from approaching it. She pulled a small detector out of one of her trouser-pockets and pointed it at the object. "OK, it's inert." She removed a black padded bag from her backpack, bent down and worked the object into the bag without touching it. She then sealed the bag with a zip and put it in her backpack. "OK, all done."

"What about our device on the window sill?" Alex reminded her.

"No, I'll leave that there as some small insurance against another Sentinel resource arriving."

Alex then dropped Gemma back at the hotel. "As we are not using mobile phones, would you like me to lend you one of the TC communications devices so you can contact me if needs be?" Gemma suggested cheerfully.

"No, I sometimes get security-searched on the way in and out of the lab so I don't want anything suspicious in my pocket," Alex decided.

"Sure. OK, see you this evening maybe around half six or seven?" agreed Gemma.

Alex decided to go into the lab briefly on his way home, to pick up his phone. As he walked in through the entrance to the building, he was dismayed to see Clements, the MI5 operative, approaching, apparently on his way out. There was no avoiding him—though Alex dreaded further questions from him.

"Good afternoon, sir," Clements started. "We managed to get confirmation from the hospital about Miss Gosmore's attendance, by the way, so all's well…"

"Jolly good…" Alex heard himself saying noncommittally. And doing his best to show a lack of concern, he walked on through. Alex wasn't sure whether he was relieved or confused. He certainly felt lucky that MI5 had apparently satisfied themselves, and he wasn't going to be faced with further questions; but confused because MI5 were usually very sharp. However, Clements had pointedly said confirmation from the hospital, not from Betty herself. Ultimately, he decided not to overthink it—if they were happy, he could focus on more important issues. Back in the office, he retrieved his phone and pocketed it. He had wondered about actioning some more photos of the boat, but decided sleep was the priority, so headed home to get a nap before the meet-up with Gemma and her drafted-in colleagues that evening.

"Grand Commander, again I apologise for the intrusion, but I have to report that there has been an attack on our units guarding the purveyance of information that I detailed earlier. The attack was organised. A swarm of six translocating devices of unknown origin approached the vessel that housed the human subject. We suspect they were intending to remove the subject rather than attack us because they were not heavily armed. All the alien devices were destroyed, as were two of our units in the exchange of fire. We sent a scouting Sentinel unit to investigate the origin of the attackers, but it was destroyed. We have now doubled the guard on the vessel."

"An organisation possessing translocating devices—how can we not have known of such an organisation as this before?"

"Presumably the organisation arose within the alternate timeline that existed during our perpetuity outage."

"Obviously it could have grown there. But how could an organisation have bootstrapped itself into existence to cause the outage in the first place? There may be a treacherous underground movement within our ranks that initiated the outage. A sweeping investigation is called for. And the purveyance of that critical information must be ensured by protecting those persons until the transfer is complete. How long does that take?"

"Initially there is a journey by sea-vessel followed by a land journey, and then some time in an establishment. We will keep a maximum number of guarding units in place around the subject at all times, but the journey by sea-vessel is the most challenging since we have no surface, other than the vessel itself, on which to position our Sentinel units. So, discretion will be difficult using more guarding units."

Chapter 7

Be strong enough to stand alone, smart enough to know when you need help, and brave enough to ask for it.

(Mark Amend)

Monday, early evening, Cheltenham

Sleep had not come easily to Alex; nevertheless, he had managed a couple of hours before his alarm woke him at six that evening. He hurriedly showered, dressed and grabbed a sandwich to eat on the way to Gemma's hotel; but he purposely left his mobile phone at home so that he could not be tracked to the hotel. He knocked on Gemma's door, but there was no answer; so assuming she had gone to meet the arriving TC operatives, he set off toward Fiddler's Green. Then, just as he rounded the first corner he saw the three of them approaching. Apart from the fact that they all had identical backpacks, they all looked strikingly different.

Gemma introduced Alex straightaway. Sveta was the Russian lady; tall, chiselled cheekbones and very smartly dressed. The standard TC backpack looked somewhat incongruous on her and she seemed to slightly disown it by having it slung over one shoulder. She had brought a small suitcase as well.

Then Gemma introduced the middle-aged scientist from Seoul, Choi Joo-Won, whose dark-rimmed spectacles lent him a distinguished air. "I am oceanographer," he stated in reply to Alex's question, having to repeat the word twice, so Alex could understand his accent. "Research methane hydrate reservoirs in deep ocean."

At the hotel reception, Alex was impressed to see that they had both brought current passports, and Sveta even managed a valid credit card. Alex helped bring a couple of chairs from Sveta's room into Gemma's so that they could all sit, and with very little preceding small talk, Gemma started briefing the others on exactly what had happened. They listened without interrupting. She described the facts without interpreting what the events meant, and without suggestions as to what should come next, such that Alex wondered if TC had taught them some protocol about how to interact in such a situation. Sveta asked about what resources Gemma had remaining, and Joo-Won asked a couple of questions about positions and times. Then Gemma passed the spotlight to Sveta, asking for her analysis.

"Firstly, it seems striking," she began, "that our adversary, shall we call it the Sentinel organisation, is showing considerable resources, in terms of numbers, at least, at the site of the boat in Constanţa as they defend their position. Whereas they were completely unknown to TC previously, despite the vast surveillance resources of TC at that time. And conversely, we know that TC now has very little in the way of resources—just our own. It seems that the Sentinel organisation has bootstrapped itself into existence at the expense of TC. So, the potential for transfer of information from the captive, Betty, to Russian intelligence, seems to be pivotal in determining the dominance of one organisation or the other—TC or Sentinel. I would suspect that the future organisational dominance arises from geopolitical differences, rather than from the actual primitive temporal information itself, because both advanced organisations' science must be way beyond that. Thus the status quo now, the current timeline trajectory, gives the Sentinel organisation advantages, both in terms of the default position being in their favour, and in terms of physical resources." Though Sveta's accent was evident, she spoke with perfect English, and precise analysis.

"It is not obvious to me," she continued, "how we could now successfully attack their position to rescue the captive. We may need to think about intervening at an earlier time, such as when the Sentinel machine was apparently on its own before snatching Betty. However, the disadvantage of doing that is that, in changing the timeline, we would lose the knowledge we now have about their organisation and their aims. That is because the timeline change would occur before we learned about those things. So, we may then just face the crisis in some other form..." She paused. "Joo-Won, your thoughts?" Sveta sat back in her chair having relinquished the focus.

"Yes, I agree all you say." Joo-Won's English was far less accomplished, but readily understandable. "But I wonder if maybe we attack their position in different way. Instead of materialise in the air near boat, we could materialise underwater and attack boat, to sink it.

Without boat, the default position of captor being taken to interrogation cannot happen, the default timeline switches to be in TC's favour, and we regain upper hand."

"That would not work, Joo-Won," Sveta cut in sharply. "As soon as they realise that the boat is sinking, they could translocate the captive away, maybe deliver her more directly to the interrogators. That is maybe not the detailed timeline they prefer, but it would likely suffice to continue their supremacy. And indeed, we would be in a worse position. At least at the moment, we know precisely where the captive is."

Alex felt alarmed at the direction the discussion was taking—sinking the boat seemed rather at odds with rescuing Betty. However, he did not feel it was his place to interrupt their discussion.

Joo-Won did not seem offended by Sveta's rejection of his idea. He nodded. They clearly were happy to brainstorm ideas. "So maybe," he suggested, "we should not see rescue as being the *only* way to defeat the transfer of information. Perhaps it would be simpler and more practical to *kill* the captive. Then, we have instantly established the default position of no transfer of information to the interrogators, and TC would be re-established. The Sentinel resources would again be minimal and overwhelmed by our TC resources. And we would be aware of their intentions, so it would be difficult for them to attempt another snatch of the captive at a time previous to her death."

Alex jumped to his feet... "What?... No. You can't. What kind of solution is that? Personally, I don't give a damn which organisation exists or doesn't exist, I am just concerned about the welfare of my friend. She is innocent in all this, abused and in need of help..."

"Alex... Betty's welfare is intimately linked with TC's existence, and the danger to her is intimately linked with the Sentinel Organisation..." Gemma tried to intervene.

"No, I'm not listening to any more of this..." Alex strode toward the door.

But Sveta rose from her chair, closest to the door, and blocked his way. She put her hands on his shoulders. "No, listen to me, Alex. You do not yet understand. If... and I say *if*, we managed to kill Betty, then, because we would then have control of the situation, we could just rescue her from a moment before she was killed. Killing her is only a tactical, temporary move. We kill her, but then we rescue her from a time before the killing, so that the killing timeline is redundant—it never then actually takes place."

"What?... So she could still be returned here and carry on with her life?..."

"Yes. Exactly," declared Sveta "But... I do not yet see a way in which we could kill her. To do that we would need to translocate close enough to determine her exact position. It is the same problem as trying to rescue her. We cannot get close enough. As soon as our devices materialise anywhere near the boat they would be destroyed by the Sentinel guards who outnumber us. Indeed, they have probably reinforced their numbers after Gemma's failed swarm-rescue attempt." Sveta gently pushed Alex toward his chair, and resumed her seat. "Or did you have a plan to get close enough, Joo-Won?" It sounded like a genuine question.

But Joo-Won shook his head. "No... I suppose if send everything we have in one attack, there is chance one device get through; especially if we confuse them by materialising underwater."

"No," Gemma interjected, "the bio-scanning would not work underwater, so our devices would still have to emerge anyway to try to locate Betty."

"Ah. Of course." Joo-Won nodded again. He adjusted the cushion on his chair.

"So," Sveta put in, "there is the possibility that I spoke about with you, Gemma, the other night. If I translocate to somewhere near the boat before Betty is sent there, *before* it all gets infested with Sentinel devices, then perhaps I could befriend this Kuznetsov to gain access to the boat, and when Betty arrives, I could..."

"I can't see it working, Sveta," Gemma cut in, shifting the position of her legs. "Though it is very brave of you to suggest it. You would have to leave all your equipment well away from the boat because otherwise the Sentinel devices would detect it when they arrived. Kuznetsov is unlikely to let you onto the boat, and would certainly check you for a weapon anyway. But *you* know how ruthless and careful these people are, better than we do, Sveta. And there's no way we could rescue you after the Sentinel devices arrive."

This time it was Sveta who nodded, acknowledging her idea was defective. "So then," she continued, "if we conclude there is no way to get close enough to the captive on the boat, then we must revert to trying to prevent the capture of Betty in the first place. From what you said, Gemma, Arbuckle's single Sentinel device was exposed for a second or so just prior to the abduction, in the pub? Perhaps we should translocate a couple of our devices into that room, to a time before the abduction takes place. Then our devices would be in a position to destroy the Sentinel device when it appears. Of course, it is not ideal because then you, Gemma and Alex, would not know how or why that had happened, you would not know the possible threat of the Sentinel organisation, or any of the details which have emerged, and so Betty would probably still be vulnerable to another attack at a later time. We would be restarting the timeline from that point—Betty would temporarily be safe, but the future would be uncertain." Sveta took a sip from a glass of water.

"Yes, that's true," Gemma took up the narrative. "But I fear even that action might be difficult. Now that the Sentinel organisation has the upper hand and significant resources, it might well have positioned its own guard devices back in time, to critical points like the abduction of Betty in the pub, specifically to prevent us carrying out the action you have described."

"Oh, I had not considered that," sighed Sveta.

"But," argued Joo-Won, "there must be limits to their resources. They could not possibly place guards around Betty at all points in the past. There must necessarily be times when she is..." he paused, glancing furtively in Alex's direction. "... when she is accessible to us."

"True," replied Sveta, "but the earlier in time we make an intervention, the less would then be understood, in that altered timeline, about the threat from the Sentinel organisation, so the more likely would be another abduction attack from them."

"Oh dear, it seems intractable," concluded Gemma. "Perhaps we should break for some food now and resume later when our minds have mulled it all over?"

They retired to the hotel restaurant where, now in public, they could talk about anything except the taboo subjects of TC and Sentinel. As they ate, Alex and Joo-Won engaged in a discussion about their scientific interests, although Alex steered clear of the *i*-vector theory. While he had earlier felt that Joo-Won was rather simplistic and cold in his analysis of the situation, his respect grew as Joo-Won generously credited the work of others in his field, and of some of his graduate students. Ultimately, he felt that Joo-Won's analysis had probably been right, bearing in mind that Joo-Won had no direct knowledge of Betty and thus no vested interest in her welfare. Later, as happens with an unfolding meal, the conversations switched round and he started talking with Sveta, who, he learned, was a hospital doctor in the suburbs of Moscow. She seemed interested to learn about Betty, and Alex found himself recounting stories of how they had met, some of their early work together, and how Betty had other interests like drama and music. Gemma occasionally flashed him a reassuring smile, though he could sense that she was uneasy with the lack of a clear plan emerging from the previous discussions.

After the meal, they trooped back up the carpeted stairs to Gemma's room. "So, Joo-Won, any further thoughts?" asked Gemma.

"I have no new ideas," he replied. "It is a choice of full-on assault, hoping one of our devices can get through; or intervention at an earlier time. No option seems good. Not even near-good."

"Sveta?"

Sveta shrugged. "Maybe we should send some reconnaissance probes back to assess potential past critical times, like when the Sentinel appears in the pub, to check whether there is now an additional guarding Sentinel presence, before we decide?"

Gemma glanced over at Alex briefly, but then looked away when he said nothing…

"… Actually, I do have a suggestion." Alex's voice was small; as if he didn't really want to speak. "But can I just ask you to clarify a couple of things for me first?"

"Of course," Gemma beamed reassuringly at him, as the others turned their gaze on him.

"Well," began Alex, "Sveta said earlier that you could successfully rescue Betty even if she was killed, because you could rescue her from a time *before* she had been killed. Is that right?"

"Yes," replied Gemma. "The reason we can't just rescue her from the boat *now*, is that the Sentinels seem to be in total control of that environment. But if we could find a way to kill her, then that instantly changes the future, because she would never then be able to give the critical information to her captors. It's that giving of information to her captors that causes the world to evolve in a way that ends up with the Sentinel in charge. So, if she dies, then the Sentinel organisation ceases to exist; in the same way that TC ceased to exist when the Sentinel device snatched Betty from us. And, as soon as Betty dies, all those Sentinel guards round the boat cease to exist—well, almost all of them. We know from the Arbuckle experience that there might still be a handful operating; very much like us in this room are the remnants of a ceased TC. Anyway it ought then to be easy for us to rescue Betty from the boat at a time preceding her death. The Sentinel guards will be gone from the boat both before and after her death in that altered timeline. However, the problem with all that," added Gemma, "is that right now, it is difficult for us to access Betty on the boat, whether we wanted to rescue her *or* kill her, so I think it's a moot point... unless... weren't you explaining earlier today that although TC translocation technology works with a measurement uncertainty to the destination place and time, your rudimentary technology works on completely different principles, and is *exact*, in respect of coordinates?"

Alex nodded. "Yes. You've anticipated me, Gemma." Alex felt rapt attention from Sveta and Joo-Won. "It seems from what I understand of your discussions that the difficulty in accessing Betty is because your translocations can only get to somewhere *near* the boat, due to uncertainty in the translocation exit. And as soon as your TC devices appear, they are subject to observation and attack by Sentinel guards. But, it would indeed be possible for me to send a precise zap using my equipment... That is an energy bolt," he explained, turning to Sveta and Joo-Won. "An energy bolt directly to an exact place and time. So if directed at Betty, it would indeed kill her. But you must understand that it would be impossible for me to commit to doing that to my dearest friend, unless I am completely confident that you can then rescue her from a time before her death and bring her back here."

"Yes, Alex," Gemma was now kneeling up on the bed, her posture showing a shift out of her unease when the situation seemed intractable. "Yes, that's the answer. To be absolutely fair and honest with you, nothing is guaranteed—but from everything that we understand so far, Betty's death should see the Sentinel guards gone, and then we just have to get past Kuznetsov—but we have bio-signature locators and weapons, and we outnumber him."

"Actually," Alex interrupted, "he's not a problem—I can send a zap for him too. He deserves it. In fact, he did get zapped, that's before Arbuckle's Sentinel changed the timeline." Alex suddenly wondered if he shouldn't have said that, as it was probably confusing to Sveta and Joo-Won, but they seemed to take it onboard easily enough—presumably accustomed to thinking about timelines, mused Alex.

"And," Joo-Won put in, "although, as Gemma says, we could not guarantee rescue Betty, you should also consider that her life, if she lived on, would not be of good quality in hands of her captors."

"That's not helpful, Joo-Won," Gemma said flatly in the same tone she had used to Vallini when he had been overly blunt.

Sveta intervened. "This has the makings of an excellent plan, but there are some details we need to consider carefully." She leant forward in her chair. "From the moment of Betty's death, we assume that the bulk of the Sentinel guards will vanish. But if there are any Sentinel devices remaining, and we must assume that at least Arbuckle's Sentinel might be still there, those devices will become aware that their organisation has ceased to exist. It may not be immediately apparent to them *why* that has happened, but they will work it out at some stage, not least with bio-signature scanning. Then the option for *them* is similar to how it is for us now. They could try to rescue Betty from a time before she dies, and, worst case, translocate her to wherever the boat was going to take her; again reinstating the timeline that favours their Sentinel organisation. So we will need to act precisely and quickly to deprive them of any opportunity to respond in that way."

"OK, well, let's think it through," enthused Gemma. "If we rescue her from some arbitrary moment on the boat, then all the time she was on the boat prior to that, she is still accessible for the Sentinel devices to execute a snatch."

"True," Sveta started. "So we need to decide when would be the best moment for our rescue. Doing it early-on would minimise the amount of prior time into which the remaining Sentinel devices could insert an attempt at a counter-snatch. But, doing it early would also lose us a lot of our knowledge learned during her time on the boat; particularly what we learned about the substantial Sentinel resources when you launched the failed swarm-rescue attempt, Gemma. Doing it later during Betty's time on the boat, allows us to keep all that knowledge, but opens up a longer prior period for remaining Sentinel resources to insert their attempted counter-activity."

"But," Joo-Won intervened, "as soon as Betty dies, we can... we must, place our own guard devices around boat, from the very beginning when she arrive there, until such time we rescue her. And we should place as many devices as possible to guarantee that any residual Sentinel devices who try to intervene during that period are destroyed. If we do that, it not matter whether we kill and rescue Betty early or late; our devices will be there during the whole period, and the period be long or short does not make them any less effective. So, answer is: we should kill and rescue Betty late—*after* the failed swarm-rescue attempt that Gemma launched. Then we still have in our minds all the knowledge we have learned in this timeline, but also defend our position strongly."

"That makes sense, Joo-Won," agreed Gemma. "And of course, following our intervention, I would expect newly re-instated TC operatives with unlimited resources to come to our aid pretty quickly anyway. I will make sure all the details of what we know, and how we are intervening, are recorded into my comms-device to be sent the instant that contact is re-established with the re-instated TC central."

"Yes, that all sounds good," affirmed Sveta. "How soon can you do this, Alex? My only worry now is of some other unexpected intervention by the Sentinels."

Alex had felt duty-bound to make his suggestion because of his understanding of the logic involved, but had been half-hoping that he would not be asked or required to carry it out. He shifted uneasily in his seat. "Well, I would need to take several views of the scene to locate Betty precisely at a certain instant in time. Each view takes me about a half-hour to run, process and then calculate the re-adjusted coordinates. Then I would have to do the same for Kuznetsov. Then the… final runs would each take just over an hour because the equipment has to become more fully charged for a zap. If I start first thing tomorrow morning, I should be able to complete it by lunchtime."

There were immediate looks of concern on the faces of Sveta and Joo-Won, noticeably replacing their upbeat enthusiasm for the jointly developed plan. Gemma took the lead again. "You see, Alex, there is some urgency. For example, if the Sentinel organisation decides to send a greater number of devices to resume retrospective surveillance of the graveyard this afternoon, then we would eventually be in trouble. If they locate you and me planting our devices in the graveyard, then we are toast—then and for always. So… could you perhaps do the work this evening?"

Alex took a sharp breath. Gemma had scared him and he was still very tired. "But Harriet runs an overnight shift on the equipment…" he heard himself protesting. Though he had already accepted that he must do this.

"I'm sure she would help you, if you tell her how important it is, Alex?" suggested Gemma.

Alex nodded, not wanting to open pointless conversation explaining that it might be difficult because Harriet was not party to knowing the full capabilities of the equipment. "OK, give me the precise time you want Betty zapped," he said uncomfortably, but decisively.

"Let's see. Gemma pulled her data screen from the side of the bed. That video we watched of the abortive swarm-rescue ended at 17:32, 1st January. So, 5 or 6 minutes after that…"

"No, wait," interjected Sveta, "if you hit Betty just *before* the abortive rescue, then that would clear the area of excessive Sentinel devices. So that the swarm rescue should then actually turn out to be *successful*. And that means we wouldn't need to launch a rescue ourselves."

"No, no," protested Joo-Won. "In such case, devices would rescue a dead body."

Sveta palmed her forehead. "God, yes, of course. These timeline changes do get so confusing sometimes. Sorry… carry on Gemma."

Gemma grinned. "But you're right to remind us about the abortive swarm-rescue attempt—I will need to send instructions to our swarm of devices to lay-by instead of going ahead with the rescue, so that they don't complicate things… So, Alex… use your technology… er… on Betty at 17:38, January 1st." She wrote the time and date on a piece of paper and handed it to him.

"And what about Kuznetsov, shall I hit him at the same time?" suggested Alex.

"Whoa, no," objected Gemma. "Because we have to mount our rescue in the minutes *before* 17:38, before Betty is killed. So hit him at 17:34—that gives us a 4-minute slot to get in to rescue Betty without him in the way."

Sveta put both her hands in the air. "Wait! I hope I'm not wrong again, but if you kill Kuznetsov at 17:34, then it's probable the boat trip would be impossible, since *he* was the yachtsman. Which would, in turn, change the timeline to remove the Sentinel organisation, just as would hitting Betty. But unfortunately, that would then alert and allow any remaining Sentinel devices to execute what we assume is their plan-B, and translocate Betty directly to the interrogators, before we get a chance to do a hit and rescue."

"Yes, you're right Sveta. If we kill Kuznetsov *before* Betty, it just gives the Sentinel devices a warning and a head start. And it's no use killing him *after*… No, leave Kuznetsov to us, Alex, we'll just have to deal with him in real-time." She reached over and squeezed Alex's arm.

"Ring us with an hour's warning of when you will be ready to action the timeline change, so we can get prepared. Then ring us again so we are on the line when you press the button, or whatever you do on your equipment. That way we can translocate the moment you make the timeline change. I'll switch my phone back on."

"Do you want me to translocate with you?" asked Alex.

"No. We need to jump *immediately* Betty is zapped and the timeline changes. You'll be at your lab. But you will have played your part. You will have done more than your fair share." She hugged him, and Sveta and Joo-Won shook his hand warmly.

So Alex tucked the piece of paper containing the time and date in his pocket and hurried off back home to pick up his phone, then on to the lab, trying to work out what he would say to Harriet.

After Alex left, the three of them continued to discuss their strategy. "So, our biggest problem, I think," stated Gemma, "is that the jump from here to Constanța, combined with a jump of a month in time, is going to give a large uncertainty to the jump exit point and time, just when we need to get into that 5-minute window. Spatially, we are limited to the length and width of the breakwater, so the exact *time* is the issue. But if we all jump independently, then, on average, I guess one of us should get close enough, that with just one extra small jump, he or she should land into that time window."

Sveta nodded. "And I, for one, will be jumping surrounded by my swarm of devices, particularly the guard ones, in case there is any offensive action from any residual Sentinel devices."

"Gemma, are you confident," asked Joo-Won, "that Alex will be able to achieve what he promised? Because if he does not, we will all be jumping into very great danger."

"Oh, I think he knows what he is doing," she replied. "He managed to bring in pictures this morning of Betty in the boat. The technology that he and Betty have developed must be fairly pivotal, otherwise there wouldn't be so much depending on the outcome of its dissemination or otherwise. I know Vallini was impressed at what they have been able to achieve at such an early date."

"OK. Well, commented Sveta, "I'm going to go and lie down for a few hours—you'll let us know when Alex gives us the hour's warning?"

"Of course."

"Hi, Harriet."

"Oh, hi, Alex. You're in late again. Do you need me to do some more pictures for you?"

"No. Well, yes. Well… Look, I'm afraid it's really important Harriet. Do you mind if I take over the equipment tonight?"

"Oh." Harriet looked at the notes on her pad. "Well, of course, if it's that important… But I'll stay and help—you look as if you're still very tired. Have you had any sleep?"

"I did manage a couple of hours this afternoon but… Yes, actually if would be great if you could help, Harriet." Alex reckoned that with Harriet's expertise and accuracy they could probably get the pictures done more rapidly, and then he could just take over at the end, to action the zap without explaining it to her. He retrieved the piece of paper from his pocket. "Here is the time. The place is still: the boat. We can assume Betty is held captive there at that time, and we need to find out exactly where on the boat."

"Captive!" Harriet gasped. But she quickly recovered her mental composure and considered for a moment. "Well, from the layout of the motor yacht that I explored last night, I would expect a captive to be detained below-decks, in the berth, the bunk room? Let's have a look." She pulled up a file on the computer screen of the coordinates she had been working on the night before, and keyed into the machine. "Actually, your timing is perfect, Alex. I had the equipment all charged-up ready to go, so we can action this new picture straight away." She stabbed a button, and when a flow of data appeared a few seconds later, she directed that to the graphics computer for processing into a picture. "OK. Just a few minutes and we'll see. And meanwhile, I'll just start the preparation for the next picture so as not to waste time," she stated, pressing some more buttons.

Alex, grateful for her efficiency, attended to the coffee machine, hoping to wake himself a little more.

"So, Alex, are you going to explain to me what's happening? This is, or was, happening way back on January 1st, when Betty was allegedly somewhere else?" Harriet insisted.

Alex sighed. He suddenly felt rather closer to Harriet than to the TC crowd with their impossible, implausible gambits. At least Harriet lived in the same world that he did, understood things the same way… mostly. "Well, Harriet," he began, "you already know that there are more things in Heaven and Earth, as they say… because you are taking pictures from the past. You already know there is more possible than we see ordinarily. Well the last couple of days, I have found out that there is even more than I ever thought possible. And it seems Betty and I have run afoul not only of foreign agents, but of an organisation from the future."

Harriet's brow was furrowed as she tried to understand what Alex was getting at.

"So," he carried on, "Betty has been kidnapped again, but bizarrely she has been taken back in time to the 1st January." There were tears in his eyes now. "Fortunately, there is an organisation that is trying to help us get her back, but they need us to do… what we are doing now… these pictures, to help. There is no way I can fix it on my own. It is way beyond me." A tear rolled from his exhausted eyes and ran down his cheek.

Harriet was at first nonplussed. And then slightly frightened—she had always regarded Alex and Betty as pre-eminent in science, robust and capable beyond the boundaries. But her immediate instinct now was to comfort and reassure Alex. She went over to him and put her arms on his shoulders, allowing him to cry gently. "I'll do whatever I can to help. I'm sure it will work out, Alex. So does that mean there are now two Bettys back in January? One in Villach and one on this boat—is that how it works?"

"I guess so," Alex responded. "Since there is one Betty missing from here, now."

"And what is this organisation that wants to help?…"

But they were interrupted by the processed picture scrolling up onto the computer screen. Almost as one, they rapidly moved to the desk to examine the picture. "That's strange," commented Harriet, squinting at the picture and then bending her neck to look at it from the side. "It seems like the boat must be the opposite way round and a metre or so shifted from the pictures I did before. Oh well, I'll adjust the coordinates and run again." She wasted no time in calculating and re-keying. Then there was a long half-hour wait before they could see the adjusted picture. Alex tried to evade more questions from Harriet, and she could see that it was not the time to press him. In any case, she was interrupted twice by phone-calls from her military colleagues.

At length, the long-awaited picture scrolled up on the computer

112

screen. Harriet had been right. There was Betty lying on a bunk, her hands and ankles apparently tied.

"What's that across her middle?" asked Alex.

"It's a lee cloth," supplied Harriet. "It's used to secure a person against the roll of the boat when it's sailing. But it looks like it has been used to hold Betty down. OK, so now we know exactly where Betty is— what else do you need?"

"We need to ascertain the exact coordinates of her head. Can you adjust the coordinates from this picture to get there?"

"Her head? Well, I don't usually work so close up, but I can try. You won't get much of a picture though—parts of the picture are blacked out if they're inside anything solid."

"That doesn't matter," Alex reassured her. He watched as she overlaid the picture with a software ruler and made some measurements.

"Now what can I use as a reference? Do you know how tall Betty is?"

Alex stood. "She comes up to about here on me," he indicated with his hand. "I'll get the tape measure from the shelf in the equipment room."

"OK, now I can get the perspective angle from the relative width of the bunk at each end." She did some more measuring on the screen, and jotted some trigonometric calculations on her notepad. "OK, I think these coordinates should centre on Betty's head. Do you want me to go ahead and get a picture to verify that—the equipment has about another 5 minutes charging to do…"

"Yes please," answered Alex. "I want to be totally sure the coordinates are spot on."

They sat back to wait.

*   *   *

Perpetuity Palace—Year 2792

Has there been any further attack on our position?

No, sir.

Then I think it is time for you to send an armed squadron to investigate the translocation-source of that failed swarm-attack—at least probe how strongly they can defend themselves there.

Yes, sir.

Chapter 8
One brief moment and all will be as it was before.

(Henry Scott-Holland)

Monday, late evening, Cheltenham, Alex's lab

Alex's phone rang.

"Alex? It's Gemma. Hey, listen, we have a big problem. My detector has just picked up multiple Sentinel arrivals at the graveyard. We have to assume they are back in force to resume a time-surveillance of this afternoon there; and as I said earlier, if they find you and me during those few minutes when we were planting our swarm, then we are done for. Are you anywhere near being ready to send that zap yet, otherwise I guess the three of us will have to head to the graveyard to see if we can ward them off but...?"

Alex snapped out of his haze. "Oh God, right, no... I mean yes. I can action it in... say 20 minutes? Would that be OK?"

"Oh Alex, yes please. Just do your part as fast as possible. Hopefully that will be OK. We'll head out to Fiddler's Green right now then and prepare to jump for the rescue. Remember to get me on the phone before you press the button so we can translocate as soon as you..."

Alex saw the amber light on the computer screen change to green indicating that the equipment was charged sufficiently for the next picture. Harriet bent forward reflexively to press the action button.

"*No! Harriet,*" Alex shouted urgently, as he bent forward and grabbed her arm.

"What's the matter?" she asked, jumping back from the keyboard.

Alex held onto her arm. "No, not you, Gemma. That's fine. I'll phone you in 15 minutes or so... OK. Bye."

"Sorry, Harriet," he apologised, releasing her arm. "Change of plan.

115

It's suddenly become very urgent—we don't have time for another picture to check the coordinates. I'm going to override your normal software in order to allow the equipment to prepare for even longer." He took over the keyboard and made some cryptic changes. The green light changed back to amber.

"But surely if you increase the energy for longer," protested Harriet, "you'll just get over-exposure. In fact, I seem to remember Betty saying that after a certain time the whole process just goes unstable?"

"Yes, that's right, at least for *your* pictures, that is. But on this occasion, I need to activate with high energy at Betty's exact coordinates in order to facilitate her rescue by these other people who I was talking to on the phone. I need to make a bright energetic signal at her exact position so they can locate and rescue." Alex found that by lying to Harriet, or at least being obscure, he was also giving himself an alternative narrative; burying his own misgivings and gut reaction against what he was about to do. "Now are you content with those coordinates as they are, Harriet? There's no second chance, and no additional picture to check with. Do you want to make any adjustments?"

Harriet thought for a moment. "No, I think they are as accurate as I can make them," she confirmed. At that moment she got a phone-call from one of her military satellite team, and had to switch her attention to dealing with that. Alex was grateful for the interruption as he did not relish further questioning from Harriet for the next 15 minutes. He waited tensely for the equipment to generate a powerful enough particle cloud to create a zap, worrying whether the newly-arrived Sentinel squad might perhaps discover him and Gemma that afternoon, *before* his zap was ready. If they did kill him, he mused, would he just disappear in front of Harriet, or would he never have come here this evening? It was all getting a bit complex for his tired brain to untangle. Perhaps he should ask Harriet to press the activate button for him if he should disappear? Would that help? He was beyond trying to work it all out. The screen was now showing 5 minutes left to charge. Harriet was still discussing something about suspect ground mobile-weapon movements with one of her colleagues. He phoned Gemma back. She sounded breathless.

"Yes, we're nearly in position, Alex. How long?"

"About four minutes. Listen… Betty is lying on a bunk below decks, with her hands and ankles tied. And she is held-down by a canvas across her middle. Oh, and the boat has turned around."

"Sveta, you head over in that direction a bit." Gemma was organising. The three of them spread out a little distance apart on the grassy area. And they each laid out their share of the remaining remote devices around them for defensive cover if needed when they arrived. There were last-minute checks on the programming in their handheld devices, and synchronising with the remote devices. "OK, we're ready Alex… You can meet us back here if you want, or I'll give you a ring when we return with Betty…"

Alex was watching the indicator light that would change from amber to green telling him that the equipment was ready to deliver a lethal zap to the coordinate position that Harriet had keyed in—Betty's head.

Green! Alex stabbed the action button. "Go!" shouted Alex into the phone.

"OK. Go!" Gemma shouted across to her comrades. And within a second, Fiddler's Green was again a dark, deserted parkland area.

The phone went dead. For Alex, it was an anti-climax. There was no indication that anything had happened. But he had completed his task, and he suddenly felt very tired. He gave a thumbs-up and mouthed: "Thank you," to Harriet who was still engrossed on the phone. She acknowledged with a wave as he left the office.

The horrible thought that he had just killed Betty wouldn't leave his mind though. Hopefully, Betty's death had changed the future, such that there would not be Sentinels present around the boat, thus allowing Gemma and the others to translocate to the boat at a time just before the zap, reach Betty, and save her from that very zap. If they were successful, Betty's death would essentially never have happened. That part of the timeline would have been superseded, made redundant, become no longer real.

Alex's scientific and emotional minds were in heavy conflict though. If all went well, the killing was 'temporary'; he tried to tell himself to calm his inner turmoil. But no narrative of logic could avoid the fact of what he had done. And for now, all hopes that his action would eventually be immaterial were just that… hopes.

He thought he would maybe get some sleep knowing that Gemma would contact him as soon as there was any news. Alex headed toward home, but he knew, before he got there, that he would not be able to sleep—his mind was racing; imagining the possible scenarios unfolding. So he decided to head back to Fiddler's Green—Gemma had said 'you can meet us back here'. She had not specified a time, but Alex saw no reason why they would not return to a time soon after they left, leaving a respectable gap to make sure they didn't bump into themselves leaving though, he mused. Anyway, walking was better than lying in bed worrying. He took the long route there to pass the time. Would they come back with Betty, or with solemn apologies? Had Harriet's coordinates been accurate? Otherwise, they may have translocated into mortal danger from superior Sentinel resources. Would they get overcome and maybe not come back at all? As he strode along, one step after another giving a sense of purpose in an effort to calm his mind, he remembered the last time he had walked in this way. Petra had been about to give birth to Charlie. But there were complications the doctor had said. He wasn't allowed to be with Petra, and he couldn't wait in the claustrophobic hospital waiting room. So he had set out walking—just like today. He had been told it was serious—in an hour's time he might learn that Petra had died, or that the baby had died, or both; or that they were both alright. The options had been stark and contrasting—just as now. In the end, it had all turned out OK for Petra and Charlie and himself—more than OK. He was blessed with a wonderful family. But there had been a time, then, walking, like now, when he did not know what the outcome would be.

*   *   *

Sunday 1st January, Constanţa 17:30

Kuznetsov had been to the local store to stock up on provisions, returning to the yacht with two full bags. He had been reluctant to leave his captive alone on the boat, even for the half hour, but was confident that she was securely bound below-decks and probably still unconscious from the sedative. He left one of the bags on the breakwater above the boat and carried the other, using just one hand on the ladder down onto his yacht. He retreated inside the cabin with the bag and immediately went below to check on the Englishwoman. Yes, she was still secure.

It was at that point that Gemma's swarm of devices arrived in a failed attempt at a rescue. Of course he knew and understood nothing of this—his perception was simply of flashes and cracking sounds outside, and some small thuds as pieces of destroyed devices rained on his boat for a couple of seconds. Alarmed, he warily pulled out his gun and re-emerged from the cabin door, looking around to try to ascertain what was happening. He could see nothing out of the ordinary. But the brief fracas had made him fearful of a possible attempt to deprive him of his prize captive - after all, he remembered, she had arrived in strange

118

circumstances… He quickly made the decision to leave immediately for the Crimean peninsula to ensure he could deliver her. Delay might invite problems. He rapidly pulled in the mooring ropes and re-entered the cabin where he fired up the engines and pulled out of the berth, turning, and then heading out toward open water. But after a couple of hundred metres he remembered that he had left the other bag of provisions on the breakwater. Cursing, he throttled the engines down to idle, wondering whether it was worthwhile returning to pick up the bag. He grabbed his binoculars from next to the wheel and intently scanned the area around the berth he had just left. There was no sign of anyone, no hint of activity, and the bag was sitting there where he had left it. Perhaps it had just been fireworks, he considered—after all there had been fireworks the previous evening, New Years Eve. And his whisky and cigarettes were in that other bag. He decided to quickly return to pick it up.

But he was cautious now, and headed into the berth prow first so that, from the cabin window, he would be able to see anything suspicious happening on the breakwater. But, as he nuzzled the prow gently against the concrete, he heard a sharp cracking sound from below-decks. Alarmed again, he drew his gun and rushed down the steps to the bunk-room. There, he was shocked and dismayed to see his captive's head engulfed in flames. Somehow, in Kuznetsov's mind, she, maybe with the help of an unseen accomplice, had managed to kill herself. And that deprived him of his prize—she was only worth anything alive. Only an alive captive could be tortured to extract information. She was worth nothing dead. His emotions oscillated between rage and despair, as he grabbed the fire extinguisher to save the boat.

*　　　*　　　*

Sunday 1st January, Constanţa 17:45

Gemma flexed her knees on landing and glanced around quickly. The breakwater was immediately familiar, cold and damp. She had landed close to the far end of the breakwater, near to the water's edge. There was no apparent reaction from any Sentinel devices. She looked at her handheld controller for the local time—it was only seven minutes after the target time-window. This raised her spirits—she would easily be able to get into that window with one more jump—200 metres and ten minutes—and could expect to land fairly accurately on target. She quickly re-affirmed the coordinates on her handheld controller and re-synchronised the small swarm of remote devices around her. And

119

jumped again.

Sunday 1st January, Constanţa 17:34

Even as Gemma flexed her knees, there was a flash from close to the wall that sent one of her autonomous devices spinning across the concrete and into the water, and almost immediately another flash, a response from one of her own devices. She checked her controller—two minutes into the target window. Perfect. The lack of any further Sentinel attack confirmed to her that Alex had successfully completed his part of the plan—the Sentinel organisation had ceased to exist—apparently only a single ancient-built Sentinel, like Arbuckle's, had remained guarding the boat. So the current timeline included Betty getting killed in a few minutes time. She just now needed to rescue Betty before that happened.

But what had Alex meant about the boat being the other way round?—it looked the same as yesterday, other than a bag sitting on the side of the breakwater. Except, there was a man standing on-deck, dragging in a mooring-rope. The access ladder had already been pulled inboard. Damn, she thought—he had obviously been spooked by the lights and sound of the abortive swarm-rescue that had, in his time-frame, taken place just two minutes ago, and he was about to take-off. She should have anticipated that. As she took a step or two toward the water's edge and the boat, he saw her, instantly pulling his gun and firing in her direction. She heard the first bullet smash into the wall behind, and instinctively she turned away from him. The second knocked her off her feet. But she could feel no pain. Then hearing an alarm bleep from her handheld device and glancing at its cryptic message, she realised that the bullet had lodged into her backpack and disabled one of the devices. Survival instincts now. The boat was below the level of the breakwater surface, so, as long as she stayed low, he would not be able to see her from the boat. She quickly crawled along the far side of the breakwater next to the wall to get some distance away, then retrieved her own weapon from a pocket. If he put the ladder back up and climbed it, she would get the first shot. She waited a few seconds.

Then she heard the boat's engine roar into life. She gingerly crawled back across the breakwater surface toward the edge to look over at the boat. But it was now powering away, just breaking the last mooring rope that he had not bothered to release. He was not in sight—of course, he would have to be at the controls, she realised. It was too late to physically jump onto the boat, though that would have been risky anyway. She quickly tapped into the handheld controller to initiate another translocation jump. But how far? She guessed 20 metres and pressed the button. No response. The device was programmed not to jump her into water. She tried 30 metres.

This time she landed with a sprawl on the roof of the boat, the uneven pitching and rolling knocking her off her feet. She desperately grabbed at a strut to keep herself from sliding off the wet slippery surface. Kuznetsov had evidently heard the thud caused by her fall, as a bullet cracked through the roof close to where she was lying. Still holding her weapon with one hand, Gemma rolled onto her side to get the bio-signature detector out of its pocket. Another bullet ripped into her backpack, causing her to slide back whilst two more bullets cracked through the fibreglass at the position where she had been. Her controller bleeped another fault code. The engines sounded as if they were throttling-down. He's coming to investigate, Gemma thought. Finally, she had the bio-signature detector in her hand, but she was slipping again. She jammed an elbow against another strut to hold herself steady. The detector showed a figure crossing to the starboard side at the front of the cabin. Without delay, she triggered her weapon in that direction. The TC device blew a hole in the roof as the beam cut through to its target. The figure on the detector stopped moving. Gemma wanted to wait to see if there was any further response, but there was no time to lose—she only had another two minutes to rescue Betty. She scrambled across the roof to where she knew the door was situated, triggering the weapon two more times to make sure Kuznetsov was no longer a danger. Then she jumped down onto the deck, and looked through the nearest window. Yes, there was his crumpled body just inside the door. It took her more precious seconds to ram the door open against the heavy body.

The boat was now heading toward a jetty on the opposite side of the harbour, with a collision imminent. Gemma realised she had to attend to that first—she didn't know how to work the engines but the steering was obvious. She wrenched the wheel about and put the boat into a sharp turn. Meanwhile, she glanced at her handheld controller. It showed that her translocator was disabled—it must have been hit by that second bullet that hit her backpack, she reasoned. Without a translocator, she would need Sveta or Joo-Won to return Betty and herself. That meant getting the boat back to its original berth where her colleagues would hopefully be arriving. She looked around. The boat had turned well away from the impending collision, but it was dark, and difficult to make out landmarks. She thought she could discern the end of the breakwater, and tried looking along the line of yachts for the gap they had come from. She straightened the boat up with the wheel to head in that direction. She looked at the other boat controls—there were two sticks with handgrips on the left-hand side, and two on the right. She decided to experiment with the leftmost one. It wouldn't push any further forward. She pulled it gently back, nothing at first, then a click and the boat veered to port. She quickly put it back to how it was, and used the wheel to correct the heading again. She tried the lever on the extreme right—pushing it forward a bit, the engine sounded as if it throttled up, but the boat again veered to port. She restored the lever and corrected the heading with the wheel. Then it occurred to her—the handgrips on the pairs of levers were angled close toward each other—perhaps you were meant to use them together? A quick try with the right-hand pair confirmed that—forward to speed the engines, back to slow them. But she had no more time to experiment. The berth at the breakwater was fast approaching. And there were two figures standing there—presumably Sveta and Joo-Won.

But when she glanced at her handheld controller, panic almost set in. Only 40 seconds left to rescue Betty, before the zap would hit her. Seeing that the boat was heading straight in now, she pulled both the throttle levers fully back to reduce the speed to minimum, and rushed to the back of the cabin and down the steps to below-decks. As she reached the bottom there was a crunch; the bow of the boat hitting the breakwater, fibreglass yielding to concrete, throwing her forward. And she suddenly realised why Alex had said the boat was pointing the other way. Now, it was. But she had found Betty. There was a sheet of canvas across her body, holding her down. Gemma grabbed her penknife from its pocket, and cut along the canvas edge as fast as she could. The seams were frustratingly tough. Finally, she was able to put her arms around Betty and drag her away from the bunk, onto the floor; just as a loud crack sounded and a disc of light enveloped the pillow on which Betty's head had just rested, setting the pillow on fire. Gemma felt elated and started working with the penknife, but more gently, on the ties restraining Betty's wrists and ankles.

Betty herself seemed barely conscious. She was muttering. "That sounded like a zap... What's going on?... Gemma?... Where's Otto?"

"Everything is OK, Betty. We are rescuing you. Just relax."

There was noise from the cabin, and Sveta appeared, jumping lithely down the steps, dressed in the jumpsuit that she had changed into. "Ah, thank God you made it in time, Gemma. We were watching the seconds tick away and were worried... Hello, Betty—I've heard a lot about you... Look we've raised some unwanted attention up there; I think we'd better jump back straight away."

"Is Joo-Won up there?" Gemma enquired urgently. "My translocator is not working—it got damaged in the fracas. Can *you* jump Betty back; I don't think she can stand on her own; and I'll go with Joo-Won on his translocator?"

"Sure."

"Betty, can you try to stand?" They both put arms around Betty's middle and pulled her up. Sveta already had her controller prepared in her hand. Gemma took a step back. Sveta, hanging on to Betty's unsteady body, pressed a button and they vanished.

"Joo-Won," Gemma called, as she started back up the steps. He was bending over Kuznetsov's crumpled body and looking nervously at two or three people who had assembled up on the breakwater. But the ladder was not in place so they could not easily get onto the boat without jumping. The boat itself was still trying to burrow into the breakwater, but the stern had swung around and was touching the boat moored in the next berth. Joo-Won stepped over to the controls and turned the boat's engine off. Gemma smiled at his evident, easy familiarity with the boat's controls, in contrast to her own naïvety. "Joo-Won, my translocator is damaged so can you help me get back, please? The others have already left."

"But of course," he replied, adjusting the reading on his handheld device for *two* people. He moved to the back of the cabin out of view of the spectators and beckoned her over. They put arms around each other and Joo-Won activated the translocator.

Monday, late evening, Cheltenham, Fiddler's Green

Sveta flexed her knees on landing, but could not hold Betty's weight and they tumbled down in a heap together onto the grass, Sveta laughing. It was dark, late evening. She sat up and looked at her controller to learn the time. "Ah, the uncertainty has brought us back quite early. We may have to wait a while for the others. Look, there is a bench over there, not far, let's see if I can help you to walk there?"

Betty shivered, both with cold and weakness. "OK. But who are you?... Where are we?..."

"I am a TC colleague of Gemma's. My name is Sveta. We are at a place that Gemma called erm... Fiddler's... something."

"Fiddler's Green? What, in Cheltenham?"

"Yes, back in Cheltenham. Gemma would have brought you here herself, but her translocator had sustained damage, so she will be back soon with another colleague. I don't know how much you remember of what happened?"

"Not much. I feel vague and confused. But I do know this feeling— I felt like this when I regained consciousness a few hours after I had been drugged—After I was kidnapped. Has it?…"

"Yes, I'm afraid it happened again. Do you remember Arbuckle and his Sentinel device?"

"Yes."

"The Sentinel translocated you away to a boat in Constanţa."

"Uh…"

"We have just rescued you from there—well, Gemma did it really. Don't worry about the details at the moment—it's rather complicated. But you are safe now. Though I would really like to get you away from this area. We have rooms at the Jurys Inn, about 5 minutes walk. Do you think you can manage that far?"

"Yes, I'm very stiff, but I think I'll loosen up if I walk a bit; and hopefully I'll warm up with the exercise," she said, shivering again. "But I thought Gemma was staying in the hotel next door to the 'Red Lion'?"

"Ah, she has had to move hotels twice since then. Once to avoid being close if Arbuckle's Sentinel returned; and again, at Alex's suggestion, to avoid your security people being able to locate her. I think they were giving him a hard time about your disappearance… I'm sorry I have no extra clothes to give you right now, but back at the hotel, you can have a hot shower and I will lend you some clean and warm clothes."

Betty smiled at the idea. "Yes, the thought of a hot shower should motivate me to walk faster. And I think I must have spilt champagne all down this outfit." Sveta pulled Betty's arm over her shoulder and put an arm around her waist to steady her. The two made their way back to the hotel.

*   *   *

Gemma and Joo-Won made a well-choreographed landing, but right at the far end of Fiddler's Green. Joo-Won looked at the local time on his handheld. "Relatively late. Others already back, I am thinking," he commented. "Which way?"

Gemma looked around for landmarks. It was dark. They were standing in a field, but not the same one they had jumped from. The area was flat, and tree-lines obscured the view in all directions. It was obvious where the town was, from the dull glow of the street lights into the sky, but Gemma had to revert to using her controller to work out the direction back to where they had jumped from, and thence their exit to the road that led to the hotel. She pointed out the direction. They strode purposefully off.

"So," continued Joo-Won, "you make strange manoeuvres with the yacht, coming in. I realise you had no time for niceties like backing into berth, but why the two turns before you came in?"

Gemma laughed. "Not intentional, Joo-Won. I was just trying out the controls to see what did what."

"Ah, but you throttled down on final approach OK."

"Yes, I finally realised that you had to work both the levers together."

"Twin screw throttles," explained Joo-Won, with a smile that betrayed pride in his nautical proficiency. "It's good you make throttle down, otherwise prow would been smashed, hitting concrete breakwater hard—probably sink. As it was, you make big cracks but I think it repair OK." He laughed out loud. "And your translocator? What happen?"

"I think it took a bullet from Kuznetsov's gun."

"Oo... too close." He put a hand on Gemma's shoulder and gave an affectionate rub. Neither of them mentioned Kuznetsov himself—that was the least palatable memory from the successful episode.

*   *   *

There had been no sign of anyone walking across when Alex had looked in from the gate at the entrance to Fiddler's Field; but he was well into the rhythm of walking now, so he decided to walk across town and maybe pay Arbuckle a visit before the day was out, to see if he was OK. It might at least break the repetitive anxious thoughts by giving his mind something to focus on.

A little while later, as he approached the hotel, he glanced at his phone wondering if he had time for a quick drink before the visit—and there was indeed half an hour before the pubs would be closing. He was also rather curious to visit the 'Red Lion' to see whether the half-sofa that had remained after Betty's departure the previous night, was still in place. It was almost a mission to quell his disbelief—the whole episode still seemed rather like a dream, and he felt that perhaps seeing that evidence would at least clear one part of his mind.

He pushed open the door of the pub and strode over to the alcove that had, the previous evening, been the scene of the abduction. He glanced inside. There were four people sitting there on chairs, chatting— no sign of the damaged sofa. The landlord would have removed it, he reassured himself; no reason to question his memory.

He walked through to the bar at the back to order himself a beer, but stopped short. There, at the bar, was Arbuckle himself. And he seemed to be in some kind of altercation with the bartender. Alex wondered at first if Arbuckle might have been associated with the damage to the furniture the previous night, but as he listened discreetly, from some distance away, he realised that was not at all the problem.

"No, sir," the bartender was insisting. "I am not serving you any more drinks tonight."

"I promish you this will be my last..." Arbuckle was slurring his words and appeared to be steadying himself on the edge of the bar.

"No, sir."

"But I was gen'rous earlier in the ev'ning. Carn't you be gen'rous to me now? Ah tell you what, my friend—I will pay double for this glassh."

"You *were* generous earlier—buying drinks for everyone, yes indeed, sir. But you have drunk enough for yourself tonight—look, you can hardly stand. I am within my rights to use discretion about serving people, and I am now asking you to leave, sir. Please."

Alex was initially surprised, then amused, and finally felt sorry for the old fellow. He walked over and put his hand on Arbuckle's shoulder. "Hello, Reverend."

Arbuckle looked at him with blank eyes, not recognising him at first. Then: "Oh, my good fr'en', Mr Shmith. Hello sir. Do join me for a drink. I was just ashking this good barman here..."

"No, no," Alex interrupted. "I'm going to walk you home. Come." He put an arm around Arbuckle to steady him, but found he in fact also needed to pull Arbuckle's arm over his shoulder to keep him upright.

"He was in here all lunchtime opening, and all this evening," the bartender advised Alex discreetly, shrugging his shoulders and grinning. Alex looked back to the bartender and smiled, nodding his understanding. They started the walk to the front door very slowly. It seemed to take ages, and Alex felt somewhat embarrassed as several people turned to watch the snail-paced procession.

Outside, the fresh air hit Arbuckle. "Ooh, I don't feel too well," he muttered in a small voice, staring down at the pavement. It was fortunate that the hotel was only next door, Alex mused; otherwise he would have had to go and collect his car. As it was, it took several minutes to guide Arbuckle back into the hotel, and along to his room. The reverend fumbled in his pockets for the key, but eventually found it, and Alex helped him across to the bed where Arbuckle collapsed down. Alex loosened Arbuckle's collar and took off his shoes.

"You know, my fr'en', the Shentinel never came back fo' me..." he spoke very softly with his eyes closed.

"That's OK," Alex said reassuringly. "I have friends who will take you back home." But Arbuckle was already snoring.

Alex left the hotel, still relishing the idea of a quick drink himself, but wondering if he dared go back into the 'Red Lion'. It was too late to find any other pub; they would all be closing in a few minutes. He decided fortitude was a virtue and went back in and ordered himself a double Black Sambuca—quicker to drink than a pint of beer. The bartender seemed happy enough to serve him. "So, you know the old fellow then?" he asked.

"Yes, just a little," Alex responded, giving nothing away.

"He's certainly a character; somewhat eccentric. Does he live around here?"

"No, he's just staying here for a few days..." At that point, Alex's phone rang giving him a welcome excuse to exit the conversation. He sat down at a vacant table and took the call.

"Hi, Gemma."

"Oh, hi Alex. Just wanted to let you know everything is fine—we've got Betty back—she's here at the hotel. She's had a hot shower and she's going straight to bed in my room—she's exhausted, poor thing. Thanks so much for doing what you did—I'm not sure we could have managed it without your intervention... Vallini—he's with us again, by the way—doesn't want anyone using any equipment tonight that might give our location away—just a precaution; so we're all staying here tonight. Would you like to come over for breakfast? I'm sure Betty would like to see you. So would I… and, of course, I might not be here in Cheltenham much longer."

Alex sipped his liqueur as Gemma related the reassuring news to him. Through the combination of alcohol and comforting words, he suddenly began to feel a lot more relaxed. And with the relaxation, the tiredness crashed back, but not in an unpleasant way. He remembered he hadn't slept much the previous night. He realised his walking for the evening was over—so called for a taxi home and was soon asleep in bed.

Chapter 9

Beyond is the infinite morning of a day without tomorrow.

(W.S. Abbott)

Tuesday morning, Cheltenham

As it happened, the next morning Alex decided to have breakfast with his family first and then get over to the hotel. He caught Sveta and Betty just finishing their coffees. At Vallini's request, Gemma had gone off to organise a small hotel conference room for them—the group was now six—so that they did not have to cram into one of the bedrooms to discuss plans. Alex was not sure why plans would now be necessary, but he went along with the others. Everyone was very upbeat, including Vallini who thanked Alex enthusiastically for what he had done.

"So, listen everybody," Vallini raised his hands to get attention and close down the informal chatter. "Yesterday was, of course, fundamental in rescuing Betty and re-establishing the TC organisation, but today we must organise some further actions to consolidate the position. At present, it is not safe for Betty to stay here, and she will never be safe whilst Sentinel resources still exist. So most importantly, I must transport Betty to a completely safe place for a short time, whilst myself and TC set about eliminating the remnants of the Sentinel organisation." Alex glanced across at Betty's face. Her look of surprise and concern suggested that Vallini had not previously talked to her about this.

"After Betty and I have translocated away," he continued, "then Gemma, Sveta and Joo-Won can translocate home, a job well-done. But please not before. The reason is that my detectors have recorded Sentinel devices in pursuit. Two devices landed in the Fiddler's Green area late yesterday evening, and another overnight. They can at present have no idea of Betty's exact location, but are no doubt waiting to detect any subwave transmission by us that they can home-in on, or a translocation by us that they can then follow. If any of you translocate first, then

129

devices are likely to follow. Although they may pose no particular threat to you, that would mean we would lose track of those specific Sentinel devices. So, I need the translocation by Betty and myself to be the *first* one, the one that they follow. We will be translocating to, and through, a series of TC Way-Stations that are secured. I have already alerted those Way-Stations so that they are expecting our transit and are prepared to destroy, or inactivate and capture, any devices following us. It is important that TC trap at least one of the Sentinel devices so it can be reverse-engineered and analysed giving TC better intelligence about what we are dealing with. Then, with that intelligence, TC will have ways of locating any other residual devices and destroying them. So, that's the general plan."

Betty, unsurprisingly, was concerned. "But how do you know we will be safe at these Way-Stations, Vallini?"

"Well, we are essentially luring the Sentinels there," explained Vallini. "Because the Way-Stations are the equivalent of… What might be a good example in your times?… The equivalent of a battleship, a military base maybe. We, you and I, will only remain at each Way-Station for a couple of seconds before translocating to the next. We'll be jumping out again so quickly that the Sentinels would have no time to do anything offensive, even if they were not immediately immobilised by the TC weaponry that is anticipating them."

"What I don't understand, Vallini," asked Gemma, "is why you are assuming that all the Sentinel devices will follow the translocation by you and Betty. Isn't it likely that some devices might wait and follow us? Indeed, they might even expect the first translocation to be a decoy?"

"Yes. Well-analysed, Gemma. The reason they will follow us is that we will *let them know* that it is Betty translocating. We will let them *see* Betty translocate."

"I don't like the sound of that," responded Betty. "How can I possibly be safe if they can see me?"

"OK," Vallini explained. "Because I will set my translocator to jump us to the first Way-Station on a hair-trigger, so to speak. As soon as it detects any action from any Sentinel device, it will automatically activate our jump. So Betty and I will walk into Fiddler's Green together, getting closer and closer to the Sentinel devices until one of them identifies Betty, at which point it will either communicate to its peers or try to translocate toward Betty. Either way, a millisecond after the first sign of any activity, we are gone. And the only logical thing for them to do then, is to follow us."

Alex was still worried. "Isn't there some way you could let the Sentinel devices know it's Betty by using the data from Betty's bio-scan? We know they have that information and could recognise it. Wouldn't that be safer?"

"There will be such a way, yes. That's why we want to reverse-engineer one of the Sentinel devices. If we understand their communication protocols then we could do things like that—but we can't as yet, not at this stage. So, Betty. This requires you to be bold, but I will be with you."

"I'm not so sure about walking toward the Sentinels. Where would you be taking me, anyway? And for how long?"

"I'll be taking you through a series of eight Way-Stations, forward to *my* time. You can keep company with my newly-arrived cousin for a couple of days until I can get to spend time with her. So you'd be doing me a favour as well."

"Wha..." Betty's mouth opened. A big grin crossed her face. "OK, then," she chirped.

The others had not been party to the conversation between Betty and Vallini the previous day when he had talked about his cousin, so they assumed that Betty's sudden enthusiasm was simply due to a promised visit to the future. And, in truth, that probably would have been enough to enthuse Betty.

"OK, then," Vallini continued. "So, Gemma, will you monitor when our jump from Fiddler's Green occurs. Give it 5 more minutes after that; then you can all translocate home. But Gemma's translocator is not functional, so Sveta, will you jump Gemma home first, and then you can return yourself? I'll visit you all sometime soon to replace any missing bits of kit, and with a new translocator for you, Gemma... So, can we all say our goodbyes now..."

"Wait a minute," Alex interrupted. "What about Arbuckle? He needs to be taken home as well."

"Oh. Yes, you're right, Alex. We need to resolve that anachronism too. Is he still at that hotel? Do you think he will cooperate with us?"

"Yes, he's still there. Umm... he trusts me, but he doesn't know anyone else."

"Well, perhaps you could go along with Joo-Won to see him?"

"Sure."

"Can I go home to get some clothes first?" asked Betty.

"No need, everything will be provided for you."

"And you can keep that outfit," added Sveta. "It rather suits you."

There was a flurry of goodbyes and promises of being in touch. "Here, take my jacket—you are going out into the cold… Perhaps I can come and visit you sometime soon," Gemma suggested to Betty. "But it will be a slightly older me—remember I came here from three years ago." Gemma seemed quite tearful.

Alex gave Betty a hug. "See you in a couple of days then… Take care."

Vallini finished keying coordinates and instructions for the series of jumps into his equipment, then, still holding his handheld controller, he slung his rucksack over his shoulders, and handed his room key to Gemma. "All good?" He offered his arm to Betty and they walked out through the front entrance, Betty glancing back once to wave.

*   *   *

Vallini's stride was confident and steady. He occasionally glanced at his handheld. Betty found herself oscillating between dreading the walk into the vicinity of Sentinels, and joyfully anticipating the journey and the experience promised after. Like a child being taken to the dentist, who has been promised an ice cream sundae afterwards. A couple of times when the dread was uppermost, she was embarrassed to notice that she was gripping Vallini's arm very tightly. He made no sign of noticing and said nothing until they got close to the entrance to the Green.

"Now Betty, it is important that you keep good physical contact with me the whole time. Probably best if you come round the other side—that way the Sentinel device will be able to spot you more easily. That's it—either put your arm around me or hold my arm tightly. I can see the positions of the devices on my handheld. I won't walk straight toward a Sentinel—that might look a bit suspicious, but I'll lead us on a trajectory past one—close enough. When you feel the jumps starting, just bend your knees a little to make the landings smoother. Then each time we land we will try to run forward a few paces before the next jump kicks in—the changes in our position just put a bit more calculative burden on any devices following us. If you stumble, just hold onto me, don't let go. We need to be in physical contact the whole time so my

132

translocator can do its job with the two of us. Don't worry about what's going on around us—there may be flashes and noise. The series of jumps is all automated in my translocator; so once the process starts, the whole set of jumps will all be over in about 20 seconds. Any questions?"

"No." Betty's voice was small. She was focussing only on the instructions. Her heart was beginning to race.

"Keep your head up now as you walk. You want to be seen."

They walked on through the gate into the field, and Vallini guided them diagonally across the grassy field. Betty decided to put an arm around Vallini's waist, as well as hold his arm. She no longer felt any embarrassment showing him her dependence. They were halfway across the field now and still nothing had happened. She glanced quizzically up at Vallini.

"Not long now," he whispered.

Suddenly the field seemed to disappear and Betty felt a puff of breeze brushing her face. She remembered to bend her knees, but still staggered as her feet re-met the floor. She clung tightly to Vallini's arm to stay upright, as he pulled her forward a few paces. She glanced around. They seemed to be in a massive empty warehouse. There were a couple of flashes and cracks a little way over to one side. Then the warehouse disappeared, another pulse of air, and another landing. This time she judged the small drop OK and danced a few steps forward with Vallini. Again the warehouse disappeared and they were jumping into yet another. This time a large flash close to her side sent something skidding across, catching her leg as it careened past. It put her off balance as the next jump started, and on landing, she toppled, but was held by Vallini. Each time now, they seemed to be landing in a different position within the warehouse, or was it a stadium. She noticed no more flashes. They landed again.

"That's it," declared Vallini, holding Betty back as she reflexively made as if to run a few steps. "Is your leg OK? It looked as if it got hit by debris?"

Betty bent down and rubbed her shin. "No damage—maybe a bruise tomorrow. So where are we?"

She took a look around them. It was a massive floor-area, like an empty exhibition hall, maybe a half kilometre in each direction, devoid of anything except themselves. The flooring was… well, not concrete, she decided, more like tiling except that it was continuous; and the walls mostly featureless.

"We're in the Way-Station in the year 2243. That last jump was just a small adjusting one to land us at the right date and time. Apart from being secure, the Way-Stations have a focussing effect so that we can accurately jump much more time in one go, without the uncertainty landing us outside."

Betty noticed an opening had appeared in one of the walls and something was emerging from it. "What's that?"

"That's our transport. Spatial translocation only. We use the spatial element of translocators to get around, but time translocation is not available or allowed for ordinary people for obvious reasons."

"What obvious reasons?" asked Betty, thirsting for information.

"Well, to avoid confusion and chaos in everyday life—we need to have a sense of linear cause and effect. And for preservation—to avoid people trying to change the past, which, as you have already experienced, is disruptive or destructive to the future. A few persons like myself are privileged users of temporal translocation, to guard and maintain that sense of linear cause and effect."

The transport was drifting silently but quickly across toward them. Betty noticed it had wheels. "Hang on Vallini, if it's a translocator, why does it have wheels?"

Vallini nodded and smiled slightly, acknowledging Betty's fast assessment of the environment. "Two reasons. Firstly, we don't allow spatial translocators to operate within the Way-Station perimeter -it is a highly specialised and controlled environment. But secondly, all translocations are not exact, so we use the wheeled vehicular aspect to travel from our jump landing to where we actually want to get to. Otherwise, it would be chaotic with transports repeatedly materialising at closer and closer points to popular destinations."

The transport halted smoothly next to them. There was a woman inside, dressed in the same strange material that Vallini had been wearing when Betty had first met him. She gave a small wave. "Ah, is that your cousin?" she asked.

Vallini smiled amusement. "No, no. That is Silvana, one of our TC operatives." He motioned for Betty to enter the pod through a door that had opened, into what was effectively a rear seat, and he followed, sitting down next to the operative in the front. Betty sat and looked around the interior. It was about the size of a large car, very minimalist but definitely comfortable and aesthetic, all greys and whites and creams. Instinctively she reached for a seatbelt. But there was none. The transport had already started moving smoothly back toward where it had entered.

"Why does the…" started Betty.

Vallini raised a hand politely. "I'm sorry Betty. You will have to hold the torrent of questions for a few minutes whilst I get a briefing."

The TC operative had handed Vallini an electronic tablet displaying data about the induced pursuit. "Essentially five alien devices destroyed and two immobilised. The furthest penetration was to the fourth Way-Station. The last device appeared some time later at the first station, and was destroyed."

"The *fourth* Way-Station! I had not expected they had that much resilience—but still, well within margins for us. The immobilised alien devices have been sent for analysis?"

"That is in progress, Vallini."

"Oh," Vallini reached into his backpack. "And here is another that was rendered inert back during our operations." He pulled out the black padded bag that Gemma had given him containing the damaged Sentinel device that she had retrieved from the graveyard.

The transport had exited through the opening in the wall of the warehouse area, emerging into sunlight, and it parked alongside an adjoining building complex. Betty noticed an elegant logo close to the entrance with the words 'Temporal Continuity' next to it.

The TC operative had made to exit the transport. "Thank you, Silvana," remarked Vallini. "I will return when I have escorted our guest here to complete safety."

She nodded. "I will see you soon then, Vallini." She turned and smiled at Betty in the back seat, "I hope you enjoy your stay." Betty noticed her glancing curiously at her attire—actually a mixture of Sveta's outfit and Gemma's coat, she remembered.

The door of the transport closed. Vallini's seat swivelled round to face Betty. Betty laughed. "Ah, I was going to ask you why the seats all faced the front when the transport doesn't really have a direction, and presumably is instantaneous anyway!"

"Oh, there is a reason why they are normally arranged like that," replied Vallini. "Social ease. The same as when you are in an elevator. It can be disturbing to be facing strangers directly. But as you see, they are configurable. Anyway, Betty, I'm afraid I am going to have to ask you to do a bio-scan. It's so that I can get you through security checkpoints. I know you had a bad reaction with it last time, in Arbuckle's hotel room, but now you know what it is, and that it is for a bona fide cause, it shouldn't be alarming?" He offered her the tablet he was holding, that displayed an outline of a hand and some text that Betty didn't bother to read.

"OK. I'll treat it like a vaccination." She took a breath and placed her hand on the tablet. She shuddered slightly at the tingling sensation. It momentarily resurrected memories of Arbuckle's hotel room. But it was trivial enough.

"Thank you." Vallini keyed into the small control panel of the transport. "Now we will translocate to the spaceport."

"The spacepo..." But the sunshine and surroundings had disappeared for a second, before a new vista was apparent. Betty glanced around. There was a modernistic building complex a little way over to one side. Every other direction seemed fairly desolate. The transport now glided along on its wheels toward the building complex. "Where are we Vallini? What is this place? Is your cousin here?"

Vallini chuckled. "I am taking you to the safest place possible. Can you deduce where is the one place that no-one can translocate to, neither TC nor Sentinels?"

"I don't know—somewhere you put a protective field around?" Betty tried.

"No. That's not possible. But the one place that you cannot translocate to is... orbit. Any vehicle in orbit around Earth is travelling at maybe 30,000 km per hour to maintain that orbit. You already know that translocation involves an uncertainty of both location and time in its destination, so as you can imagine, trying to translocate into a vehicle in orbit would be an absolutely hopeless prospect. And if you simply translocated a vehicle up to orbital height, it wouldn't be moving at orbital speed, so it would just fall straight back down again. Anyway, so no Sentinel could possibly get to you in orbit. Add to that, the spaceport has the tightest security of personnel and freight anywhere, so there is no way that even a future-wise Arbuckle could reach you there. It is the safest place for you to be, bar none. And you remember me telling you that my cousin had arrived on a freighter from the Pericyon system? She was offloaded to the Orbital Rehab Station earlier today. I remember, at the racecourse with you, when I was bemoaning the fact that I could not be there to meet her, you asked me why I couldn't just go back in time to the day she arrived, after I had finished the operation? And I said it would not be correct for me to do so as an officer of TC? However, of course, it is quite in order for me to do it as an *operational* move—to keep you safe. So this serves my purpose too. I can now greet her soon after her arrival, you are safe, she keeps you company, you keep her company; whilst I go and sort out the elimination of any further Sentinel threat."

"Oh. Oh, I presumed that when you said your cousin had arrived, that you meant she had arrived on Earth."

"Ah, no. When people have spent many years in hibernation on a space transit vessel, it is necessary for them to regain strength in the low gravity of an Orbital Rehab Station before being ferried down to Earth."

"I see. But, if we can't translocate into orbit, how do we get there?"

Vallini's eyes shone. "Good old-fashioned chemical rocket power. It is irreplaceable for gaining orbit. There have been some efforts to use magnetic rail-guns, but for a variety of reasons, they were never as successful as rockets. You can perhaps imagine that, having replaced all those relatively exciting driven-vehicles like cars, in your day, with dull silent automatic utilitarian transports like these," he gestured disparagingly at the transport as they stepped out, "we rather celebrate exciting energy modes like rocket; and when on holiday we like to race cars and speed-boats." Vallini grinned as he led Betty through the entrance into the spaceport. It was uncrowded, functional. He glanced around locating the sign that he was looking for. "So we want the Rehab 3 Ferry." He pointed at the large illuminated sign and led Betty in that direction. "We check-in here."

They were greeted by an attendant who asked for ID and glanced at Vallini and Betty's attire with some surprise. Vallini was still wearing the clothes that Gemma had chosen for him in Cheltenham. He showed the attendant some sort of ID pack from his inner pocket that Betty noticed had the TC logo on it, and the attendant suddenly became very helpful—clearly, Vallini's position held some weight. He placed his palm onto a reader and faced a camera, before instructing Betty how to do the same. Green lights allowed them through after Vallini's backpack had been quickly scanned.

There seemed to be a small food counter over to the side. "I'm afraid we have no time to eat, but it has barely been an hour since breakfast anyway. There is only one of these ferries each day, and I have timed it tightly. They walked straight through to a larger transport—the equivalent of a bus. There were a dozen or so people already sitting in the vehicle. Betty again felt eyes looking at their unusual clothing, and she was glad, as Vallini had indicated, that the seats conventionally all faced the front so she could avoid the gazes. She, herself had already got accustomed to seeing the light flimsy-looking shiny material that everyone here seemed to dress in, generally subdued shades of grey and cream, apart from the ones who were obviously in uniform. A few more people joined the transport before an audible warning sounded, the doors closed and it translocated instantly to fairly near what was unmistakably a rocket. The transport glided on its wheels the final distance to the servicing tower. A short ride in an elevator up the tower and they were ushered across a bridge to an entryway into the top stage of the rocket. Betty looked down and saw long plumes of vapour streaming out of release valves. Now into a tiered seating area. The seats were reclined, arranged in a circle of about twelve, with heads in the middle, feet facing a small window at about eye level, at least for the passengers on her side. Betty could see only a little cloud and sky, and she decided the windows probably served more purpose in relieving claustrophobia than for viewing. An attendant was coming round fastening the seat straps for the passengers. Betty was able to talk to Vallini—his head fairly close to hers, though their feet pointed apart, separated by a luggage locker into which Vallini had placed his backpack. Vallini reassured her the recliners were well sprung and that these personnel ferries only accelerated at a maximum of 2.2g. Asking about the windows he told her not to worry because there would be ample time for great views from the cupola of the Rehab Station. She noted that above each person's head was positioned an individual screen for entertainment. Her screen was currently informing her that takeoff would be in 5 minutes, and docking to Orbital Rehab Station-3 would be in just over 2 hours.

It began to feel rather dreamlike to Betty; it was all happening so quickly. Because the people of this era did not seem to have the long periods of travel-time, during which reflections could be made, and memories consolidated, the series of events seemed to follow each other without allowing time to process and savour them. She suddenly longed to have her phone with her so she could take some photos. But her phone had gone missing sometime during the abduction. Idly, she wondered if Vallini would have allowed her to take the images home, anyway.

"How do you get the entertainment on the screen, Vallini," she asked, noticing that his screen was now showing lists.

"Just speak to it," he replied. "Say something like 'Video options' or 'List entertainment'.

Betty experimented and was intrigued by the unfamiliar titles.

A countdown imposed itself across her screen, and she lay back, anticipating the launch. When it came, it was marked by deep vibrations and just a gentle pushing upward from the recliner. Then, after a few seconds, that pushing became more pronounced as the engines throttled up, and Betty relished the feeling of being accelerated. In her Cabriolet, she could floor the throttle and get that feeling for a few seconds. But here, the acceleration just went on and on—she could only imagine the speed that they were attaining. Frustratingly, there was still only sky visible through the small windows, though when she craned her neck round to the other side, there were maybe glimpses of Earth. After a couple of minutes of acceleration, the screen informed her that 'Main Engine Cut-Off' and 'First-Stage Separation' were coming up soon. The feeling of acceleration was replaced for a few seconds by a quick sensation of falling, like speeding over a humpback bridge, and then the push upward from the recliner resumed as the ferry's main engine fired up, with a more mellow vibration.

After a few more minutes, the novelty was beginning to wear off, so she shifted her attention to the screen again. Vallini turned his head in her direction. "Just a suggestion, but there is actually a re-make of a classic from your time, if you would like to watch that. Ask the screen for 'She spoke with harmless shadows'." It was not a title that Betty recognised, but she requested it be played and allowed herself to be carried along by the narrative and the images. It was not a story she remembered, and it was sometimes difficult to follow the futuristic style in which the story was told, but she felt a strange sense of déjà vu about it.

*   *   *

In fact, she had been so absorbed in the video that she had hardly noticed the transition into near-weightlessness. When the video finished, she savoured the new feeling for a few minutes and started thinking again about the journey she was on.

She turned to Vallini. "Vallini, can you tell me something about your cousin. I'm a bit worried that I won't have anything to talk about with her if I don't know anything about her life."

"Pause," he directed to his screen. "To be honest, Betty, I know very little about her either. I have never met her, of course, and communication with the colonies is very technically fraught. I have not had any meaningful communication with my uncle since he left, and I was just a teenager then. But I tell you what. You can read the communications between her and her parents since she left—they were copied to me as her new legal guardian. That will give you some flavour of her situation." He released the belt on his upper torso and floated to a sitting position from which he could open the luggage locker. He pulled out a tablet, turned it on and opened a file. He handed it to Betty, pointing to the text, pulled himself back into a recumbent position and re-fastened the belt. "Continue," he instructed his screen.

Betty was initially a bit surprised and uncomfortable about being given someone else's personal communications. Perhaps that's just a cultural difference between my time and now, she mused; it sounded like the messages had been formally copied to Vallini. And she wouldn't have to mention it to... She realised she didn't even know the cousin's name yet. She wouldn't have to mention to his cousin that she had read these messages. She started reading off the tablet:

Earth-Standard StarDate 2237.302

Hi my dear Astrid,

*Well, another year has gone by, and as you know, I always message you on the anniversary of when you left, even though I realise you will probably still be in hibernation. Or maybe not, now. The estimate of hibernation for the journey was around 16 years, so you might just have arrived by now, although this message may take another few years to reach you at or near Earth. And, although I only message you **once** every standard year, you can be sure that I think of you **every** day. Your mother, unfortunately, is still in a coma in hospital, but she would otherwise also be thinking of you today.*

I have had to retire from working at the quarry this year—the dust has finally compromised my lungs too much. So, since I cannot expect to live many more years here (we knew our life expectancy on a non-terra planet would be shorter), and because I know it is now around the time you will be arriving, I thought I would write a longer communication to explain why we sought to send you back to Earth to live your adult life, and why I am now sure we were right to do so. I have also paid what I consider to be an exorbitant fee to have this message multiplexed into the priority comms channel, because I have heard reports from friends that the ordinary comms are not reliably being received at either end.

I am so glad that we decided to send you back to Earth whilst we still had the opportunity—life on this planet has deteriorated markedly. It all seemed such a good idea to emigrate here when your mother and I were young—the opportunity to participate in the mining of lanthanides from a planet bedecked with quality deposits seemed like an enduring future. We didn't realise until you were coming of age that exporting millions of tonnes of the stuff, excellent as it was, would soon depress the market price, gradually taking the sheen off our golden opportunity. Wages were beginning to fall even before you left and I could see that the will and financial resource to develop the planet further was already beginning to wane. So, we bought the transit ticket for you whilst we could still afford to raise the mortgage for it. I suspected that there would be little future for you here on this backwater planet as our only real resource became devalued. And events have proven that to be right. There has been no official statement, but I think the perchlorate oxygen generators are not in such good condition these days—I find myself having to breathe harder, especially during our so-called summer when the UV levels are high; though I guess that might also be because of my lung troubles. Richer folks have started building habitation pods closer to the perchlorate plants—I guess the oxygen levels are more pleasant there; and some expensive oxygen-bars have opened in the main mercantile super-pod. It seems to me crazy that the authorities would not spend money on maintaining and upgrading the oxygen generators—but maybe it's because we do not have extensive manufacturing capability here. The parts have to be ordered from Earth or other planets where they have a significant industrial base, and the delays, even to the nearest colony planet, are formidable. Trouble is, once they have all the lanthanides they want, we have nothing left to trade with. So yes, in retrospect, it was a stupid idea for your mother and me to relocate here, and I apologise to you for that, though your education was, I think, reasonably good. But now, the schools here are, I gather, beginning to deteriorate—like everything else on a planet in decline.

So, as I said, I think we made the right decision to send you back home to Earth. I have no regrets. Well, of course, I do regret not being able to enjoy seeing you mature and perhaps have your own family. Ah, how I wish we could have all gone back to Earth, but the transit fares were enormous. And had we left it any longer, we would not have been able to afford even your fare. So it was done. I know you were not entirely convinced at the time, and I had to be somewhat dictatorial about it, but hopefully you will forgive me that, and realise in the fullness of time that it was the right decision. I just hope that you will be received with hospitality back on Earth—born on a distant exotic planet, and, by their standards, technologically naïve, especially after a long hibernation on the ship. But at least you have had a reasonable education and should somehow be able to get decent employ.

The hospital says your mother is unlikely ever to improve, but they can keep her alive indefinitely, which is wonderful. One piece of good news is that I have been able to acquire a marvellous piece of marble for our gravestone—for your mother and me. It's a fluorescent-veined travertine. I know you think it's strange that I am fascinated with the ornamental stone that is also quarried here, but I really think you would be impressed by this slab.

So I am not sure whether you will ever receive these comms messages from me, and I suppose it is unlikely I will still be alive to receive a reply from you, considering the probable long delay for each communication. But I would like you to know that I love and miss you, and still think of you every day. And I hope you will find a worthwhile life back on mother Earth.

Take care, dear Astrid,

With love from your Pappy xxx

Earth-Standard StarDate 2243.214

Hi, my dearest Pappy and Mammy,

We just arrived, well at least we have been resuscitated and are in Earth orbit—6 years late! Apparently, one of the ship's drives developed an anomaly during the journey and the AI thought it best to put that drive down to half-power—hence our arrival 6 years late. The engineers have just looked at the data and thought the AI was a bit over-cautious, but better safe than sorry, I suppose. We are all unsurprisingly very weak—mentally OK, but physically weak after such a prolonged hibernation. We are staying in orbital LGR (Low Gravity Rehab) for at least a couple of weeks to build up strength before transferring to FGR (Full Gravity Rehab) and then finally getting ferried down to the surface.

As you suspected, the regular comms had not been getting through, so the only message awaiting me was that dated 2237.302 but nothing dated before or since.

Of course, it only feels to me like yesterday when I left Pericyon c, and, although I knew to expect that, it is still bizarre and very sad to hear from you, knowing that you are so much older and frail. What happened to mother to put her in a coma in hospital?

I am also sad to hear that the planetary economy is beginning to fail, but it makes me feel very grateful and understanding of why you sent me here—I'm sorry if I upset you arguing against it. I have been brushing up my language skills with the rehab agents—trying to get my vocabulary a bit more in vogue, and my physio has told me that several of the colony planets have run into sustainability problems; one or two have actually been abandoned and evacuated.

So, I wonder if you will receive this message—another few years in transit—that means it would arrive with you maybe 25 standard years since I left you. Oh dear. Tears... Time and distance are so cruel.

But you will be pleased to know that I messaged the family contacts on Earth that you gave me and, considering the 38 years two-way hibernation time protraction, it is not surprising that your brothers and sisters have all passed on; but Pappy's brother's son, Vanilli, has replied, and said he will take me under his wing when I land on the surface, after I come out of FGR. He is an operative in Temporal Continuity—whatever that means. So, I am not alone—I have at least one cousin on Earth.

All my love,

Astrid xx

Betty's eyes welled up with tears of sympathy at Astrid having lost her family and presumably all her friends, and now being so alone. But she also saw how Astrid's life would probably now be much improved by her parents' decisive sacrifice.

And what idiosyncratic points of social history Betty realised she was gleaning. She wondered idly if history was the right term to use for things happening in the future; she decided it must be, because history is a description of events, not dependent on the timing of the audience. She read the messages again, making sure she had taken in all the nuances.

Betty's screen informed her that docking to Rehab Station-3 was now in progress. Vallini seemed to have finished watching his entertainment, and he was fiddling with his seat straps. "It's a good idea to loosen the belts a little now, Betty—so you begin to get used to the weightlessness." Betty did so and was surprised at the difference—she had hardly noticed the uncommon feeling of weightlessness with the straps holding her in place.

"What are the Earth-Standard StarDates in those letters, Vallini?"

"Ah. Well, it's just the Year, a dot, then the day of that year; for us on Earth anyway. Off-world, they use clocks that are synchronised with that, so we can all keep track of the sequence of events," he explained.

Betty looked around. "How long now, Vallini?" she asked.

"About ten minutes, I should think. They have to equalise the pressures, open the docking hatch and then we can go on through into the Station. But there's one thing I need to talk to you about first, Betty. I know you are a scientist, and probably very curious about how everything works, but you must resist the temptation to understand the technology. The reason is that you will be going back to your own time afterwards, and if you took any advanced theory or information back with you, then there would be the possibility of you inadvertently or purposely changing the future. Which we don't want, because it might be very destabilising. You have already seen how the transfer of your own knowledge to another part of the world, even in your own time, would have drastic consequences for the future. You will have access to automated services here, so I'm going to have to ask you to not to try to advance your scientific knowledge by asking for education in any technological subjects. It's OK to make full use of the entertainment, and I'm sure you and Astrid will talk about social history and so on. It's just the areas in which you have technical expertise, and our modern technology generally that I'm concerned about. It's OK to learn about how we use things, but not how they work or how we make them."

"Oh. That's disappointing of course," admitted Betty. "Still, I understand what you're saying Vallini. But what if I overhear or learn something by accident?"

"Well, we have no way of erasing memories, so then you wouldn't be able to go back home!" It seemed from his tone that Vallini was joking, but the idea was chilling nevertheless, even more so because Betty couldn't be sure whether he was joking or not, with so much at stake.

"OK, I get the message Vallini. I'll be good. But when *will* I be able to go back home again?"

"Well, I'm thinking two or three days? You see, although the reverse-engineering of the Sentinel devices may take months or years of work, they will feed-back the results to me today, from the future, when they complete the analysis, so any operations we need to conduct can be done imminently—during the next couple of days. I'll message you when I think it's completely safe to take you back. To be honest, you would probably be safe going back now, but I would like a little time to make sure we completely eliminate any surviving Sentinel remnants before we return you to your own time. Does that sound OK?"

"Yes. One other question—how do I access what you called 'automated services', and what are they?"

"Oh, I'll let Astrid explain things like that, and there are rehab agents who can explain how to do things; though basically, it's just asking—as you did with the flight entertainment." He pointed at the overhead screens. "Right, it's our turn..."

The attendants had been working their way round the passengers, one by one, releasing their straps and guiding them in the direction of the docking port. She watched as Vallini struggled to get his now-weightless backpack over his shoulder; he was helped by the attendant who knew exactly how to anchor, push and pull to get the passengers and their luggage sorted out. Betty, without any luggage, found it much easier, as the attendant indicated to her to take hold of each handrail and gently pull herself along toward the docking port, gliding in midair. It was simple, but also very easy to overdo it, and more than once she nearly barrelled into Vallini in front, as she followed.

The docking port was the only narrow part, and once through, it opened out into a large room-sized reception area where the arriving people were each being met by Station workers, Betty assumed. They were dressed in a different sort of uniform from the attire she had seen on the ground—more like cotton jumpsuits, light-blue with black beading and sewn-on badges. She waited as Vallini showed his documentation to one of the workers. "Do you mind if I go on to meet Astrid by myself first," Vallini asked.

"Sure, Of course."

"You can sit over here," suggested the worker, gesturing to a seat on the side with a belt, freely dangling.

Betty strapped herself in and watched the arrivals still coming through the hatch. Most of them must be workers, she mused, noting that they greeted the others and went straight on through to the rest of the Station. Others, she suspected, must be visitors to those being rehabilitated. Or maybe they were coming to be habilitated to weightlessness, before journeying off on spaceships, she wondered. There had only been about eighteen arrivals in all, and they had all been disembarked and taken wherever in just a few minutes. Then came the cargo. Large packs, the size of a fridge. Their surface looked like canvas, with lots of straps. Each was pushed through from the ferry by one of their crew and then guided away by one of the Station crew. There was no way to tell how heavy each package was as it floated, weightless, except by watching how much effort the crew put into pushing or pulling the pack into a change of direction; one arm on a handrail and the other clutching a strap. And also expertly hooking their feet into the rails for stability, Betty noticed. Then finally a stream of departing passengers, more than had come up, she judged. She tried to view their faces as they pulled themselves along the handrails with accomplished ease. Most, like Vallini, looked inscrutable, though one or two smiled at her, on noticing her watching; and looked quizzically at her clothing.

Betty watched intently as one of the workers now went through a ritual of inspecting the lining around the edge of the hatch, before pushing it shut and pressing some buttons on a control panel to establish the pressure-sealing. He noticed Betty watching avidly. "First time?" he asked.

"Yes, very much so," she said, then wondered if she should have left it at a simple 'yes'. He beckoned her over, and explained how the pressure was being slowly released on the other side of the hatch, showing her the instrument readings and the checks that were registering on the panel.

"So where are your strange clothes from?" he asked.

"Oh... I don't think I'm allowed to talk about that," she muttered apologetically.

He laughed. "That's OK," he reassured her, "I expect you think my uniform looks weird? Anyway, we will kit you out with a more practical outfit for your stay." He gestured to her dress; actually, Sveta's dress, which, in this weightless environment, was no longer hanging, but tending to balloon up toward her waist.

Vallini returned. "You're not trying to learn new technology already?" he quipped.

"It's a pressure seal hatch, Vallini. Hardly bleeding-edge technology. I already know how these things work." Then she noticed there were tears in his eyes. "Oh... OK, will you introduce me to your Astrid now?"

"Yes." He pulled his ID from his jacket pocket and flashed it to the worker. "Sorry, I will be back in three minutes."

"Ah. Yes, sir. Certainly." The worker, without any protest, pressed some buttons on the control panel to commence re-opening the hatch.

Vallini led her, pulling on the handrails, gliding through a tunnel that joined to the rest of the Station. As Vallini exited the tunnel in front of her, she realised that the massive open cylindrical area beyond was slowly revolving relative to her. Slightly unsettled in her stomach, she followed Vallini over the edge of the tunnel opening and grabbed one of the revolving handrails. Then she trailed him along the handrails towards the outer edge of the massive cylinder. As she got closer to the outer part, she felt the centrifugal force pulling her down slightly. She copied Vallini in turning her feet to face the outer wall, and clambering the rest of the way feet first. When she reached the outer wall where Vallini was waiting, she found she was again able to stand, and appreciate why this area of the Station was called Low-Gravity. She experimented with a small jump. It was like slow-motion and the landing was very soft. "So, what's the strength of the pseudo-gravity here, Vallini?" she asked knowingly.

"About 0.33g in this section," he replied. "In the next part of the Station it is 0.67g, and in the furthest part a nominal 1g. All three parts rotate as one unit at the same rate, but the larger diameters, further along, mean the centrifugal force on the rim is greater there."

They began to walk the great circle, Betty resisting the urge to make long bounding strides. At intervals, corridors led away from the circle with rooms to either side, in similar fashion to a hotel. "This is corridor 'E'. You and Astrid will be staying in room 9 along here." He led the way. "Another thing, Betty. I have already talked about not trying to glean the technological principles employed in this age. But it is also important that you do not enquire personal details—births, deaths and marriages of yourself, descendants or those close to you—it would compromise your life back in your own time and could also lead to changes to the future."

"Are those details available now then? Surely they would all be ancient history?" Betty countered.

"Absolutely they are available. Your time is only two hundred years ago. Think about it. In your time you could easily access genealogical records from two hundred years previous—from the early 1800s."

"You're right," conceded Betty. "I suppose in the scheme of things, two hundred years is not a long time—just three life-spans. Yes, sure Vallini. I will resist that temptation too."

He had pressed the door buzzer, waited a second and then slid the door panel aside and entered. "Astrid... Betty..." he introduced them formally. Astrid was sitting in a posturally-correct chair, and she strained to stand to greet them. "No, don't get up..." Vallini reassured her.

"Yes, I must keep making effort," she countered, finally pushing on the back of the chair to attain a full standing position. She was tall, but very thin and alarmingly pale—her skin almost white. Although her face, in youth, lacked wrinkles, her cheeks were so hollow they reminded Betty of an old woman. "It's great to meet you, Betty." She extended her bony hands and took Betty's in greeting. There was warmth to her touch, but a lack of strength. "Vanilli has, intriguingly, told me just a little about you, but I have a million questions."

Betty laughed. "Me too," she replied. "It could be a very long question and answer session." Astrid smiled, cocking her head slightly to one side.

"OK you two," Vallini interrupted. "I must hurry to get aboard the return ferry now. Astrid, we will talk at much greater length when I return. Don't worry about anything. I will be here for you. And Betty, I will come to fetch you in a couple of days. Relax and enjoy your stay. You have VIP status as a guest of TC. Just ask for anything you want. And you are completely safe here." He kissed Astrid on the cheek, then shook Betty's hand. But she couldn't resist putting her arm on his shoulder and kissing his cheek. She hoped she had not committed a cultural faux pas, but Vallini just smiled at them both and slipped quickly out of the room.

Astrid still had hold of the other of Betty's hands. "Your bedroom is through the door on this side," she stated, leading Betty slowly across. "Mine is on the other side; and we share this ante-room. There'll be some clothes laid out on the bed for you if you want to change." She looked closely at Betty's jacket and stroked it to sense its feel. She shook her head. "I've seen pictures of old-fashioned clothes of course. But I didn't imagine them quite like this. Presumably, Vanilli wears normal clothes when he's not visiting back-times?"

"Oh yes," Betty laughed. "A friend of mine kitted him out in those clothes because he was standing out like a sore thumb in my time. But can I correct you on one thing?"

"Yes. Please do. I have so much to learn here."

"Well, your cousin's name is Vallini, not Vanilli."

"Oh. Goodness. Vallini... Vallini... Right. OK, I'll remember that. I hope he didn't mind. I've never heard the name before, it sounded strange to me."

"But *your* name is cool," Betty commented.

"What, Astrid? No, it's not—it's corny as hell. *'She of the stars'*. I can see why my parents chose the name; they were so overly idealistic about everything." The door buzzer sounded. "Oh, that'll be my physio, back for another session."

"Right. I'll have a shower and get changed," said Betty. "Oh?"

"Yes, the shower does work in low gravity—it's pumped downwards and vacuumed out. Come and join us when you're ready. We can still talk whilst I am doing the exercises."

Betty closed the door to the ante-room and looked around her bedroom. Sure enough, there were Station-style clothes and towels on her bed. She slipped off the clothes she had been travelling in and walked over to the shower. No controls were evident. She looked around, grimacing and thinking she would have to re-dress and go ask Astrid. Then she remembered Vallini saying *'Basically, it's just asking'*. She spoke: "Turn on shower."

"What temperature would you like the shower water?" A soft, helpful, but disembodied voice.

"Umm... Medium please," Betty requested, not knowing what the heat that she usually enjoyed was, in degrees. The shower burst into life, and she bounced lightly in, the door automatically closing quickly behind her to keep the spray, that was voluminous in the low gravity, from splashing out into the room. "A little hotter please." A grin spread across her face. This was going to be fun.

Chapter 10

I didn't come here of my own accord, and I can't leave that
way. Whoever brought me here will have to take me home.

(Rumi)

Earth-Standard StarDate 2243.215, TC HQ

Vallini stepped out of the transport back at the TC Headquarters
building to be greeted by a TC operative thrusting a set of clothes into
his hands. "Ravel, the Head of Analysis is waiting for you in your office."
It was a less than subtle message that he should dress appropriately
before seeing the analyst. Vallini went somewhere private to change out
of the outfit Gemma had made him wear, though he had become
somewhat fond of the padded black jacket. Ravel was actually an old
friend, and, as Head of Analysis, enjoyed equal status to himself as Head
of Operations; he felt no need to dress formally to meet him, but Vallini
liked to conform to how the operatives wanted the show to run.

"Hi, Ravel."

"Vallini! It's so good to see you again. I know from your point of
view you saw me only last week, but I have been in isolation with my
team for four and a half years analysing those Sentinel devices that your
people just 'recently' captured. You can probably see my hair has gone a
bit more grey at the temples? Though it's more a result of the isolation
than the work." Vallini nodded and smiled his sympathy. "Anyway, I
have just translocated back from four years on, to share the completed
report with you, and advise on actions if you want." They both sat, and
Ravel pulled up data onto a big screen. "We have had to work in
complete isolation from TC because otherwise the results of the actions
that you take today, if they were known to us, would have prejudiced and
perhaps de-motivated our analytical work. Too much of a feedback loop.
Anyway, but you know all about such problems.

So, the easy part was reverse-engineering the hardware—no

151

particular surprises there. A fairly standard implementation of translocation technology, though all done with components completely unfamiliar to us; and they use the standard subwave channels for comms. The harder part was deciphering their communications protocols, and testing, in a limited controlled environment, how we could communicate into their network. And then reading out all their information." He displayed some diagrams on the screen. "The most exciting part was discovering that each device had access to a complete history database that is stored in a shared server somewhere. And when I say complete history... I mean centuries and centuries of detailed records of events—political, scientific, social history and detailed records of people and places etc. Of course, it's more sketchy in ancient times, and indeed their records are exactly in accord with what we know, right up to the early 21st Century—the time period you have just visited. Then very slowly their history begins to diverge from ours. Geopolitical power differences first, social awareness divergence, then the whole fabric of the structure of society, And... well you already know the outcome—no TC organisation. But instead, a rather more hierarchical society, with an alternative organisation to restrain temporal translocation, they call it Perpetuity Enforcement, set up for the same reasons that we do it—to maintain the consistency of the future—self-preservation if you like. I'll have more to say on that a little later."

He shifted in his seat. "Their version of history goes on way into the future, and it gets increasingly difficult to understand—my guess is that these Sentinel devices are optimised to work on a stretch of history over a few hundred years. The ones that your operations captured were manufactured in very early times, presumably to defend against the possibility of a change being made to time which rendered their organisation non-existent. They obviously considered the possibility of such an event, just in the same way that we did, and so manufactured and left devices in early years that were designed to re-establish their timeline and organisation, if such a demise ever occurred. For the same reason the history database server must have been manufactured and established in early years as well, though the devices seem to access it in real-time. They seemed to favour leaving the devices as autonomous, unlike the way we have trained human agents with each translocation device."

"Anyway," he continued, "that annihilation event did happen for them, and there were just a few of their Sentinel devices left trying to work out what had happened, and how to put it right—from *their* point of view that is. Helpfully for us, the active devices recorded everything that they did into their massive database. So, it seems that the process they went through was comparing their history, as it should have been, with the history that actually did exist—they were able to tap into the 21st Century internet to read that. And eventually, they discovered that the deviation all started with an Eastern espionage group failing to acquire sensitive information about early temporal science from a Western geopolitical research group. That resulted in the Eastern geopolitical block substantially lagging behind the West in surveillance capabilities. Anyway, the names and places were all recorded in their historical records. It seems the Sentinel could not deduce exactly *why* the dislocation in events had occurred, but it knew the name and location of the spymaster who was to receive the kidnap victim with the technological knowledge, and it knew the victim's name. So it set about trying to locate her with the intention of translocating her directly to the spymaster."

Vallini nodded and Ravel took a sip of water before carrying on. "As we decoded the AI reasoning, we saw that although it understood the syntax and semantics of social history, it was a bit basic with the pragmatics, at least as social practices changed through those early centuries. It enlisted the help of a Vicar—a religious authority in the 19th Century. And although that authority would probably have worked well in his own century, it was not well suited to the 21st Century. However, one way or another they succeeded in getting the Sentinel device into close proximity with the intended victim and... well you know the rest. By the way, we even found an image of you in their database—it was gathered in the instant before it spirited your Betty away—you and your operative, Gemma, were sitting in chairs next to Betty." Vallini felt uneasy hearing that. "And so, TC ceased to exist. I think we were extremely fortunate that Gemma was so resourceful and swung the balance back for us—we could so easily have been lost forever."

"Which brings me to the biggest questions in all this," declared Ravel. "The Sentinel did not just empirically know that it needed to relocate Betty. That insight came from a comparative study of the then-current history with its own history database. But a history database would not, could not, just exist in isolation. Therefore the implication is: the Sentinel's recorded history must have been an actual reality at some stage. It must have existed at some stage *before* the Sentinel arrived to track down Betty. Just as *we* know that *our* history existed before the Sentinel snatched Betty in order to re-establish their Perpetuity Enforcement timeline. We know that, because Gemma used knowledge of *our* history, and devices from *our* history, to re-establish our own TC

153

existence. But the mystery is that we have no knowledge in TC about any actions of ours that caused a previous incarnation of Perpetuity Enforcement history to be replaced by ours. Unless you discovered the reason for that in your operation?"

Vallini nodded his understanding of the issue. "Off the record?" he requested. "At least for the time being?"

Ravel looked excited to hear the explanation. "As you wish, Vallini."

"It seems that Betty and her colleagues had enough capability using their primitive temporal science to change the course of events to defend her against being kidnapped by the Eastern Intelligence group that you mentioned earlier. You see, it was not just a case of 'receiving sensitive information' as you described it earlier; it was a kidnap and torture extraction of the information. So it seems that Betty's colleagues simply acted in self-defence. They had absolutely no idea of the forward consequences of that action, or that it would have consequences beyond saving Betty."

Ravel inhaled sharply. "But do you see what that means, Vallini? It means that the *original* history was not ours, it was that of Perpetuity Enforcement society. Our organisation has always been founded on the principle that we uphold and maintain the natural, original, rightful chain of events that constitute history. Our whole ethos is based on not allowing changes to the course of time. But now we discover that our own timeline is not the *original*, pure history. It is built on a deviation."

"Indeed." Both men were silent for a moment. "This is an existential question, Ravel. On the one hand, our pure ethical inclination might be to give back the course of history to Perpetuity Enforcement because it is the original. That means you and I would no longer exist. Or do we choose existence? Do we continue to maintain defence of our own timeline and course of events just because we obviously choose being alive? I suppose there is a third way—that we evaluate the merit of our society versus the merits of Perpetuity Enforcement's society to determine which should have precedence."

"No, I think that third way is problematic," declared Ravel. "History is ever-evolving. There are dark periods when wars or oppression take place; and more enlightened times with progressions that approach utopia. Are we to evaluate the endpoint, which we can never know, or the average merits of the path. There is no way of making such a judgement."

"I agree," Vallini stated. "This is why I suggested we keep it off the record for the moment. When we have dealt with any residual threat then we can discuss it further. My own view is that I choose to exist. But I would not seek to keep the truth from the Seniors of TC, and I would expect them to consider and perhaps come to the same choice. But I accept that there will be angst involved—that we may need to completely rethink the ethos of our organisation. I wonder also if a more pragmatic TC might want to conceal the messy truth from the public. It might prejudice our authority and ability to enforce the 'no temporal translocation' rules, if it was understood that the status quo that we are so avidly protecting is actually an arbitrary one; rather than the unmodified, original, pure course of events. On the other hand, we might be more supported by the public if they understood that their own existence could even be up for question. Ultimately, it is human nature to protect one's own way of life—choosing to exist over questioning one's right to exist."

"But..." Ravel started.

Vallini raised his hand. "I am happy to discuss this with you at length in due course, Ravel. But right now, we should first do our duty: which is to urgently address any residual threat from the Sentinel devices. Let's postpone our angst. What are your proposals arising from the reverse-engineering of the devices and analysis of their functioning?"

Ravel eased back in his chair. "Yes, as you wish, Vallini." He caused some further diagrams to appear on the screen... "So firstly the devices have a simple 'Enquire/Acknowledge ID' protocol. If we transmit the properly encoded ENQ signal on the subwave comms channel, then we should receive back a simple ACK with an ID message from each of any devices that are still operational. We would need to do this in present time, because we obviously are not interested in replies from devices that have already been destroyed. We should activate all deep-listening stations so that we can get a location fix on where any replies arise."

Vallini raised his hand again, promoting a pause in Ravel's reasoning. "Let me get the necessary resources in preparation." He spoke to the screen. "Voice link to operations control room."

After a few seconds: "Operations control responding, Vallini. What can we do for you?"

"Hi, Bram. I'm just giving you some advance warning so you can get the network prepared. We are going to broadcast an encrypted message on subwave, and we expect short immediate replies from some alien devices. So we need worldwide deep listening stations on alert—

hopefully we can get triangulations to the locations of all those devices."

"OK, Vallini. In present time?" asked Bram.

"Yes, in present time, please."

"OK, Vallini. Give us an hour to prepare," concurred Bram.

Vallini turned his attention back to Ravel, and gestured for him to continue.

"Yes. I guess it may be useful to learn their current locations but it may not be necessary because..." He paused initiating more explanatory graphics on the screen. "Another simple protocol that is implemented on those devices is a 'Summons and Search'. We can send a 'Summons with ID' message to each of those devices, to lure them to a place where they can be destroyed. I would suggest not using one of the Way-Stations since that might appear suspicious following their loss of contact with other devices translocating to those when they pursued you and Betty. And I further suggest appending the Search command protocol, including Betty's bio-scan data, which should parse as all the more credible to the devices."

"Do you have a location in mind?" asked Vallini.

"Well, bearing in mind that the remaining devices may have fragmented data about the pursuit of you and Betty through the Way-Stations, it would probably seem most plausible to them that Betty had ended up somewhere not too far away from here. Other than that the choice is arbitrary."

Vallini looked thoughtful. "There is a disused airfield some 20 km north of here. We could use that as the summons target location." He again addressed the screen: "Voice link to operations control room."

"Bram here, Vallini; sorry, we are not ready yet."

"No, that's OK, Bram. We need you to set up an additional, offensive operation. We are proposing to lure the alien devices to the disused Nikenfeld airfield by broadcasting a summons to them. I need you to set up a ring of offensive resources around the perimeter of the airfield with instructions to destroy on detection. Bear in mind that there are some dilapidated buildings on site. But please do not use translocation transports to get our offensive devices there—I don't want to give any indication of translocations in the vicinity. Have them physically transported."

"Physically transported! That will take some time. Can we use flotation conveyors?" asked Bram.

"Yes, that will be fine. But also maintain subwave silence in the vicinity. We want to reveal no clues of activity."

"I'm just looking at the plan of Nikenfeld now," commented Bram. "We don't have enough stock weapons to cover the whole area—can I take the fixtures from the Way-Station?"

"Yes, but you can translocate in offensive stock from other Way-Stations as well—it's only the Nikenfeld area that must be free of afterbeats. How long do you envisage that will take?"

"We can be ready for your deep listening exercise in less than an hour. But the Nikenfeld operation will take 24 hours to put in place."

"OK, Bram. Set the arrangements in progress, and then join Ravel and myself for a detailed briefing," Vallini concluded. He broke off the conversation and picked up a coffee that one of the operatives had just brought in for him.

Ravel had already started on his. "So, the third part of the strategy," Ravel picked up the lead again, "is just in case we have not destroyed all the alien devices with a summons; or indeed to be absolutely sure no device could possibly threaten us in the future. We can send a set of amendments to their historical database storage centre. Those amendments would be designed to overwrite any data about Betty, her colleagues, the Eastern intelligence operation etc., and confound and confuse any attempts by Sentinels to re-analyse the desired steps for re-establishing their own timeline."

"Excellent Ravel. I assume you have pre-prepared the data to overwrite the historical database?"

Ravel laughed. "Yes, we have spent the last few weeks of our analysis time preparing that. But I must just give a couple of provisos. We have been able to test out the other protocols—ENQ and Summons—on the captured devices whilst they are in isolation so that we know they will work. But we have not been able to test writing to their database. It would have been unwise to trigger any possible responses before planning today's actions. And indeed I do not know where this database physically resides. It is possible it will respond to the ENQ command that operations control is preparing for now. But it is equally likely that it may not, since it is a not a *standard* Sentinel device like those we have been analysing. We have been able to read their history from it in great quantity, so my guess is that we can determine its location by requesting history and triangulating to the subwave response. I suppose ultimately we should destroy the database server to finally eliminate any possible threat. But it would be responsible and useful to read and store the entire history before we do that—I'm sure it would provide much fodder for academic studies, and indeed inspiration for literature for years to come."

*   *   *

Tuesday morning, Jurys Inn, Cheltenham

Alex still hadn't got used to the way people just disappeared when they translocated. It was even more of a wrench when you knew you might not ever see them again. Though Gemma had promised to keep in touch, it seemed doubtful that he would see Sveta again; he was certainly not planning any trips to Russia, especially after Betty's frightening experience abroad. But, working through a crisis together, he had grown fond of all these people.

"Well," said Joo-Won to Alex, "I guess we better go sort out your friend, Arbuckle, back to the past, now?"

"Yeah, that will be a relief for him, I know," Alex responded.

"How far his hotel?"

"About a 20-minute walk." Alex swung on his coat. They dropped off all the room keys at reception on the way out. As they walked, Joo-Won filled Alex in on some of the details of Betty's rescue. It all sounded a bit crazy and unsafe, and Alex counted himself lucky to have had the stay-at-home job, though he knew that too had been pivotal.

As they walked up the road to the hotel that Arbuckle was staying in, Alex suddenly remembered Betty's missing car, and that he had not mentioned it to her when he had seen her this morning. Perhaps it was for the best, he thought—she could enjoy her trip without worrying about it.

He knocked on Arbuckle's hotel-room door. There was no answer. He knocked again. Finally, the door opened and Arbuckle appeared—dishevelled and looking the worse for wear.

His greeting was not as bright as usual. "Ah, my friend. Come in, Mr Smith. You must forgive me; I have a frightful headache. I think I saw you last night?" He creased his forehead trying to remember. "I'm afraid the evening is a bit of a blur."

Alex managed to suppress his inclination to smirk. "Oh, I'm sorry to hear that, Reverend. Can I introduce you to my friend here? This is Joo-Won." Joo-Won stuck his hand out politely and Arbuckle shook it but looked puzzled and dubious. He retreated back into the room and slumped into a chair.

"So, I have some good news for you, Reverend," Alex continued. Arbuckle looked at him quizzically. "Yes. Joo-Won, here, can take you home." Almost at once, Alex could see that Arbuckle was going to be difficult.

"Oh, I don't think so. The Sentinel has not returned yet. I should wait until it returns. It would be insulting to the Lord not to wait patiently."

Joo-Won gave Alex a concerned look.

Alex went over and sat on the bed, close to Arbuckle. "You see, Reverend, you have been deceived, taken advantage of. The Sentinel is *not* operated by the Angels," Alex tried to explain.

"Oh, but I met the angel first-hand. He said his name was Uriel. He said his job was to maintain God's will and correct it when it was transgressed..." He trailed off, not sounding as if he was convincing himself.

"No." Alex was trying to break the news gently. "It was nothing to do with *God's angels*, and it's not coming back for you."

"Uh." Arbuckle slapped his forehead as if he was suddenly realising something. "Uh. You mean as was prophesied in Revelations 16:14. '*Satan's angels will also appear as godly clergyman, and Satan will appear as an angel of light.*' Oh. I have made a terrible mistake." He slumped forward with his face in his hands.

Alex was torn between amusement and pity. He swallowed back the mirth before continuing gently: "No, no... The Sentinel has nothing to do with God's angels, *or* Satan's angels. The man pretending to be Uriel was an impostor, just an *ordinary* man, with some fairly clever machinery from the future. He needed someone's help to locate Betty. He was just a charlatan who tricked you into helping him.

"So it's not my fault?" Arbuckle raised his gaze to Alex.

"No, that's right. It's not your fault. You were an innocent victim of trickery."

"Ooh, my head."

"Look, I think we'd better get you a good breakfast before we take you home, eh?" Alex noticed Joo-Won glancing at his wristwatch.

Arbuckle nodded gently. "That would be most kind."

Alex helped Arbuckle to his feet. Aside to Joo-Won he whispered: "He had rather a lot to drink last night." Joo-Won rolled his eyes impatiently. They led him out to reception where Alex asked for some aspirin and fed the tablets to Arbuckle to try to ease his headache.

"Will you be staying another night, sir?" the receptionist asked Arbuckle.

Alex answered for him. "No, I'll be checking him out later this morning."

"Very good, sir."

*   *   *

Alex was a little concerned whether the full English breakfast that Arbuckle was avidly consuming would make him feel better or worse. Alex's own experience with hangovers was fairly limited, but he could remember at least one occasion when food had definitely not been the answer. However, the speed at which Arbuckle was eating suggested that perhaps he had not had a meal the previous evening. Alex sipped at his coffee. Joo-won had finished his, and Alex noticed his foot tapping impatiently.

At length they all trooped back to Arbuckle's hotel room, the Reverend declaring that he felt much better. "OK," said Joo-Won, taking out some equipment from his rucksack. "So where he need be taken?" he asked Alex.

Alex turned to Arbuckle. "Tell me your address, Reverend."

"I live in the Rectory at Winterbourne Steepleton," he replied.

"And that's in the county of Dorset, isn't it?"

"That's right my friend. I am most fortunate to live in a beautiful part of the country."

Joo-Won looked flustered. "Here. I think it best you search on map, Alex. Wait. I change alphabet from Korean Hangul to English." He made some keystrokes on the screen and turned it to face Alex. "You write address here." He tapped a box on the screen.

Alex duly typed in the name of the country where it was indicated, then stopped at Zip Code or Postcode. Clearly, it would be no use asking Arbuckle—he long preceded such designations. Thinking for a second he pulled out his phone and tried the address in Google Maps. It came up with 'The Old Rectory, Winterbourne Steepleton'. "Is it called the *Old* Rectory?" he asked Arbuckle.

"No. Just 'The Rectory'. There is only one Rectory there," the old man answered doubtfully. And he retreated into the bathroom.

Alex decided it must be one and the same. If it was called *'old'* now that would fit with Arbuckle's time. He copied the Postcode across into Joo-Won's screen, and was relieved to see that the map displaying on Joo-Won's screen seemed to match that on his phone. It was clearly a very rural area, the village consisting of a scattering of buildings along a single winding road. "So, it seems to be that building there." He pointed the spot out to Joo-Won, who now looked somewhat relieved. Alex realised he must be struggling with the unfamiliarity of English names.

"Excellent. Thank you Alex. And we will need date and time for return him to."

Alex walked over to the bathroom door and knocked. Arbuckle opened the door. He was half-way through washing his face. "Sorry. We need to know the date and the time that you left the rectory."

"Oh, yes. Let me see now. The year—that's easy; 1853. Now, I had just finished breakfast, so it would have been about 8:30 in the morning. And the date… It was May. The last sermon I had given was about The Ascension; it was following Ascension day. And it was the following Friday. Ah, yes. It was Friday the 13th. I remember Mrs Dobbes, my housekeeper, making a joke about it before she left." He started drying his face on the towel. "She said: 'Watch your step today, Reverend. There will be ill luck for some poor soul this day'. So there you have it, my friend: May 13th 1853, and I left with the Sentinel at about 8:30 in the morning." Arbuckle declared it proudly, as if it was a matter of some achievement to remember such precise details.

Alex relayed it to Joo-Won from the door of the bathroom: "May 13th, 1853, 8:30 am."

"Whoa, slow, please… Century?" requested Joo-Won.

"19th."

"Year?"

"53."

"Month?"

"May"

"May—that is English for month 5, right?" Joo-Won checked. "And day of month?"

"13."

"And the time he left, you said 08:30, yes?" Joo-Won read the numbers back to Alex to confirm. Joo-Won was double-checking his data on the screen. "So that's a Wednesday?"

"You remember me talking about Mrs Dobbes?" Arbuckle was saying from the bathroom sink.

"Yes," said Alex, returning from the bathroom door.

Arbuckle followed him. "She is a blessing, no man could ask for a more loyal housekeeper."

"OK, Mr Arbuckle," Joo-Won addressed him directly for the first time. "When we soon leave, we will need make two successive translocations, because, although place not so far away, it is very big time interval. First jump will get us *near* date and place. Then second jump should land us on target."

Arbuckle's brow furrowed and he looked to Alex for explanation. "So, in a minute you should pack your bag, ready to return to the Rectory. You will stand away from the furniture, holding on to Joo-Won like this. He demonstrated. Then you will travel, just like you did with the Sentinel. But it will take two journeys, one after the other to get you back home. OK?"

"Oh, no. It only took one journey to come here…"

Joo-Won sighed. "That because," he explained, "when you come here, it not matter exactly when you arrive, one day, the next day. But getting you home, we must arrive correct day. Not day before, because you would see yourself already there. Not day after, because Mrs Dobbes worry where you are, when you not eat breakfast."

Arbuckle opened his mouth to say something, then closed it again, reconsidering. "Without doubting this gentleman's integrity, Mr Smith—your friend, I am certain is entirely honourable. But I am not confident or willing to travel with him in this way. I hardly know the good fellow, and you have already told me I was foolish to trust that Uriel fellow, or whoever he was really… No. But I trust you, my friend, Mr Smith. You have always demonstrated kindness to me. Why don't you take me back yourself? I will happily travel with *you*."

"I'm sorry. I'm afraid that's not possible," reasoned Alex. "I do not have the equipment to enable it, and nor am I trained to use the equipment."

"Then I will wait for the Sentinel," stated Arbuckle stubbornly.

Alex looked at Joo-Won, who was again showing signs of impatience. "Is it possible for you to automate the jump so that I could take him?" asked Alex. "I made a short jump with Gemma and she gave me a duplicate controller in case I wanted to get back independently..."

"It not allowed," said Joo-Won, shaking his head. "It complex. Many possible things to go wrong. Many things need know about." Alex, disappointed but realistic, nodded his agreement.

Joo-Won stood. He proffered an ultimatum to Arbuckle. "You must come with me now, if you want go home," he said firmly.

But Arbuckle sat resolutely in his chair.

Alex thought for a way to break the impasse. "Is it possible," he asked Joo-Won, "for the three of us to go together? Obviously, you can do it for two; so, can three people translocate together?"

Joo-Won sighed again. "It possible, but it drain the equipment of energy. Let me calculate... Three people, two jumps to get there; that make six units. Two people, two jumps to return; another four, make ten units. Then two jumps for me get home, make twelve units altogether." He looked at his handheld controller and tapped a couple of buttons. Then he drew in air through his teeth. "Uhmm... Maybe just possible... small margin. Yes, we try that?" He looked at Arbuckle questioningly.

Alex spoke to Arbuckle. "So, if I come too; if we all travel back to your home together; is that OK for you?"

Slowly, a smile spread to Arbuckle's face. "Yes, my dear man. If you are accompanying me, then I will feel safe. Perhaps I can make us all a nice cup of tea when we arrive."

"That's the spirit," Alex responded brightly. "Right, get your bag packed so you are ready to leave." Then he paused to think. "Ah, but, Joo-Won, if we are *all* going then I will have to checkout the room key first. I'll just dash down to reception now."

"OK." Joo-Won slumped back down into his chair signalling his increasing impatience. Alex took the key-card and walked through to reception. He was disappointed to find that he had to pay for the two previous nights as Arbuckle had not done so with his bundle of cash. He walked back to Arbuckle's room and they let him in. Arbuckle had, by now, packed his few belongings into his leather travelling bag.

"So, you hadn't paid your room bill with your cash?" Alex asked Arbuckle, with just the merest hint of reprimand in his voice.

"Oh. Oh, I'm sorry. Here, let me repay you." He pulled out a small untidy bundle of notes. How much is it, my friend?"

"No," Joo-Won butted in. "You must give back all money. It is not permitted take things back to the past."

Arbuckle looked slightly disappointed, but obediently handed the entire bundle to Alex, and followed it with a large fistful of assorted coins. Alex sorted and pocketed the notes, wondering where the rest of the money had gone. The coins, he was less than delighted with. He dumped a portion onto the writing-table, muttering: "Tip for the room-cleaner," and thrust the rest into one of his coat pockets, feeling uncomfortable that the coat was weighed down to one side.

"OK, *now* we ready?" asked Joo-Won, eager to get away. The three of them stood side-by-side in the middle of the room, as Joo-Won arranged how they should put arms around each other to maintain good contact for the jump.

At that moment the hotel room door opened, and the housekeeper entered pushing a cleaning trolley. She froze, open-mouthed. "Oh, I'm sorry, sirs. I thought you had checked-out?" she apologised, glancing at the room number on the door to check.

Joo-Won let out a long-suffering sigh.

"Oh, er, yes. We are just leaving," Alex confirmed with embarrassment, gesturing to the others to follow him out. "It's OK, we can jump from the churchyard up the road. It's quiet, discreet, and not far," he reassured Joo-Won. "In fact, that's where you arrived isn't it?" he added, turning to Arbuckle.

"Indeed it is," Arbuckle replied, but with a slight look of anxiety on his face. The three of them crossed the road and strode the two-minute walk to the church graveyard, entering by the side gate.

"Over by the tree?" suggested Alex. But before they had got halfway across, Alex noticed the figure of Paul Liddington, tidying the path by the church. The vicar straightened, hearing them approach.

"Can I help you?" he enquired with normal politeness. Then he recognised Arbuckle, and his demeanour changed markedly. "Mr Arbuckle, what are you doing here? I thought I made it quite clear that you are not welcome at this church." He looked hard at Joo-Won, then at Alex.

Alex noticed Arbuckle's face going crimson. He sought to quickly abort any confrontation. "Oh, in that case, we are just leaving." He wheeled Arbuckle around by the arm and led him back to the gate. Joo-Won followed, muttering '*Shibal*'. Alex turned to him. "It's OK, Joo-Won, we can go back to Fiddler's Green and jump from there."

"Is long walk," Joo-Won complained.

"Yes, is long walk," Alex parroted, becoming rather annoyed at Joo-Won's unreasonable impatience.

"*Aish.*"

They walked on in sullen silence, Arbuckle fuming at the encounter with the Vicar. Alex tried to think of somewhere else nearby where they could be unseen for a few minutes, but he failed to come up with any ideas. Then it started to rain, quite heavily. Alex turned his collar up. He and Joo-Won were faring better than Arbuckle whose Victorian tail-coat offered little protection to his front. "Don't worry about what the Vicar said," he reassured Arbuckle. "He just doesn't know the full facts." Arbuckle shook his head without commenting. Alex mused that the cold rain was probably taking the heat out of Arbuckle's indignation. His face was certainly losing its crimson flush.

By the time they reached the entrance to Fiddler's Green, twenty minutes later, they were thoroughly uncomfortable. Alex could feel the rain squelching inside his shoes, and the lower half of his trousers were soaked through. There was nobody around, so once inside the gate, they turned alongside the hedge so that it shielded them from being seen from the road.

"OK, Joo-Won?" Alex stated passing the initiative to him.

Joo-Won flicked the raindrops off his glasses without replying and dug into his backpack for his controller. He gestured to the other two to come close to him. "Now, all hold each other tightly, bend knees a little. Ready?"

Alex almost expected another interruption, but there was none. Instead the puff of air across his face, and then they landed. Almost inevitably Arbuckle stumbled and brought down Alex and Joo-Won. But the grass they fell onto was dry and soft, and the cold wet January had been replaced with a warm, sunny May morning. There had been a loud clinking sound from Arbuckle's bag as he fell. Alex suspected he now knew what Arbuckle had been spending money on, but he said nothing as he feared Joo-Won might insist on confiscating the bottles and create more discontent. He and Arbuckle looked around as Joo-Won checked the data on his controller. They were in the middle of a pasture with gently rolling green hills in all directions.

"Good," Joo-Won reported. "Only 5 kilometres and 2 days away. One more jump do it now. Come." He hurried them back into an entangled huddle and activated his controller without delay.

Again the breath of equilibrating air. This time, Alex was ready for Arbuckle's clumsiness and managed to keep him upright. They were in a grassy field again. "Perfect," Joo-Won stated, reading from his controller. "Mid-morning, May 13th. One kilometre that way." He pointed.

Arbuckle looked around. "There is the steeple," he declared excitedly. "But I'm not sure that things… look quite right…" he added, his gaze darting around. The road was evident at the bottom of the field, so they started down toward the gate. As they passed by a small copse, a building and driveway came into view.

"Oh look," Alex pointed to the driveway. "A classic car—it's a Ford Zodiac…" He froze. "Hey, that can't be right, Joo-Won…"

"What the problem?"

"There are no cars in 1853."

"What? 1853? No… you tell me 1953." He pointed angrily to the date on his controller display. "I ask you century. You tell me 19. See."

"No, no. When we say the 19th century, we mean the 1800s," Alex protested impatiently.

Joo-Won gestured his hands outward, remonstrating the stupidity he was presented with. "*Aish!* OK. OK!" He shouted. "You want 1853. We go 1853." He stabbed numbers into his controller. "Look." He thrust the controller close to Alex's face. "May 13, 1853. That what you want?"

Alex pulled his head back a little to focus on the display. "Yes, that's right now."

"In 1853, is a Friday. See. But in 1953, is a Wednesday. I checked. I ask you, is a Wednesday? You said 'yes'."

"No." Alex was confused by Joo-Won's assertion, but he decided not to argue, and just reasserted their intended destination clearly: "We want Friday, May 13th, 1853."

"*Shibal!* Come." Joo-Won gestured strenuously for them to huddle again. Arbuckle had only half-understood the details of the argument and was hesitant to approach the animated Joo-Won. Alex coaxed him in reassuringly. When he finally cooperated by joining the huddle, Joo-Won stabbed the controller to initiate another jump.

Puff. This time, Arbuckle managed to stay upright. Cloudy skies, another field. Joo-Won studied his controller. Arbuckle looked around, and his face lit up. "Yes, my friends, we are home," he declared enthusiastically, starting to walk briskly toward the nearby building, with the spired church visible close behind.

"No, no. Stop him!" cried Joo-Won alarmed.

Alex ran forward a couple of paces and grabbed Arbuckle's arm. "Wait...Wait..."

Joo-Won addressed Arbuckle directly. "Listen. Was big jump. One hundred years. We close to your house, but we three days early. Is dangerous. Old Arbuckle maybe in house. Must not see. OK? We jump one more time to Friday 13th. Yes? Come. Quick." Alex was not sure Arbuckle understood, but Alex himself saw the danger. He hurried a somewhat reluctant Arbuckle back into the huddle and nodded to Joo-Won to activate. He also felt a pang of anxiety remembering that Joo-Won had said there was a small margin before his estimate of people-jumps would drain the equipment of energy. And they had already wasted two jumps with all three of them 'on-board'.

Puff. It was sunny. And the steeple was visible in the near distance again, though they were now in a field surrounded by small trees. But this time Arbuckle looked sheepishly at Joo-Won for permission before assuming a successful arrival. Joo-Won studied his controller. "Perfect. 11:30 am, Friday 13 May, 1853. Close to target building... You home," he announced to Arbuckle, holding the controller so Alex could read the data.

Arbuckle looked to Alex for confirmation. Alex nodded and smiled at him. "You're home," he stated. But inside, Alex was hoping desperately that Arbuckle had, in fact, got the date right. He also felt a little insecure. Now Arbuckle was home, it was just himself and Joo-Won, and they hadn't been seeing eye to eye. Might Joo-Won just leave him if the equipment had insufficient energy to get them both back; or even just leave him out of spite. No, surely not.

Arbuckle shook hands with them both warmly, effusing thanks. Then there was an awkward silence for a few seconds.

"You make us cup of tea, then, Mr Arbuckle?" Joo-Won finally asked. Alex was slightly surprised. He had expected Joo-Won to be impatient to leave.

"Oh yes, please do come to The Rectory. I would be most happy to offer you both a cup of tea. And Mrs Dobbes will have left some lunch for me—we can share it. And maybe dry out our clothes a bit..." He beamed, clearly delighted at being able to offer hospitality, and gestured the way down between the small trees toward the wooden gate onto the road, where a horse and cart were passing.

Just as they were opening the gate, a young lad, perhaps 8 years old, was ambling by, carrying a basket and a bundle of something. He tipped his hat: "G'morning Reverend. 'Tis a lovely day."

"Good morning to you Timothy. Indeed, it is a most pleasant day."

"What be ye a-doin in old Lampard's orchard, Reverend?" he continued, looking from Joo-Won to Alex and back again. "Surely it be a long wait yet afore apple-season?"

"Well now, that be none of thy business, young Timothy. But I would be obliged if ye say nought to old Lampard 'bout it, eh?" Arbuckle touched his nose knowingly.

The lad cocked his head slightly to one side, as if pensive. "As ye say, sir. G'day Reverend, sir." He tipped his cap again, and walked on.

The lane was roughly grassed over, apart from two ruts that marked the passage of numerous cartwheels. Alex noticed, now that the horse-drawn cart had receded into the distance, that there was a penetrating silence populated only by their footsteps and occasional birdsong or rustling of leaves. The calm and stillness was striking compared to the modern town that he lived in.

Arbuckle sat them down at the table in his parlour, whilst he busied himself making tea. When it turned out to be unpalatable to Joo-Won, who had a quite different idea of tea; he was not offended and made some coffee as an alternative, which Alex said he would also prefer. Arbuckle carved doorstops from a large loaf of bread, and the three of them, hungry by now, ate through some cut meat and cheese that had been left in the pantry by his housekeeper, with the chunks of bread liberally spread with country butter.

It was only after eating, that, sitting outside in Arbuckle's garden

168

enjoying the May sunshine, Alex asked Joo-Won, who seemed to have completely lost his impatience of earlier, about the state of the translocation equipment. "So, Joo-Won, you said before we set off that the equipment only had a small margin, with our planned jumps, before it would be drained of energy. And we had that... er... misunderstanding, which wasted two jumps. So, what is the energy status of the equipment now?"

Joo-Won sighed. "Very low energy. Enough maybe one person, one jump. Not enough get us home. We stranded here for now."

Chapter 11

We are miles from sea, And years from land…
Look at the space that surrounds us.

(anon)

Earth-Standard StarDate 2243.215, ReHab Station-3, Lo-Grav

"Oh, hi, Betty, this is Eva, my physio." Eva glanced up and smiled without stopping the rotation of Astrid's leg that she was working on.

Betty had showered and dressed in the provided clothes—a kind of smart but light tracksuit, that was comfortable as pyjamas on the inside; with soft stretchy shoes. They reminded Betty of ballet shoes and she couldn't resist trying a few jumps and pliés in the low gravity, memories from her younger days.

"Eva was just telling me about progress in the other colonies."

"Oh, but I'm no social historian," insisted Eva. "I'm just passing on what I learn from talking with all my other patients. We get arrivals from everywhere through this Rehab Station. So, I would say many are experiencing the same classes of problems that you have described on Pericyon c, Astrid. Most of the colonies were founded on mining something that is rare on Earth, but needed in quantity. So there was a natural trade. They sent back mineral resources to Earth, and we sent structural prefabs, materials and tooling in return. But quite quickly the resources that came back to Earth started exceeding requirements and so got stockpiled. Just like the Lanthanides that are freighted back from your planet, Astrid. And yours is not the only planet that can ship large quantities of them. There's a limit to how much is needed, even planning for the future. So, gradually the enthusiasm for colonising began to wane… Now push as hard as you can with that leg…"

"So what's the attitude, on Earth, about colonising, now?" asked Astrid.

170

"Well, the IRMC—that's the International Resources Management Council—is pushing to lower the prices paid for resources, allegedly because having artificially high prices for commodities just encourages the colonies to carry on with a blinkered approach, and not diversify and broaden their development. Though in reality, it's also becoming uneconomical for them to store the excesses. But, on the other hand, there is angst that, if we encouraged colonisation in the first place, we have an ethical duty to keep supplying them with necessities, regardless of whether they supply anything useful back... Now pull sideways... that's it."

"But the truth," Eva declared, "is that the word 'colony' is a misnomer. The intention was always that a real colony would gradually become self-sufficient, expand, develop all areas of industry, so that it could service all its own needs. But only a couple show any signs that they are going in that direction. Tau Ceti d2 is doing quite well, though they have problems with too many meteor impacts. Most of the rest are really just mining outposts, not actually suitable for sustainable living. There is a lot more appreciation now how small the margin is for natural agriculture. The star spectral type and size have to be similar to our sun, otherwise the radiation-habitable zone and the temperature-habitability zone don't overlap. And if you can't have natural agriculture, and have to revert to artificial sunlight, that's a very big strain on sustainability."

"Yes, we got a lot of that in our education," commented Astrid. "The other thing our Planetary Council used to bemoan was the communication difficulty back to Earth. If they urgently needed something for a repair, it would take years for the message to get to Earth, and more than a decade for transport. So everything around seemed to be patched and bodged, always waiting for proper materials for repair."

Eva nodded her understanding. "OK. That's all for this session, Astrid. Your joints seem to be pretty much functioning correctly. You just have to keep working those muscles to build them up again. I'll see you for another session tomorrow morning."

"Thanks, Eva."

Astrid turned to Betty. "So, are you all OK, Betty. Sorry if we were just talking shop."

"No, don't apologise—it's all absolutely fascinating to me. Tell me about the planet you lived on. Presumably, you still remember it after a hibernation?"

"Oh yes. Psychologically, hibernation is just like having a sleep. It seems like just a few days ago I left. The goodbyes are still emotionally painful." She teared-up. "But the planet itself. Well, there's not a lot to tell. A few thousand people; everything under domes. We rarely got to travel outside the domes, and then only inside sealed transports. But there was plenty of entertainment inside. All of the videos we had were from Earth, so we kind of knew what it is like—a sort of promised land, with a liberated life—you could walk around anywhere, and vegetation actually grew on the planet's surface—not just in agridomes. But it was fantasy; not many of us entertained the idea of actually coming here, it seemed kind of... implausible. Education was pretty good. We had all the technological and historical information from Earth, updated each time a freighter arrived. We learned a lot of space science of course, and all about the life support systems. We all knew that employment prospects were narrow. Most people went into agri-maintenance, engineering or mining. Friends were the most important thing there... I had to say goodbye to everyone." Her voice cracked. "And the bizarre thing is they will all have forgotten me by now. Our freighter took 22 years to get here because it developed a fault. My boyfriend will be married to someone else by now, probably with kids. They will all have forgotten me..." She cried a little. Betty realised that she should avoid asking Astrid about her old life; it was only going to bring up emotional pain.

The soft disembodied voice spoke: *"Astrid, a reminder to take your anabolite tablets."*

"Oh. Right. Excuse me a minute." Astrid retreated into her bedroom and returned with some tablets and a bottle of water.

"What are those for?" asked Betty, glad for the chance to change the subject.

"They boost muscle growth," replied Astrid, necking the tablets and sucking some water from the bottle. "The biggest problem with hibernation," she explained, "is that the muscles tend to atrophy. You see, normally muscle tissue slowly breaks down, and is re-built at the sites where exercise has worked the tissue. So without any exercise in hibernation, the muscles just tend to wilt. Even though the body is continually perfused with myostatins to suppress that natural process, and the hibernation pods do stimulate the muscles electrically a bit. But you still tend to end up a wraith—like me." She extended her bony arm to illustrate the point. "For me, it's a little worse because my old planet only had 89% of Earth's gravity. So I have grown up accustomed to

172

lesser gravity, to needing less muscle. I'm a bit worried that it will feel like hard work, just walking around on Earth."

"Oh, I'm sure you will quickly get used to it," Betty reassured her. "It would only be like walking around with a backpack of shopping."

"Yes, I guess so. Anyway, I need to do lots of exercise to build muscle mass. I'm going to have a run now; will you come and run with me?"

"Sure. So how long does the rehabilitation process take?"

"Maybe a week here in Lo-Grav. Then a week in Mid-Grav followed by a week in Full-Grav. Perhaps less if I work hard at it." Betty followed Astrid out of their room, on down the corridor to a point where it opened-out, revealing the large cylindrical inner surface of the Station, which was evidently the low gravity running track. Astrid set to work running gently round. Betty soon got bored of running gently, but discovered there were plenty of fun exercises to do, rediscovering cartwheels and even handsprings; tumbling made easy in the low-gravity environment.

*   *   *

Earth-Standard StarDate 2243.215, TC HQ

Vallini, Ravel and Bram had gathered in the operations control office, once Bram had confirmed that the deep listening network was ready. Ravel was setting up the equipment to broadcast a properly encoded ENQ signal on the subwave comms channel to cause all Sentinel devices to reply using their simple 'Enquire/Acknowledge ID' protocol.

"OK, I'm ready," he declared, looking first to Bram for his consent and then to Vallini for his formal authority. They both nodded. He pressed the button to activate sending the message, then leaned back in his chair, waiting for Bram, seated at the deep listening network console to inform them of the results.

There were flickers of data appearing on Bram's screen. "Four devices," he declared after a few seconds. "We have good fixes on them. None very close. Two in the African continent, one in Siberia, and one in Australasia. We will keep listening for the next hour in case any more respond."

"Makes sense," commented Vallini. "They probably used the nearby devices when they initially tried chasing Betty and myself. But it makes no difference. Carry on setting up the Nikenfeld airfield operation, Bram. Expect four devices initially when we address those specifically with Summons and Search. But we'll also send a general Summons in case we missed any just now."

Bram nodded. "We expect the airfield to be ready around midday tomorrow," he acknowledged.

*　　　*　　　*

Earth-Standard StarDate 2243.215, ReHab Station-3, Lo-Grav

Astrid had managed to keep the gentle run going for twenty minutes. Betty had got bored sooner, and had sat and watched Astrid running in slow circles up the wall, across the curved ceiling high above Betty's head, and then back down the wall behind her; at least that was how it appeared if she didn't analyse it too much.

It was getting to late evening on the timetable that the Station liked visitors to adhere to, so Astrid suggested they get some food. They returned to their room.

"Lex, Menu," Astrid said, turning toward the wall screen. A short list of available dishes appeared. Astrid spoke the names of two or three dishes and the screen confirmed her choice. "What would you like, Betty?"

"Asian chicken noodles, please, Lex," Betty stated.

Astrid laughed. "You don't have to say 'please', Betty. It's not alive."

The food was delivered to them by a worker, a few minutes later. Betty took a mouthful. It was the first food she had eaten since translocating here with Vallini.

"Oh, the food here is just sensational," enthused Astrid, as she tucked into the first of three dishes she had ordered. "And I've been encouraged to eat as much as I can to build up my body... Do you like the food?"

"It's good," agreed Betty. "But I wouldn't call it sensational."

"Oh, well you've probably been eating good Earth food all your life," suggested Astrid between mouthfuls. "But this is just amazing compared with what we ate back home. The variety and the flavours... We only had a few basic foodstuffs and flavourings there. Except when a freighter had just visited—then, if you were lucky, you might get some exotic sauce that had been exported from Earth… if you could afford to buy it… and if it hadn't decayed during the long journey. Anyway, this is luxury for me, and I'm going to make the most of it," she declared, scraping her fork around to get at the last morsels.

Betty laughed. "Yeah, that's a good attitude. Be sure to try porcini when you get down to Earth—that's my favourite."

"OK. Hey, before I go to bed I want to visit the cupola. Come with me and I'll see if I can point out the star system where my home was," offered Astrid. "I haven't visited the cupola yet, but it's back near the docking port, on the part of the Station that doesn't rotate. I guess the view would be a bit giddying otherwise! Actually, they told me there are two of them; one looking down to Earth, and one pointing out to space. Oh, I forgot to check the schedule—which half of the sky you can see depends on where we are in the orbit; and also, during half the orbit, the sun is dominant. But we'll just see what there is to see—we can always come back lots of times tomorrow." Astrid eagerly led Betty back along the corridor from their room to the area where the cylindrical structure was revealed, and they both climbed lightly up the handrails to its centre where the sense of gravity was lost, and along the tunnel leading through toward the docking and reception structure. Just before reaching the reception, there were two sliding doors opposite each other—one labelled 'Earthward Cupola', and the other 'Spaceward Cupola'. Astrid opened the latter, and they pull-floated through a few metres of tunnel into an unlit huge transparent dome, about ten metres across. A container at the entrance advised taking sunglasses. The sun itself was well over to one side, but was intensely bright. There were a few other people already in there, staring out into various parts of the expanse.

"Oh, good," commented Astrid, "as she studied the star map and data on a wall-mounted screen away from the dome itself. "The sun is just about to set, and Canis Minor is visible about 40 degrees across from register 132." They push-floated themselves across to the dome and grabbed holding points that were mounted on its surface. Without an atmosphere to scatter the sun's light, the blackness of space allowed an extraordinary clarity of vision; myriad steady pinpricks of starlight dotting the black canvas. They both studied the starscape in silence. Then, gradually the sun set behind the Earth, and the final loss of distracting shafts of light enabled an even clearer view. The Milky Way stretched massively from one side of the cupola to the other.

"I've never seen it like this before," whispered Astrid, wiping a tear from her eyes. "My whole life was lived under domes designed to shut out the outside. I've seen pictures of course, but…"

"Yes, it's stunning," agreed Betty, her voice cracking slightly. "On Earth, if you get away from the city lights on a cloudless night, the view is great. But this is something else entirely. Perhaps the most amazing thing I have ever seen. I shall always remember this… So where is your star?"

"Oh…" Astrid looked round the angular markings circling the edge of the dome to get a bearing, then worked her way inwards. "So… Ah, look you see the equilateral triangle of brightish stars, there. Then come down in that direction to the very bright one—yellowy white—that's Procyon. Betty nodded. Then, see there is a cluster of faint stars just beneath it—the middle one is Pericyon—that's our star. I lived on planet 'c' of Pericyon." Astrid started crying again, and Betty put a sympathetic arm around her. "I don't know why I'm crying; I'm actually so glad to be here. It's not as if… Oh, I don't know."

After a few more minutes, they floated their way back toward the living quarters and bedtime. "I'd love to know how they engineered the moving join between the revolving part and the static part, with pressure on one side and vacuum on the other," mused Betty, as they transitioned from the tunnel into the giant cylinder. "But your Vallini was very clear that I mustn't ask questions like that!"

"Oh, why not?"

"Because when I return to my time in the past, I mustn't have any knowledge that could be prematurely applied, and so cause significant changes to the future."

"But you could keep it a secret just for yourself," suggested Astrid.

Betty laughed. "I'm not sure that I could! No, he's right; that's his job to protect the integrity of the future. I must suppress my curiosity."

"Mmm… Well, they had submarines in your time didn't they?" posed Astrid. "It's only the same issue as a propeller shaft through the hull."

"Ah…" Betty nodded, appreciating the perceptive parallel, and making a mental note to google the submarine engineering.

*   *   *

Friday afternoon, May 13, 1853, Winterbourne Steepleton

"Stranded?" Alex repeated, alarmed. The sound of a horse trotting

176

along the lane had been gradually growing louder, and now it became visible pulling a gig, on which was seated a smartly dressed gentleman.

"Oh, my word. The Archdeacon!" declared Arbuckle, springing up from his chair in the garden. "I wonder what he wants?" He hurried over to the drive to meet the gig as it pulled in through his front gate. "Good day, Archdeacon," he greeted the man. "This is an unexpected pleasure, sir." The young lad that they had seen earlier ran up and attended to the horse, availing himself of the opportunity to earn an extra penny. The archdeacon, as he stepped down from the gig, glanced over quizzically at Alex and Joo-Won seated in the garden, but then followed Arbuckle into the Rectory.

Alex, amused at Arbuckle's sudden deference, looked over to Joo-Won: "I hope he is not in trouble about something." But it was lost on Joo-Won who was oblivious to the cultural titles and nuances. Alex returned to the more worrying subject. "So, what happens if we are stranded? Will TC send someone to rescue us?"

"No. Is not necessary. We wait. Enjoy nice weather."

"You can't recharge the equipment with energy here?"

Joo-Won laughed. "No electricity in this time, I think, especially here." He gestured to the fields around. "No. We just wait. Equipment charge itself."

"Ah, so how long will it take?" asked Alex, feeling relieved, but hoping the process was not too slow.

"A few hours maybe. We jump you home this evening. For me, maybe need to stay in Cheltenham one more night before enough energy to jump me home also."

"That's interesting," commented Alex. "So how does it recharge? From this thing they call the subwave?"

"I not know," said Joo-Won, shrugging. "They not explain how equipment works. They just explain to use it."

Alex acknowledged the answer with a nod, recalling that it was the same sort of answer he always got from Gemma. He looked around restlessly. "Perhaps we could go for a walk through the village?"

"TC not like it," stated Joo-Won, his eyes closed, as he relaxed in the sunshine. "Bad practice. We strange to them. Should keep low profile. Not disturb. But you maybe explore round Arbuckle's house when visitor gone?"

Alex became aware that their moods had reversed. Joo-Won, impatient to get on with things earlier in the day, was now completely content to relax, since there was clearly no alternative. Alex, himself, did not enjoy just sitting around, especially when there was not much conversation to be had. He considered asking Joo-Won about his oceanographic research again, but they had more or less exhausted that topic over dinner the previous evening.

At length, the Rectory door opened again and Arbuckle and the Archdeacon emerged, the latter gesturing toward Alex and Joo-Won and asking something of Arbuckle. "Timothy," Arbuckle called into the field opposite, summoning the boy to bring back the horse from pasture. The men strolled over toward Alex and Joo-Won. Alex could see that Arbuckle was reluctant, hanging back slightly. But ultimately his etiquette demanded that he make a formal introduction: "Archdeacon Grantly, these are my guests, Alexander Smith and er... Jewelon."

They rose from their seats. Alex held out his hand. "Very pleased to meet you, Archdeacon. It's a lovely day."

"Yes, indeed, Mr Smith. We are blessed with a quite lovely day."

Joo-Won bowed deeply. "Choi Joo-Won, sir."

"Jewelon hails from foreign parts, Archdeacon," put in Arbuckle helpfully.

"Indeed, how interesting. Pray, what country have you travelled from?" asked the Archdeacon.

"I from Korea."

"Korea! Dear me. I apologise that I am not well versed in geography. That would be in the Far East, would it not?"

"Yes," Alex chipped in. "Near to China and Japan." Joo-Won nodded.

"Fascinating. And are there Christians in Korea, Mr Won?"

"Yes. Just few. They learn Christianity from Catholic missionaries to Court in Beijing, and bring back to Korea. But mostly meet in secret. Not approved by Confucianism."

"Dear, dear. Confucianism. What does that teach?

"K'ung Fu-tzu was Chinese philosopher. He teach ethics to make life good for all."

"But not good for Christians, eh?" the quick-witted Archdeacon interjected.

Joo-Won laughed. "Followers not always understand good teachings of masters," he replied pointedly.

"So true, so true," muttered the Archdeacon. "And you, Mr Smith. You are English, are you not, though I detect a slight accent?"

"Yes, I am English, sir; from Cheltenham."

"Ah, Cheltenham. Yes, we have an Ecclesiastical College there."

"Yes, I am familiar with it. 'Francis Close Hall'. A magnificent building," waxed Alex, delighted to find he could hold conversation with this historical dignitary, after being impressed by Joo-Won's presumably accurate historical focus.

"Timothy has your horse ready, sir," Arbuckle interjected, seemingly eager to terminate the conversation, lest it stray onto dangerous ground.

"Ah! Well, A pleasure to meet you gentlemen, and I wish you good fortune on your travels."

"Thank you, sir." They shook hands again, and the Archdeacon returned to mount his gig, and encouraged his horse to turn out of the gate and take up a trot along the lane.

Arbuckle was beaming, clearly delighted that his Archdeacon had been satisfactorily entertained, rather than he himself having to answer difficult questions about his unusual-looking guests. "So, my friends, I would be honoured if you would stay for dinner? I usually eat at around 5:30."

"That sounds perfect," commented Alex, looking at Joo-Won.

"Yes, please," he affirmed.

"Excellent." Arbuckle called the boy who had been loitering near the gate hoping to get paid. "Timothy! Here." He handed a coin to the lad. "Kindly call in at Mrs Dobbes', would you? And tell her I will be having two guests for dinner this evening."

Arbuckle went back inside, and soon reappeared carrying a tray with three glasses of beer, cool from the pantry. Alex sipped at it cautiously at first, but found it very palatable, and soon started to feel a lot more relaxed about wasting the afternoon away in the sunshine.

*   *   *

Betty woke after a very refreshing night's sleep. The easy one-third gravity made the mattress feel whisper-soft, and almost any position was comfortable. She showered and emerged into the ante-room, where Astrid was already working some light weights with her arms.

"Good morning, Betty. Hey, order us some breakfast, would you. I'm hungry, but I'm not familiar with anything on the menu."

"Lex, menu," commanded Betty. She ordered a selection of food, aiming for lots of protein for Astrid.

After eating they headed to the low gravity running track. Betty wondered if she should perhaps do some serious exercise. "Do you think I am allowed through to the higher gravity parts of the Station?"

"Yes, of course," Astrid reassured her. "Just float through the central core tunnel on the other side and you'll emerge into the mid-gravity track. And then if you float through the next section of central core tunnel from there you get to the full 1g track and rooms."

Betty followed the directions and emerged into the mid-gravity cylinder. The diameter was noticeably larger, and it took longer to work her way down the handrails to the running surface. There were lots of people exercising in various ways. It took a while to adjust, but it provided a satisfying medium between being able to easily cartwheel and tumble, but having a more satisfying, firmer landing. After playing there for a while she worked her way from the other side of the track up the grip rails toward the centre and through the tunnel to the 1g area. Here, the radius was bigger again. She climbed down to the track, having to be careful on the last few rails as she rediscovered her true weight. She joined the bunch of people running. There seemed always to be a consensus about which direction people ran on these tracks, to avoid the danger of collisions, and she was happy to put in some serious exercise and overtake lots of runners.

"Well, I think you're ready for the ferry down, dear," commented one woman, as Betty overtook her for the third time.

"Oh, no, I... I'm just visiting someone here," Betty explained, panting.

"Ah. Well, that makes me feel a bit better about my own efforts then," said the woman, laughing.

After a half-hour run, she headed back to their room, collecting

Astrid on the way. "I've got another physio session a bit later," said Astrid. "How about we go and have a look at the Earth-facing cupola for a while?" They made their way along the central tunnel that led to the non-rotating part of the Station, and in through the door marked 'Earthward Cupola'. The layout was identical to the cupola they had been in the previous evening, except that the information screen displayed data about countries they were passing over, and day and night times. The dome gave a sweeping view of the Earth, which was currently in darkness. Where there was no cloud cover, the glow of city lights lit up swathes of the surface inviting identification of landmasses and cities. They both watched, mesmerised, until eventually the orbit of the Station took them across the boundary of day into night. The globe was now an integrated tapestry of blues, splattered with white cloud formations. Betty remembered the comments from astronauts in her own time that the view of Earth from outside was transformative and uplifting, the 'Overview Effect' they had called it. To the edge, the atmosphere looked paper-thin, and she found herself committing to doing everything she could in her future to foster the sustainability of the environment, to care for this planet that looked as delicate and fragile as it did beautiful. Astrid had been crying gently, finally seeing her destination, her place of destiny; the planet she had been brought up to revere as her ancestral home. Betty held her hand in sympathy; there was simply nothing to say in the face of this awe-inspiring spectacle.

Later, Astrid was about to go for another of her runs. "I've done enough running for today, thanks," Betty said, refusing the invitation. "Are there entertainment videos available on these?" She gestured to the screen in their room.

"Yes, of course," Astrid laughed. "That's what they are mainly used for. Or you can get education, or information."

"I think I'd like to watch again the video I saw on the ferry coming up here. It was really absorbing, but I found that some parts were difficult to grasp back then. I think I might understand them better having talked with you at length about present-time social attitudes."

"OK. I'll see you later after my run then. Enjoy it." Astrid left.

"Lex, play video…" Betty creased her forehead trying to remember the name. "Ah, yes… *'She spoke with harmless shadows'*."

Chapter 12
With lures of ostensible profit, they await him in strength.
(Sun Tzu)

Earth-Standard StarDate 2243.216, Nikenfeld Airfield

Vallini, Bram and Ravel had taken a transport out to the edge of Nikenfeld airfield, a barren expanse, partly overgrown with bush. Disused, flat concrete areas featured sporadic plant growth breaking through the cracks. It was hot and dusty. They parked beside the old boundary road, with a view across the dilapidated concrete toward some broken-down buildings. Bram manned a control screen in the transport.

"Can we attempt capture of any arriving devices?" Vallini asked him.

"No. That's difficult to achieve, even at the Way-Stations. But out here, with the limited equipment we have available, I wouldn't advise trying it," Bram replied.

"That's OK," put in Ravel. "It's not necessary. We have learned everything we need to know from the previously captured devices."

"Right. Set our offence for automated destruction, then," agreed Vallini. "The alien devices are arriving from far distances, so they won't all arrive immediately we send the summons command, or indeed simultaneously. So our offensive equipment should have ample time to re-focus between arrivals."

"I can send the summons command to each ID, one at a time, if we want to space them out," suggested Bram.

"No. If you do that, it might look suspicious. Send all four commands simultaneously."

"OK," said Bram. "Four Summons ID plus Search with Betty's Bioscan. Sending now…" He tapped a control on the screen. After a few seconds, data started flickering. "Yes… Three translocations detected out of their remote locations... now four." A pause of two or three minutes... Then there was a flash over to the west side of the airfield. "One device destroyed."

"Well, I hope they're all as easy as that," commented Vallini dubiously. They waited.

"Another arrival detected. But it looks like it has materialised within those disused buildings. It is out of the line of sight of our weapons," reported Bram.

"Damn. Anywhere in all these hectares of empty open field, and the uncertainty has to drop it there," complained Vallini.

"Shall I send it another summons, to get it out in the open?" asked Bram.

"No. I'll walk over there and deal with it," decided Vallini, stepping out of the transport and swinging on his backpack of equipment. He marched quickly toward the broken-down buildings.

Bram's voice came through his earpiece: "It seems to be located in the left-hand part of the building, about half-way along."

"Thanks, Bram."

Vallini had got most of the way there when there was suddenly an explosion, about a hundred metres to his right. He froze for an instant.

"Another arrival destroyed, Vallini," came the reassuring comment.

Vallini resumed walking. But then came the message he had half expected. "The device you're headed for, just translocated out, Vallini. Probably deduced a trap, after sensing the arrival and destruction of that last one."

"Damn. OK. Send a small swarm of armed automated devices after it. Are you getting good tracking data?" Vallini turned to walk back, wiping sweat from his brow. The day was hot.

"Yes. We still have deep listening active, so we can pinpoint the device's travels very accurately... Whoa, wait... The fourth device has just arrived, but our equipment has not fired offensively at it because there is a human accompanying this one. They're about 400 metres to the North-West. Do you want us to hold fire?" Bram asked.

Vallini looked in the indicated direction. Sure enough, he could see a figure, indistinct at that distance. "Yes, hold fire. Damn. That's all we need—another Victorian Vicar. OK, I'll walk over and engage. Keep tracking…" He set off in that direction. He sensed that the person was looking around, and had probably spotted him. After all, Vallini and the building were the only prominent artefacts on the otherwise flat terrain. Vallini made a slow wave over his head, as an early attempt at rapport. The figure waved back in acknowledgement and started in his direction.

"Where did this device stem from?" asked Vallini to Bram.

"South-East Africa," came the reply in his earpiece. Anticipating the possible need for translation, Vallini reached into a pocket of his backpack and retrieved a small smooth device, which he activated.

He assessed the situation. The goal would be to separate the human from the Sentinel device so that he could destroy that without injury to the person. He had an armed weapon in his pocket. This was the last of the four Sentinels to arrive, so there would be no interruption; no indication to this Sentinel that a trap was afoot. The Sentinel would pose no immediate danger to him, since it was anticipating human help to find the target, Betty, that it was searching for. There was a chance that Vallini, himself, would be recognised by the Sentinel because he remembered Ravel saying that he had been pictured alongside Betty the moment before she had been abducted. But there was no negative connotation that the Sentinel would attach to that. Indeed, it maybe gave him more credibility as someone who could help the Sentinel find Betty.

As the figure got closer he discerned an African woman, dressed in a very brightly coloured robe-like dress, with a matching bright scarf tied around her head. She was striding confidently toward him, and seemed to be holding the Sentinel device, concealed in a fold of her dress, with one arm. The other arm swung freely as she walked. They both stopped within a couple of metres of each other. Vallini bowed: "Greetings," he said, hoping to gain the confidence of the woman.

"Imibuliso kuwe. Lo mthunywa uthixo wam unqwenela ukuthetha naye Beytee Goss-maw." She had patted the concealed Sentinel on the fourth word. The diction was interspersed with strange oral clicks. Vallini smiled at her, waiting the second it took for his translation device to register the language and translate.

"Language is Xhosa: Greetings to you. The messenger of my God wishes to speak with… (Beytee Goss-maw)… object un-translatable."

The woman looked with some surprise at the speaking translation device.

"Yes," Vallini started, making a deliberate gesture of wiping his sweating brow. "I can help you. It is hot. Let us drink some water." He swung off his backpack and placed it on the ground in front of himself, pulling out a metal water bottle, as the device translated for him.

"Ewe. Ndingakunceda. Kushushu. Masisele amanzi."

He watched her eyes for her reaction. She listened intently to the device, then seemed to accept the suggestion with a grateful nod. Vallini unscrewed the cup from the top of the bottle and offered her the bottle with one hand and the cup with the other. The whole charade had been choreographed with one aim in mind. He had put his backpack down on the ground, making that seem like a safe action. He had offered her two items—the cup and the bottle—with separate hands, meaning that to take them she would have to put the Sentinel device down on the ground, to free up her other arm. Would she comply?

But she seemed to find a compromise. With her elbow, she held the Sentinel device, still under a fold in her robe, against her chest, whilst extending that hand for the cup. Inwardly, Vallini cursed—he hated to manhandle anyone, particularly an innocent woman. But the action with her elbow had told Vallini that the Sentinel needed to be held. It must therefore not be otherwise secured in the fold of her dress. So he gave the bottle into her free hand, and, as he passed her the cup, grabbed hold of that hand and pulled hard, releasing the Sentinel device from under her elbow. Before it had even hit the ground he had blasted it with his weapon, firing straight through his pocket, carefully avoiding her legs.

The small explosion and cracking sound were uncomfortably close for both of them, and for a second they both reflexively cowed away. Then the woman yelled an angry tirade of abuse that the translation device, which had been partially deafened by the loud destructive event, failed to interpret. She followed her shouted abuse by roundly clouting Vallini over the head with the water bottle that she was still holding.

Strangely, Vallini welcomed the blow. He felt guilty about tricking and physically pulling the woman, and judged the blow as partial deserved retribution for his lousy behaviour. This feeling was augmented by echoes from the conversation that he had had with Ravel, when it had become clear that TC was not the exclusive righteous arbiter of time as they had always previously supposed—just an alternative. Without the purity of purpose, missions such as this were harder to complete with a clear conscience. "I'm sorry," he began. "Please let me explain…" But the translation device was not functioning. His own ears were ringing— he wasn't certain whether that was a result of the explosive sound or the blow to his head. "Bram," he tried. "If you can hear me, I need another translation device over here. And can you call Silvana to come out here as fast as possible." Silvana was his protégé; another woman, and good with emotions, he knew. He had left her at HQ, monitoring the operation.

The woman had picked up the now-defunct Sentinel device to see if it would respond to her. Vallini told himself that the Sentinel had lied to the woman, and used her. That the fracas was the fault of the Sentinel. A consequence of *its* actions, not his own. But somehow the guilt he felt would not subside. At least, he thought, the woman seemed more angry than scared. Causing people to fear was, for him, the worst guilt to deal with.

Bram arrived close to them with the transport, and hurriedly stepped out, offering a fresh translation device to Vallini. The woman looked startled at the arrival of the transport and two more men, but she stood her ground watching.

Vallini tried again with the new translation device. "I'm sorry. I apologise for my actions, but it was necessary to quickly destroy that device. You have been deceived. The device has nothing to do with your God. The people who made the device have tricked you into helping them find someone. Someone on whom they wish harm." Vallini paused to allow the translation to catch up.

"Banokwenza umlingo. Bangakwazi njani ukuba ngo Thixo?" she gestured with both hands.

*"They can do magic. How can they **not** be Gods?"* came the translation.

"I can do magic too." Vallini gestured to the translation device and the transport. It was clear from the word 'magic', and plural 'Gods', that his concepts might not be translating well.

At that point, Silvana appeared. She had simply translocated from the HQ building, appearing within the line of sight of the African woman. But, materialising out of thin air, her white dress and long blonde hair accentuated her alien-ness to the African woman, who muttered something that the device blandly translated as 'Daughter of Light'. She knelt down in a gesture of supplication.

"No, no," Silvana remonstrated, rushing up and kneeling in front of the African woman, taking her hands. Vallini dropped the translation device into Silvana's lap. "My name is Silvana," she started. "What is yours?…"

"Igama lam ndingu Silvana. Yeyakho?"

Vallini watched in silent admiration as Silvana quickly established a rapport between them, and pursued conversation. Then he turned and took the few paces back to the transport.

"Are you OK?" asked Bram, sounding concerned. He handed Vallini a tissue and pointed to his forehead where the slightest trickle of blood has emerged. Vallini dabbed at the spot. Bram was an equipment operations specialist—he would not understand how it was to deal with people in adversarial situations, he thought. Nor Ravel, the Analyst. Though Ravel's expression suggested he seemed to have found the altercation amusing. Vallini glanced back at the women. They were already sharing a joke about something, and laughing. His thoughts drifted back to Astrid. He hoped he would be able to demonstrate enough kindness and sympathy to her. His throat tightened. He would introduce her to Silvana, he decided. Or would that just be evading his own responsibility? He snapped back to the present.

"So, Bram," he started. "What is the status with our automated swarm chasing down that Sentinel that jumped out of here?"

"They successfully destroyed the Sentinel after a three jump chase. We lost one device. The others have returned to HQ."

"Good. Well, that concludes the four Sentinel devices we were expecting. Would you like to try another round of acknowledge and summons calls to see if we can detect any further devices."

Bram nodded and stepped back into the transport and tapped on his control screen. He waited. Vallini looked over at the women; they were deep in conversation, the African woman making wide gestures with her hands, and Silvana nodding her understanding.

"Nothing." Bram interrupted Vallini's thoughts. "Absolutely no response to either command. And that is good news, I guess?"

"Which just leaves," Ravel put in from the rear seat, "the database server."

"OK," said Vallini. "So you wanted to download all their history that you haven't collected so far? Bram can action that now, while we have deep listening enabled, so that we can pinpoint its physical location."

"The download requests are in that filename starting with 'DB' that I sent you." Ravel pointed it out to Bram who actioned the request, and then watched the flickering of data on the screen.

"Well, you're getting plenty of historical data," commented Bram. "But strangely, we are having trouble pinpointing the physical source. Let me have a look at the data manually... So the signals are consistent—it's not a moving source... The South American signals are the strongest... and they are congruent... Let me have a look at Australia... Ah, yes, I see."

"What is it?" asked Vallini impatiently, his interest piqued.

Well, our deep listening stations are all on land naturally, so the system does not work very well when we get a situation like this... The signal seems to be coming from somewhere in the middle of the Pacific Ocean."

"What, a boat?" Vallini suggested.

"I don't know. I can't pinpoint it with the network composed like this," explained Bram. "I'll have to configure in some satellites to get a more accurate fix. Give me ten minutes." His fingers danced over the screen controls, adeptly selecting and connecting new nodes into the tracking nexus.

Vallini walked back over to where the two women were conversing. "How's it going?" he asked Silvana. The African woman gave him a sour face at the interruption.

"Excellently," enthused Silvana. "Her name is Nandipha," she said, taking great care over the pronunciation—a difficult task as it involved a tongue-click. Nandipha nodded appreciatively and smiled. Silvana deactivated the translator so that she could converse with Vallini in confidence. "She doesn't trust you I'm afraid. But she is so interesting, Vallini. She is a priestess in a religion that sounds like it employs a lot of intercession—called Voodoo."

"Ah. Sounds like the Sentinel organisation was betting each way on religions," observed Vallini.

"She's been explaining how they believe that everything contains spirit—animals, plants, a river, even a stone. Nandipha prepares a talisman from dried animal parts and calls in a spirit; then she gives that to someone for healing." Vallini hoped that his face was not conveying to Nandipha the disdainful scepticism he felt. "Can I spend a little longer with her?" pleaded Silvana.

"Yes, it looks as though I will have to work through some complications with Bram anyway. Perhaps you would like to take her home?"

"Oh. Yes, I would," replied Silvana eager to be entrusted with a creditable mission. "And can I have a look around where she lives?"

"No, I'm afraid not," apologised Vallini, bluntly. "Much too dangerous; I don't want to have to come and rescue you. Besides, you know TC policy—no unnecessary interactions in the past. But you can talk for a while longer before you take her home, and you can always read up on the history afterwards if it really interests you. Get the time and place coordinates of her origin from Bram before you jump; she probably does not know them in our terms. And bear in mind it will probably take two or three jumps to get her back accurately to where and when she left. Remember, make it a little afterwards, but not before." He walked back to the transport as the women resumed their translated conversation.

Bram looked up, smiling. "I have it," he said with satisfaction. "Not a boat, but an island in the Pacific Ocean, named Rapa Nui." Vallini looked bemused. "More colloquially it's called Easter Island."

"Ah, that's the island where they have huge ancient carved stone heads all round the coast, isn't it?" Vallini acknowledged.

"Indeed. But I can't pinpoint the position of the Sentinel server any more accurately without getting listening devices onto the island."

"Well, I guess we had better make the trip and investigate. Are you in, Ravel?"

"Definitely," came the enthusiastic reply from the back seat of the transport. "I'll get my history specialist to forward a background report on the island to me."

"How far is it?" asked Vallini.

"Over ten thousand kilometres travel to get there," supplied Bram. "We'll need to make the final jump right on the coast of Chile because we are targeting a tiny island, at four thousand kilometres into the ocean. Assuming we are going in present-time, I estimate five jumps, here to there, in total, if we are fortunate with the uncertainties."

"But we'll have to take a lot of equipment to cater for all eventualities, so communal transport is out of the question," Vallini considered. "Best we go back to HQ and load up our heavy-duty transport; and I'd like to start as soon as possible. Bram, could you go over and load Silvana's controller with the exact time and place coordinates where Nandipha, our guest from Africa, came from…"

Friday evening, May 13, 1853, Winterbourne Steepleton

Alex's opinion of Arbuckle was changing. Whilst, back in Cheltenham, he had seemed rather comical, capricious and dependent; by contrast, in his own domain, he was generous, entertaining and hospitable; and he seemed buoyed by the successful end to his adventure. Alex found himself wondering what sort of attitude he, himself, would exude if he did not have the comforting certainty of Joo-Won to extricate him back to his own time.

After a pleasant afternoon in the garden, chatting, they sat down for dinner inside. Alex felt slightly uncomfortable when Arbuckle insisted on saying a long grace before the meal, but could only relax as Mrs Dobbes then served up a steak and kidney pie with vegetables, which was truly delicious, followed by an Apple Charlotte for dessert. Alex and Joo-Won both earnestly praised her cooking skills, which Alex could see not only gladdened her, but made Arbuckle proud. To round off the meal, Arbuckle insisted on serving port. He kept the source concealed, but Alex suspected he knew exactly what the bottle looked like, and hoped Arbuckle never showed the dubious vintage date on the label to any of his friends or guests.

A little later, Joo-Won refused a second port saying that it was now time for them to leave. After checking that the equipment was sufficiently replenished with energy, he programmed his controller for the return trip to Cheltenham and they said hearty goodbyes, Arbuckle thanking Alex profusely for his support when he was in need at Cheltenham. Alex had grown fond of Arbuckle and found something of a lump in his throat on parting, knowing that he would never see the old fellow again.

Standing clear of the furniture in Arbuckle's parlour, Alex and Joo-Won put arms around each other and flexed their knees. Alex raised his other hand to wave goodbye to Arbuckle as Joo-Won pressed the button on his controller.

A puff of air and they landed, this time with poise, in darkness. Joo-Won checked his controller. "Yes, is close. Within one kilometre, but three days late. We jump again. Ready?" Alex nodded and they adopted the posture once more.

Puff. This time it was daylight and raining. "Ah," said Joo-Won, looking at his controller. "We very close to time we left. Same rainstorm." He laughed. "But not enough energy to get me home. I stay in hotel overnight, yes?" They hurried out of the field to the gate, and on to Jurys Inn. Alex used his credit card to book Joo-Won in for another night and made sure he had cash for meals. They shook hands.

"I'm sorry we had that misunderstanding that has delayed you," offered Alex.

"No, no. My fault. I think I not understand well the method you use century numbers?… But you confirmed Wednesday, so your fault also?"

"No…" Alex protested, puzzled. But then he let it go with a shrug which was mirrored with a shrug and smile by Joo-Won. "Goodbye, Joo-Won. Thank you for your help rescuing Betty and getting Arbuckle home."

"My pleasure. It has all been most interesting. Take care, Alex."

Alex headed home, orientating events in his mind. Now it only remained for Vallini to bring Betty back home, and all would be well. A couple of days, Vallini had said. Worth the short anxious wait if it marked the end of all their troubles.

*   *   *

Earth-Standard StarDate 2243.216, Rehab Station-3, Lo-Grav

"Well, I think my cardio condition is improving already," commented Astrid. "I managed to run the whole time this afternoon without stopping for a rest."

"Excellent," Betty responded encouragingly. She knew that it was only a small achievement considering Astrid just ran on the low-gravity track, but she was genuinely pleased that Astrid was making progress from her previous, evidently frail state.

"So did you enjoy your video?" asked Astrid.

"Yes, I understood a lot more of the references and style this time," Betty replied thoughtfully. "It's strange though. You see, Vallini said that it was a remake of a classic from my time. I sort of get a sense of having experienced the story before; it seems curiously familiar, but I can't actually recall having read it."

"Oh, well ask Lex what the original was, then you can read it when you get back home," suggested Astrid, beginning a set of stretching exercises.

"Oh, yes. Great idea... Lex, what was the original work that the video *'She spoke with harmless shadows'* is based on?"

An almost imperceptible pause. *"That video is based on an original theatrical production titled 'Speaking into Shadows' that was first staged in 2029, and novelised two years later."*

"Ah! That is just a few years after the time that I come from," observed Betty.

"Well, that explains why you don't remember it then," proposed Astrid, her leg extended high over the top of a chair.

"Mmm... But it doesn't explain why it seems so familiar," murmured Betty, shrugging.

"I remember we had to study that book at school as an early example of the pragmatic-presentist philosophy."

"Oh? What was that philosophy about?" pressed Betty, pursuing clarity.

"It proposes that the best outcomes arise by learning from the past, but then discarding it. Not letting the light of the present be overcast by emotional shadows from the past—be they tribalism, grudges, fears, failures or whatever. Memories are like shadows."

"Ah! The shadows are the metaphor in the story. I get that," Betty acknowledged.

"Ow. I've got my foot stuck over the top of this chair. Can you help me please, Betty?"

Betty went over, put her arm around Astrid's waist and lifted her clear of the chair.

"Thanks. One day maybe I'll be as strong as you are."

"It's not much effort in low gravity," Betty insisted. "But yes, a few weeks of exercise... and lots of anabolite tablets..." They both laughed.

"Lex, who was the author of the original 'Speaking into Shadows'?" Betty asked.

This time the pause was noticeably longer. *"I am unable to give you that information."*

Astrid looked up quizzically. "Lex, look in the Comprehensive Bibliography."

No pause this time. *"That information is denied to present company."*

"That's just silly," commented Astrid. Turning to Betty, she said: "I can't recall it just at the moment, but I'll keep thinking—see if I can remember it from schooldays…" She laughed. "There's a lack of consensus about whether hibernation affects memory."

"So what kind of hibernation is it—do you get frozen?" asked Betty

"No. It's analogous to animal hibernation. Chemical stimulation of a particular group of neurons induces a deep torpor. And then there is a complex automated support system; monitoring blood and vital signs, providing nutritional and biochemical support the whole time."

"And how long were you in hibernation?" asked Betty.

"Well, it was supposed to have been a sixteen-year trip, but the freighter developed a problem and it took twenty-two years. Not that I knew any difference. It still seems like last week that I left the Pericyon system."

"So how far away is Pericyon," probed Betty, looking puzzled.

"3.7 parsecs."

"What's that in light-years."

"It's about 12 light-years."

"Well, I don't get that," stated Betty, perplexed. "To do that distance in 16 years, the freighter would have had to accelerate up to near light speed… and decelerate again. But no rocket could do that…"

"Ah. *You* came up *here* on a rocket. But they are only used for precision injection into low Earth orbit because it is quite crowded with satellites and stations. For long distances, freighters use repetitive translocation."

"Oh. Like the ground transports. But why repetitive?" asked Betty.

"Well, translocation has an uncertainty principle associated with it. It's a bit like the Heisenberg Uncertainty principle which says the more accurately you know the position of something, the less well you know its momentum, and vice versa. With translocation, if you target to go just a few kilometres then you would get fairly close to your target, plus or minus a fraction of a metre. But the uncertainty scales with the square of the distance. So if you tried to jump millions of kilometres then the uncertainty dominates to such an extent that you could land almost anywhere—perhaps in the direction you want to go, or sideways or even behind where you started. So the space freighter has to make multiple iterative jumps of shorter distances. And each time it exits a jump, then it

193

has to work out its new location from the parallax changes—that's the relative apparent positions of the stars, re-compute a new direction, and initiate a new jump. Which takes time. So the design engineers do a calculation to find the sweet spot, working out how many jumps they can make each second, and then jumping as far as possible, but minimising the error, to gain the maximum useful distance per second. I think for our dear freighter which could achieve ten jumps per second, the optimal jump was around 50,000 kilometres; but the useful distance covered each jump is about half that... I hope that makes sense? I had to write an essay on it in my final school year."

"Wow." Betty's face was alight with enthusiasm as she mashed the numbers in her head. "So that's equivalent to a speed of about a quarter of a million useful kilometres a second. Amazing! But can't the translocations use backward time to make more progress."

"Well, theoretically they could, but then the uncertainty is increased even more. The intriguing thing is, no matter how you permutate the parameters, you can never get faster than the speed of light... *Travelling,* that is. Theoretically, the subwave *communications* can be instant, but they get restricted in a different way."

"How do you mean?"

"Well, the distance that subwaves transmit before deteriorating is relatively limited. So communication depends on a network of onward re-transmission. For example, if I want to send a message from the Pericyon system, it will get repeatedly transmitted until a freighter, going in the right direction, and within calling distance, receives it. Then that freighter repeatedly transmits it until it gets picked up by another freighter even further on. And so on. The trouble is there are not enough freighters to make it work efficiently, so the freighters have to store a huge queue of transmissions that they are trying to pass on..."

Betty nodded, looking pensive. "OK, so the freighters use repetitive translocation. But how do the freighters get into orbit when they arrive?" challenged Betty. "It's all very well arriving somewhere, but you need velocity to attain an orbit around a planet. If you just translocated close to a planet and stopped there, gravity would pull the freighter straight down toward the planet's surface."

"Exactly right," confirmed Astrid. "That was always my favourite bit of Space Science at school. So the freighter arrives at a safe distance from the planet and starts to fall inwards. We know what orbital speed we need, for the orbit we want to end up in. So we let the freighter fall until we reach that speed. Then the freighter calculates and executes a translocation off to the side of the planet, and to a distance *from* the planet, that matches the orbit it wants. So it actually exits that translocation *in* the desired orbit *carrying* the correct speed.

"Brilliant," enthused Betty. "Absolutely brilliant! But, because gravity itself varies with the inverse square of the distance from the Earth, the fall will be under increasing acceleration, and so the calculation involves an integral."

"Indeed. Of course, that manoeuvre won't be absolutely precise—it has its own uncertainty; so the freighter still then requires a couple of very small correctional translocations to fix the orbit perfectly. But that FDT manoeuvre—the Fall-Duration and Translocative manoeuvre—is a classic equation in Space Science. Mind you, the 'fall' is not as dramatic as it sounds. If the freighter starts the fall from a safe distance—say 50,000 kilometres—it would probably have to fall for about two hours before gaining the speed it needs for a translocation into orbit."

"So, is that procedure executed by a space pilot on the freighter?" asked Betty.

"No. It's executed by the AI running the freighter, but in coordination with the planet's STC—that's Space Traffic Control." Astrid laughed: "It would not be practicable to have a human sitting around in the freighter for 20 years just waiting for that moment. And people need some care and attention as they are gradually emerging from hibernation—they wouldn't be capable of reliable judgement at that point."

"Anyway, in practice, the calculation and manoeuvre are not that straightforward. When the freighter arrives close to Earth, it will still have the velocity that it had in orbit around the planet it came from. The translocations during a journey do not scrub off that speed. So the actual calculations to manoeuvre that residual velocity into a useful *orbital* velocity are more complex and nuanced. Of course, the whole journey and the final manoeuvres are all done in free fall, so the passengers still experience nothing but weightlessness "

Betty nodded wistfully. "So what happens when the freighter successfully gets into Earth orbit?" questioned Betty. "Are you already out of hibernation then?"

"No. Arousal is not usually started until a medical team dock to the freighter and come on board to care for the passengers. They first check the monitoring history for each passenger so they can anticipate what immediate care they will need, and then rouse each patient. Arousal doesn't take long. But it does take a while to ensure everyone is stable enough to be transferred to the medical ferry, which then navigates down to a lower orbit where the Rehab Stations are. The medical ferries are hybrids of translocation and propulsion, indeed, most of the ferries are. But the medical ferries use notoriously gentle rocket and ion thrusters, because, as you can see, we travellers are in no fit condition to experience more than fractional g-forces. So that medical ferry transfer trip to here seemed to take quite a few hours. Anyway, the rest you know…"

"And the freighter carries cargo as well?" asked Betty.

"For sure. That's their main purpose. The few passengers are cocooned right in the centre of the freighter, with the cargo all around protecting us from years of space radiation. Once the medical team has evacuated the passengers, then the cargo ferries are allowed to dock and start extracting the shipment and transporting it down to the planet surface."

"So, you said that your freighter developed a fault that made the journey longer?" recalled Betty.

"Yes. One of the Hadamard drives developed an anomaly…"

"That information is not appropriate for present company. Miss Gosmore should please disregard that previous sentence," the soft, disembodied voice interrupted. But naturally, Betty couldn't help but remember that sentence *more* vividly, now that attention had been drawn to it.

"Lex, clarify," demanded Astrid.

"TC have proscribed certain topics to their guest. Whilst your discussion of space science contained only operational and mathematical considerations, that was within constraints; but to be clear, explicit discussion of modern technology, or matters pertaining to Miss Gosmore's later personal history are prohibited."

"Oh, well, that's clear enough, I suppose," said Astrid shrugging.

"Wait. Does that mean that our whole conversation has been listened to?" asked Betty, somewhat outraged.

"Well, of course," stated Astrid. "How else could a voice control system help if it's not listening?"

"But don't you find that an invasion of privacy?" asked Betty, surprised at Astrid's calm acceptance.

"Invasion?… Well, no. We spend our whole lives with voice control

196

systems ready to respond to commands or requests. It's only there to help. I'm sure there are good reasons why Vallini established limitations. Our conversation doesn't get reported to anyone else, it's just being evaluated in real-time to check for appropriateness. Did you not have voice control in the time that you come from?" asked Astrid curiously.

Betty thought. "Well, we do. It's more limited, of course. And I guess we are just more paranoid about privacy. Worried about our data getting into the hands of someone who might use it against us."

"Astrid, a reminder to take your anabolite tablets." Lex sounded entirely unconcerned. Betty laughed, having half-expected a spirited defence, from Lex, of the benefits of voice control.

"There, you see. Lex has my best interests at heart," quipped Astrid as she walked to her bedroom to collect the tablets.

"You said that there is education available on these screens didn't you?" Betty asked, as Astrid returned with her tablets and a bottle of water. "I'd like to learn more about your Space Science if I'm allowed to?"

"Sure… Lex, put Space Science 101 up for Betty."

"I will furnish an appropriately-redacted version. If the redaction of technology renders any sentences unreadable, then please ask for an alternative explanation."

Betty rubbed her hands together in glee, beginning many hours of absorbed enjoyment working through several educational units.

Chapter 13
Step softly, a dream lies buried here.

(Yates)

Earth-Standard StarDate 2243.217, Santiago, Chile

The heavy-duty transport, about the size of a large motor-home, was now sitting in the jump-port area near Santiago, Chile. Vallini looked at the clock. It had taken them several hours to get this far. Not so much because of the six jumps they had made, but because preceding each jump, Bram had been negotiating clearance procedures with the various regional authorities, and checking their proposed landing areas for any dangers. Vallini did not often venture this far round the globe. He looked up to the sky, remembering that Astrid and Betty were somewhere above, orbiting in the Rehab Station. Idly, he pulled the coordinates of the Rehab Station onto the screen; but it was currently over Canada—nowhere near.

"I'm ready to initiate the jump to Rapa Nui," Bram announced, looking round at the other two men. "Because it's such a long jump to such a small island, there is a 30% chance of uncertainty placing us over the ocean, in which case the translocation pre-processor will abort the jump and try again." Vallini nodded. This was all standard practice. "Do you want to ready any weapons, before we jump?"

"I can't see the need," replied Vallini. "There are communal tourist transports making the jump every day. But..." He patted his pocket.

"OK. Here we go." Bram initiated the jump. The transport lurched a little to the left as it landed. The ground was not flat. They looked around. Hills, some greened, some just bare rock. To the right, the slopes leading up to a large outcrop, were adorned with several stone heads, with tourists standing and walking around and between.

"OK, I'll set up the first of our listening devices here," stated Bram, stepping out and unloading a metallic cylinder. A man was marching up

198

toward them from the group of tourists. He seemed rather irate.

"We do not allow private transports on Rapa Nui," he barked.

Vallini pulled his ID from a pocket and showed it to the man. "Temporal Continuity," he explained.

"I don't care who you are," shouted the man. "This island is a nature reserve. Tourists must come by the communal transports which are then parked in the authorised lot."

"We are *not* tourists," insisted Vallini. "We are here officially, on an important mission."

"Anyway, we're just leaving," interjected Bram, who had already positioned his listening device. And he climbed back into the transport. "Now we'll jump to the other side of the island to position another device to enable triangulation," he informed the others.

"Hey. You can't leave that here," objected the man, whom Vallini had deduced was a tour guide from the badge on his clothing.

Bram just ignored him and initiated a jump across the island. "I hope they are more friendly on the other side of the island," he quipped, as the transport landed on more level land, close to the sea. This time there were only a couple of walkers in sight. Bram quickly unloaded another cylindrical listening device. Then he returned to the control screen within the vehicle and watched the data. "Well, that was straightforward," he concluded. "The triangulation to the subwave signals coming from the database pinpoints a place on the map that is in the foothills of a volcano called Rano Raraku." He stepped out and retrieved the listening device. "So, do you want to risk the wrath of the tour guide to recover the other device, or shall we go straight to Rano R... Rano Raraku?" he asked, studying the displayed map to get the name right.

"No, let's keep it tidy," decided Vallini. "Let's reclaim our equipment first." Bram tapped the screen a couple of times to effect a return jump. They landed just a few metres from their device and quickly repossessed it. The guide had walked back down to his tourists, but gesticulated when he caught sight of them again.

"Right. Rano Raraku," declared Bram, preparing the jump.

"Actually, jump us a kilometre or so inland, and we'll walk down from there," said Vallini. "It looks from the map as if it will be another tourist magnet, so let's keep out of the way."

Bram studied the map. "I'll land us behind the volcanic crater's rim, on the opposite side from where the tourists will be."

Bram's prediction appeared correct as, when they landed, no-one was in sight. The three men walked for several minutes around the volcano rim and came in sight of an impressive display of 15 carved stone monoliths standing in a line atop a long stone plinth, close to the sea's edge.

Ravel had been mostly quiet during the preceding part of the journey whilst he studied the background report that had been prepared for him by his history specialist. "So, that line of monoliths," he explained, pointing down toward the sea, "is called Ahu Tongariki. The stone figures are called moai. Although it looks very impressive, even from a distance—and indeed it is a tourist magnet—it has in fact been completely reconstructed. Actually, almost all the Ahu sites have been reconstructed to some extent, because there was a civil war on the island in the late 18th Century when rival tribes toppled each others' monuments. Ethnically the inhabitants originated from different areas— the Polynesian Islands, and distinct parts of South America. But additionally, Ahu Tongariki, over there, was hit by a tsunami in the 20th Century and then rebuilt after that. The interesting thing, though, from our point of view, is that the only moai left *standing* after the civil war, were these ones in the area we are walking to, on the slopes of this volcano."

"Ah," declared Vallini, immediately seeing the implication.

"The island," continued Ravel, "seems to have had a very turbulent history with more than one population collapse. Apparently, at one stage they had cut down *all* the trees on the islands for building, burning, and using as rollers to transport the stone blocks to position the moai! It has been hailed as a prime example of unsustainable practices getting out of control." Vallini laughed. "They have managed some reforestation now, as you can see, but it is difficult because the rainfall disappears quickly into the porous lava rock, so saplings are prone to dry out."

They had reached the moai on the slopes, which were dotted around in great number. Tourists were ambling between them and taking photographs, but there were so many moai over such a large area that there was no sense of crowding.

"Many of these are just head and shoulders," commented Bram, "compared to the full torsos down by the sea."

"In truth, they are probably *all* full torsos," Ravel corrected him, "but hundreds of years of rolling rock erosion and vegetation has added a few metres of topsoil, burying most of the torso."

"Wow, you only really appreciate how huge they are when you get up close," commented Vallini admiringly. "This one must be eight or nine metres tall."

"This one looks like it's only half-finished being carved," called Bram from a few metres away, examining one lying on its side.

"Almost all the stone for the moais was quarried from this volcanic crater," Ravel informed them. "So this is also a workshop area for carving. Then they would roll the carved moai on tree trunks to its intended position, erect it, and then carve the back surface to complete the job."

Vallini noted, with some apprehension, a tour guide approaching them.

"Hello. You gentlemen must be the ones that ran into Uki, our tour guide over at Ahu Vinapu, judging by his description," he laughed.

"Oh, er yes..." Vallini was not sure how to respond. "We left our transport well out of the way, behind the volcano."

The man laughed again. "It's OK. He reported you, but was told by our boss that you had been cleared, and have every right to travel round the island. Temporal Continuity isn't it?" Vallini relaxed and nodded. "We don't get many official visits out here," he continued. "Uki is a bit defensive. One of the traditionalists. He believes the spirits of our ancestors deserve not to be disturbed. You're lucky he didn't attack your transport... Throw rocks at it or something... Like the Mana incident." He laughed again.

"What's the Mana incident?" asked Vallini, confused.

"Ah. Well, Mana is the sacred supernatural power supposedly running from the godhead, through the ancestors' spirits. So, back when translocation transports were first invented... Well no, when they first bothered to visit this remote island... We had tourists and supplies come in by aeroplane before then... So, anyway, this is about a hundred years ago, they wanted to start bringing tourists in by translocation instead of by aeroplane. It was OK for about a month, they were landing at various indeterminate places all over the island, as you know is inevitable. But then one day, a transport happened to land here for the first time, at Rano Raraku, just a little way down the slope there, but the spirits had had enough of the intrusion and in their wrath they released a swarm of

Mana manifestations that attacked the transport and destroyed it, killing a load of the would-be tourists. There was a big furore and investigation—they had to call in the military. The military transport was fine when it landed centre-island, but as soon as it jumped out here—to Rano Raraku, it got attacked as well. But being the military they responded hard. Drones it was, they said. The military destroyed them all. No-one could ever explain how they came to be here. And we never had any more trouble of that sort. But it took a long time before the tourists felt safe enough to come again. Anyway, the incident is pretty much forgotten about now, but people like Uki think it justifies a hostility to transports, in the name of our ancestors... Right, I'd better get back to my party. Nice to meet you fellows. I hope you enjoy your trip."

"Well, it sounds like 'the military' did our job for us," remarked Bram, watching the guide walking back to a gathering group.

"It sounds like they destroyed the Sentinel defences," Vallini clarified. "But of course the database server is still functioning."

"So, bearing in mind the history," Ravel suggested, "the Sentinel organisation knew that this site is the only one that is undisturbed by the civil war, and therefore not subject to reconstruction. And being a conserved site of historical value, it would never be demolished or otherwise developed; particularly on a remote island like this. So going back in time, and building their facility underground here, long before the island became inhabited, would ensure it survived through hundreds or even thousands of years of civilisation aboveground."

"Agreed," said Vallini. "And presumably lava rock from the volcano would be easier to cut and dig making it an attractive site to install something underground."

They caught up to Bram who had been wandering, his controller in hand. "This close to the subwave source I can locate it directly," he explained. He took a few more paces forward and back, and shuffled sideways. "Here," he pointed at the ground in front of a massive moai. "Directly beneath here."

Vallini backed off a few steps and looked up at the moai face, several metres above, staring out resolutely toward the shoreline. "I wonder if they considered the particular features of the actual moai that would be standing here," he wondered out loud.

Bram made an adjustment to his controller and scanned up and down the statue. "Nothing special about the statue. Solid stone. No metal."

"Well, I assume you're not considering digging? In a global heritage area?" posed Ravel. "Perhaps it's best to just leave it be?"

"I would feel happier if we destroyed the Sentinel facility," replied Vallini thoughtfully. "Bram, could we try a directional emf-pulse downwards?"

"No chance," came the reply. "None of our non-disruptive weapons would penetrate through metres of soil and rock."

"Any other ideas then?" asked Vallini, anticipating Bram's technical expertise.

"Well... The only way I can see of disrupting something *down there*, without causing disruption *up here*, is to translocate stuff into 'down there'."

"Ah, translocate some rocks into it, you mean?" Vallini asked.

"Well, that would probably do it, but I'd be a bit worried about whether increasing the volume of what's down there, would raise the surface a bit up here. In other words, it might be disruptive to the ground the moai are standing on." There was silence for a few seconds while Bram considered... "It might be better if we translocated *water* down there. Water would be destructive to any sort of machinery or equipment, but it would dissipate easily into crevices and porous rock, so it shouldn't be too disruptive volume-wise to the structure of the ground. Trouble is, the sea is a bit far away."

"There's a freshwater lake inside the volcano crater," Ravel suggested helpfully.

"Ah. That would be a lot nearer, though it's out of the line of sight. But with the three of us, we should be able to coordinate that. Yes, that sounds like the best idea," concluded Bram. Vallini nodded his agreement.

"And presumably you want to translocate back in time and destroy it early on?" Bram asked.

Vallini considered. "Well, ideally it would be good to destroy it early on, but we are constrained. Because, if we destroyed it before Betty's kidnap by the Sentinel, then the Sentinel devices would have had no way to understand and locate Betty, so we would be erasing that kidnap incident from history. And more important, therefore, we ourselves would know nothing about the Sentinel organisation, so we wouldn't be here to destroy their database device—in other words, we would create a paradox. Ravel is going to rewrite the critical pieces of recorded history in their database facility with false narratives anyway. If you do that just after Betty's episode, Ravel, then we are protected from that time on. So I think for completeness we destroy the Sentinel database facility today, but knowing it's really just overkill."

"I'm afraid," interrupted Ravel, "it's not quite that simple. If I overwrite their critical history just after Betty's episode, then that history wouldn't have been available for my team to analyse in present time, so again we would be creating a paradox. Remember that I have come back to you from four and a half years in the future, after my team have analysed the Sentinels and their communication protocols. So if we destroy this database facility now, then that four and a half years work would not be possible—again we would create a nasty paradox. It seems to me the only neat way to do it would be to travel four and a half years into the future and destroy the facility then."

Vallini thought about it, then nodded wearily. "Agreed. It's less than ideal. If we have in fact eliminated all the current remaining Sentinel devices then we are safe anyway. But leaving the database intact for so long is a vulnerability."

"We can minimise the vulnerability by permanently listening for any activity," Bram put in. "In the unlikely event that we ever hear any device sending to or receiving from this facility in the vulnerable years, we can respond immediately."

"Good thought," acknowledged Vallini. "OK, then. Let's translocate four and a half years into the future and put an end to it. Ravel, can you give Bram the exact date we need to get to. We'll need to do it after dark though. We'd attract far too much attention otherwise. Ravel, have you extracted all the historical data from it that you want?"

"Yes. We've read and stored 500 years plus. We could get more, but, to be honest, it's fairly indecipherable that far ahead—we don't understand enough about the conventions and subject matter for it to be meaningful at those advanced dates. But, I have got one suggestion. Instead of translocating ahead into the dark of night, why don't we spend the rest of this pleasant day having a good look round—it's such an interesting place?"

"Good idea," agreed Vallini. He ran his hand over the rough stone of the moai they were standing next to. "So how long have these things been standing here for?" he asked Ravel.

"The oldest ones—maybe a thousand years," was the reply.

"Impressive… Maybe we should get a tour guide?" Vallini quipped.

*   *   *

Earth-Standard StarDate 2248.032, Rapa Nui

It was dusk when they arrived, again on the far side of the volcanic crater rim. "That's good enough," Bram commented, looking at their position. "I need to do a bit of preparation first. I'll have to override the normal safeguards on a translocator that _prevent_ it jumping stuff into a collision, and _prevent_ it jumping to below ground-level; since that's exactly what we _do_ want it to do.

They set off shortly afterwards, on the walk around to the foothill under which the Sentinel facility lay. Pretty soon it became very dark, and they had to use flashlights to illuminate the rock-strewn path. Bram left the other two there, and continued, with a bulky backpack, on to the path that they had earlier identified was the easiest access to the lake inside the crater. Vallini and Ravel sat down to wait for Bram to get to the lake, with their backs against one of the moai.

"Wow, look at those stars," enthused Vallini. "Without any sky shine from city lights, you can see so many more." His mind flashed briefly back to Astrid, and he decided he must learn how to locate her star system in the sky so he could point it out to her on clear nights.

"Yes, amazing," agreed Ravel. "In fact, some of the ancient civilisations, the Incas for example, for whom a vivid sky like this was normal; they used to identify and name constellations not only as a join-the-dots group of stars, but also as the shapes of darker patches you can see in the Milky Way, where dust or gas obscures any stars." He pointed to the vast swathe of the galaxy overhead in which there were dark zones. The two men were pensive and quiet for a while.

Finally, Bram's voice coming through their earpieces, broke the silence: "Right, I'm in position at the edge of the lake. I've immersed a five-litre jump container in the water, so each time I action a translocation, it will deliver those litres in your direction. I've encoded the coordinates to the moai that is over the Sentinel facility as accurately as I can without direct line of sight, but we'll need to do some test runs first. So if you and Ravel can observe, I'll jump a fill of water over to there, at a height of five metres above ground, and you can tell me if I need any fine adjustment to hit the spot we identified as being directly above the Sentinel facility. From this close, the uncertainty will only be a few centimetres so we don't need to worry about that. But listen, you must stand well away from the spot, because I've disabled those safeguards on the translocator, so it would be lethal if you got in the way."

"Understood, Bram. We're backing away now. Wait till I give you the signal." Vallini waved Ravel to get twenty metres away South, *down* the slope; as he did the same East, *across* the slope. That way they could assess the necessary correction in both spatial dimensions. "OK Bram, we're ready. Take your first shot."

It was, of course, difficult to see in the dark. Even though Vallini had flashed his torch in the general direction, they heard, rather than saw, the virtual bucketful of water hit the ground.

"OK, hold off, Bram. We're going to investigate." Vallini thought he had caught a flash in his beam so followed, in that direction. But ultimately, it was by finding wet ground that they located the first shot. "OK Bram, adjust one and a half metres to the East, and half a metre North. We've backed off, so you can try again now." This time they stayed a bit closer, widened the flashlight beams and played them where the water was expected. They waited a few seconds whilst Bram adjusted his parameters.

"That was spot on, Bram. Now you can start translocating the slugs of water to underground coordinates. You're going to start at three metres down, right? Ravel is listening for any disturbance in the subwave signal."

"Will do. I'll start at three below and go down an extra half-metre each shot till we get some action," came back Bram's voice.

Vallini was surprised to hear a muted thump. He glanced questioningly at Ravel, who shook his head. "It's still transmitting the signals."

"Then I guess that's just the muffled shock from rock breaking, when the translocated water forcefully penetrates it," commented Vallini. There followed several more dulled and indistinct thuds each separated by the seconds it took for Bram to readjust the coordinates.

Then: "Hang on," said Ravel, "I think the signal faltered, then picked up again."

The timbre of the sounds had changed. Still very deadened, but with a hint of stricken metal, and grinding. A few more seconds and Ravel declared that the transmission had stopped. "OK, Bram," said Vallini. "We have hit the target. The transmission has stopped. But can you do a pattern of hits around that area, spreading out a metre in all directions to make sure we hit everything that we can damage?"

"Will do," Bram acknowledged.

Vallini and Ravel sat down again leaning back on one of the moai, the silence punctuated by the strange unpredictable muffled noises from below.

"So," Ravel mused with some sadness. "I think we just destroyed the last remnants of a civilisation. I hope it was the right thing to do."

Vallini looked up at the myriad stars. "I have given this a lot of thought over the last couple of days. There is no 'right', Ravel. Only a multitude of possibilities. Is there a right or wrong about which sperm gets to fertilise an egg? Isn't that single sperm denying the possibility for millions of alternative babies to be born? We just chose the possibility that includes our existence, and tried to ensure its longevity. It's as natural an event in evolution as any other…"

Suddenly there was a massive thud from below, causing the ground to ride up and fall by a few centimetres. The men felt themselves bounced. There followed a loud crack, and the head of the moai above the Sentinel facility slid and toppled in their torchlight beams to land, ignominiously, nose-first into the grassy slope.

"Oh no…" started Vallini in exasperation.

"Whoa… My guess is the containment of their power supply just ruptured," proposed Ravel.

"Do you think we should get Bram to stop?" asked Vallini.

"No. I reckon that would have to be the main disruption. The last couple of thumps have been much less pronounced. But I'm not sure we'll be able to fix that moai; the head must weigh a few tonnes, and I think the torso has shifted. Maybe Bram will have some ideas?"

Vallini had stood up and was now playing the flashlight over the fractured monolith, shaking his head. He noticed the way the dignified effigy lay with its forehead resting on the ground, like a face palm. His breath seemed to catch and then he found himself laughing at the incongruity. And he found himself laughing long and hard.

"What is it?" asked Ravel, bemused at his friend's uncharacteristic reaction.

"Oh... I'm sorry, Ravel. It's just the way such a serious face is staring into the ground. It's... And it's made me realise that maybe I have been taking this job too seriously. I have always cherished the role because TC seemed like an ideal; like an unquestionable truth. Then this mission came along and, like we were saying yesterday or the day before; if anything, it is the Sentinel organisation that has the prime rights to existence. We are just another alternative, and all the efforts and struggles I put into the job are just that, and not a precise, correct, grandiose drive of guardianship."

"Ah... Well, I think you are being a bit hard on yourself," countered Ravel. "You have always done a meticulous job, and you are indeed a guardian of *our* existence. *Of course* we have a vested interest in our *own* existence. Like you said it's an evolutionary imperative. And you are usually protecting the integrity and quality of our existence by chasing down the rogues; it's just this particular mission when you are enforcing our *right,* or ability to exist... Personally, as a scientist, I choose to work for TC because it gives me access to the most interesting technology; not because I see any particular ideal in it. Though I can appreciate that as an agent, you have to be a bit closer to the ethics of an organisation."

Vallini nodded. "It just seems like I have never had to compromise before; the course of action has always been very obvious and clear. Now, with this mission, I am forced into serial compromises. So I suppose we will have to leave this statue in its sorry state. It doesn't really change anything for the world. There are several others lying around unfinished or broken." He sighed. "You know," Vallini continued, "when this operation is finished, I am going to take some time off. I have a young cousin who's just arrived at a Rehab Station from the Pericyon system. I want to spend a lot of time with her, help her understand and discover life here on Earth. She's the only family I have now. I am really looking forward to it."

"Ah, yes. I remember you telling me years ago that you had been notified that she was in transit. What is her name, again?"

"Astrid."

"Well, I'll look forward to meeting her. But she will be four and a half years older then, because I have to go forward to my regular time again after this escapade. I have really missed our friendship whilst I was locked away doing the analysis, so I am looking forward to spending time with you again—but that's the *you* of four years hence, of course! *You* are going to miss *me* for four years now, whilst I am in isolation!"

"Uh... Yes, it can be cruel, messing with time," acknowledged Vallini.

"Before I return to my regular time, I would quite like to meet Betty, though, if that's possible? I'm intrigued, having spent so much time working on issues where she was pivotal. I assume you will be bringing her out of the safe place you have hidden her, imminently?"

"Yes. We can arrange a meet-up, of course. She is delightful; very free and lively; and very intelligent too..."

Vallini yawned. "I'm tired, we have been working for too many hours. Though I'm glad you suggested staying for a while to look around the moai and learn about their history, it was refreshing and thought-provoking.

The muffled underground noises had long-since ceased, and soon Bram's return was heralded by the rhythmic wavering of his flashlight in the distance, as he walked. Vallini and Ravel rose to greet him. "Great work Bram. Here, let me carry your backpack—you've had more than your fair share of walking tonight." Bram wearily handed over his backpack without argument. "Let's go home."

Chapter 14
For all we know this might only be a dream,
we come and go like ripples in a stream.
(Nat King Cole)

Earth-Standard StarDate 2243.218, TC HQ

After a good night's sleep, Vallini headed into his office and tried to book a seat on the shuttle to Orbital Rehab Station-3; but he found it was already fully booked. He sat pensive, considering. Then he decided that because it *was* official business, he would pull strings. He translocated himself back to the previous day, having considered carefully where he would have been, so that he did not inadvertently encounter himself. As expected, he found that the shuttle then was not yet fully booked, so he reserved a seat for himself, and a returning trip seat for both himself and Betty. Then he sent a message to Betty telling her that he would be coming to collect her the next day. Finally, he translocated himself forward a day, and prepared to head off to the spaceport.

*   *   *

Vallini bounced his way along the Lo-Grav corridor to Astrid's room and knocked. Astrid answered and embraced him. Betty hung back. She had realised over the last couple of days just how much Astrid would depend on Vallini, how completely lost and alone she was.

"So, how are you getting on?" Vallini asked.

"Good, Vallini," she responded enthusiastically. "See, I have learned to pronounce your name properly. And I have gained a lot of strength during the last few days. My physio says I am well on course for a room in Mid-Grav next week." She performed a couple of jumps to demonstrate. It was, Betty mused, a major step forward from that first day when Astrid had struggled even to stand. A triumph both for her laudable dedication to exercise, and for the unexacting anabolites. Betty smiled at the juxtaposition.

"Sorry, I'm not ignoring you, Betty. We can talk later, but I only have a few minutes with Astrid before you and I have to catch the return ferry. Have you enjoyed the stay?"

"Emphatically yes, Vallini," Betty replied. "Thank you. It has been an exceptional holiday from which I can take back many very special memories; and it's been lovely to get to know Astrid."

"Yes, may I communicate with Betty after she goes back in time, Vallini?" requested Astrid fervently.

"Oh… Well, that's difficult. Messages through time are normally limited to TC operatives," asserted Vallini.

"Please… You could send the messages for me, couldn't you?" begged Astrid.

"Well… I suppose so; occasionally. On two conditions. First, that you refrain from researching any history about Betty's life, so that you don't inadvertently tell her things that might provoke her to *change* the course of her life."

"OK, I promise. What's the other condition?"

"And second, that you only message each other in synchronised elapsed time. In other words, if you send a message three months from now, Betty will receive it three months after she arrived back, and vice versa. As if you were living concurrently. No sending messages to older or younger versions of each other."

"Agreed." Astrid beamed.

Betty found it amusing that Vallini had been compromised by Astrid's innocent manipulation, but she didn't let it show on her face. "I'll just go and finish packing my bag," she said, considerately leaving the two of them to spend the remaining minutes of the visit together. In truth, she had little to pack—just the clothes she had arrived in and a few mementos she intended to take home—23rd Century toiletries and such.

A few minutes later Vallini knocked on her bedroom door. "We need to go now, Betty."

She hugged Astrid an assertive goodbye, as they knew they would never see each other again. Betty was encouraged to feel some little strength in Astrid's arms.

Then Astrid hugged Vallini. "Remember," he said. "I will be back next week, and I'll stay here for a few days so we can talk and really get to know each other."

Betty followed Vallini back to the ferry, eager to experience the novel descent down to Earth. In truth, the return was disappointing after the views from the Rehab Station. Although there was some thrill from the feel of the deceleration during re-entry and landing burns, the lack of any direct visual experience, through the inaccessible tiny windows, made the process less than exhilarating. The camera relays through the passengers' overhead screens provided only a proxy version of the reality. Indeed, it was all over in twenty minutes. Nevertheless, Betty was still buoyed by the totality of memories she was carrying home as they exited the spaceport and took a transport back to TC HQ.

*   *   *

Vallini left Betty listening to Silvana, who was telling her the story of Nandipha, the African voodoo priestess who had held a roughly equivalent role to Arbuckle in TC's recent foray. Vallini went to find Ravel.

"Just before we go and have lunch with the others," Vallini said to Ravel, "there is one issue I wanted to discuss with you. I'm thinking that it is very important that you not only rewrite the Sentinel database history to replace Betty's name, whereabouts and general details with something fictitious, so that any Sentinel agent, if one happened to still exist, would not be able to find her again; but that you also do the same in the final version of the report that you file with the TC Seniors. I will copy your false data for *my* report to them. That way the only people who know the real details about Betty are your small team and mine. It's not that I mistrust anyone within the TC organisation to cause mischief, but just to ensure that those pertinent details are *never* externally available *anywhere*. Indeed, I presume that the TC Seniors would expect us to do that."

Ravel nodded his agreement. "Except, of course, as we discussed last night at Rapa Nui, I could only amend the database after four and a half years from now, otherwise the Sentinel events, and our knowledge of them, would never have happened. But, at that time, the database server has been destroyed anyway. So the amendment can't actually be done. Though, yes, I will falsify Betty's details in my official reports."

This time it was Vallini nodding his assent. "Yes, I agree that is the correct way forward. It's a pity we cannot eliminate the risk entirely. But I guess we can bolster our number of agents like Gemma with equipment, back in the past, as a further precaution against the Sentinel, or indeed any other alternative organisation, trying to take over again. And Bram has implemented a protocol to listen for any requests sent to the database… Anyway, let's go and have lunch now…"

"Not so fast, Vallini," Ravel put up his hand in a delaying gesture. "I also have something of importance to make you aware of. At least I think, although this is possibly important, we probably do not need to do anything about it."

"So what is it?" insisted Vallini, his brow furrowed with curiosity.

"Right. Well, I have just received a report from six years in the future. From my history analyst, who has spent a year or so studying the divergence between our own history, and the history encoded by the Sentinel organisation. As we expected, the histories begins to diverge as a result of geopolitical differences—the result of Betty's technical knowledge either being or not being available to Eastern governments. But my history analyst suggests that that's *not* actually the *main* source of divergence. She makes a strong case that the main driving force behind the divergence is that Betty writes a very influential novel, kick-starting a whole genre of cultural activity that in turn propels a change in social and political attitudes over a century or so. It is certainly possible that the particular genre—the pragmatic-presentist philosophy—might have arisen and flourished anyway, without her publication. But it is very noteworthy that this distinct genre and philosophy never arose within the Sentinel-led society; their society and philosophical approaches developed a much more hierarchical structure based on rule-following and enforcement… So my historical analyst's conclusion, and she is very capable in historical interpretation, is that Betty's role as author is actually more pivotal than that lack of knowledge transfer resulting from her not being kidnapped… Though of course, it is axiomatic that she would not have been able to do the literary work if she *had* been permanently kidnapped."

Vallini was quiet for a moment, taking in the significance of what he had been told. "Yes, I don't think it makes any difference to the actions we have taken, or need to take… Strange though—I don't remember her name from the reading and studies I undertook on philosophy when I was younger."

"Ah," supplied Ravel. "That's because she used a pen name."

"Don't tell me," replied Vallini quickly and bluntly. "I don't think I want to know right now."

Surprise showed on Ravel's face, but he was silent, respecting Vallini's wish.

"And absolutely don't say anything to Betty about this," asserted Vallini.

"No. Of course not; that would be reckless," affirmed Ravel. "So let's go and have that lunch now; I am even more intrigued to meet Betty after hearing from my history analyst."

*   *   *

After lunch, Vallini led Betty back to his office. "So, now I have to take you back to your own time, Betty. Let's see." Vallini consulted his notes. "We brought you here from the Tuesday morning, so I should return you to the Thursday as you have spent two days here."

"Oh…" Betty initially looked disappointed, then determined: "No, I need to go back to the Sunday before."

"What? We can't do that, Betty. You were already there on the Sunday—we can't have two of you wandering around."

"Well, no," Betty argued, "technically I wasn't there from the Sunday evening when I got abducted, until the Monday evening when I was rescued. So if you take me back to the Sunday evening that would be fine."

"…Until the Monday evening when there would then be two of you," Vallini countered. "But why would you want to go back then? What's so special about Sunday?"

"Uh…" Betty sighed heavily. "Can we sit down for a moment. There is something I need to explain to you," she requested.

"Sure…" Vallini acquiesced by taking off his backpack, putting it down beside one of the chairs and taking a seat.

Betty sat down opposite him. "You see," she began, "One of the things that I presume you don't know about me is that I have a serious genetic disorder. Called Huntington's disease. Are you familiar with it?"

Vallini shook his head. "No, I can't say I've ever heard of it."

"Ah, well, that's actually good in a way. It probably means that this particular hereditary disease, at least, has been eliminated during the last two centuries." Vallini nodded his understanding. "The symptoms start manifesting about my age, and the decline is relentless. I watched my father suffer terribly. I had made my mind up that when the time came, I would end my life with an assisted suicide. My symptoms started recently, but then, just weeks ago, a clinical research trial began on a possible treatment. It's based on antisense RNA that theoretically could silence the aberrant gene. So I managed, with some difficulty and string-pulling, to get myself included in the clinical trial. And so far, after a couple of treatments, it does seem to be holding the symptoms at bay. But my third assessment and treatment were due on that Monday, and I desperately don't want to miss it, because then I might lose my place in the trial. It's literally a matter of life and death for me..." Betty wiped away a tear with the back of her hand.

Vallini sat silently, thinking through what Betty had explained. Yet again, this operation seemed to be pressing him in the direction of undesirable compromise. "You see, Betty, apart from the issue of two incidences of yourself, the danger of dropping you back on the Sunday or the Monday, is that if Gemma or Alex saw you, or suspected in any way that you had returned, then that would reduce or destroy their motivation for pursuing your rescue. The whole sequence of events could unravel—you might remain abducted and this world as we are experiencing it now, with me and TC in it, would not exist, replaced by a world overseen by the Sentinel organisation. Do you see how high the stakes are in risking something like that? For us and for you."

Betty nodded. Another tear appeared as the intense enjoyment of the last couple of days was suddenly and rudely replaced by the stark reality of her life's difficult circumstances.

Vallini was now factoring in what Ravel had recently told him about the pivotal importance of Betty's life. Could he trust that her medical issues would be solved in some other sufficiently timely way; or was it critical and imperative that he help her to be present at this appointment with all the attendant risk?

"Look," Betty suggested in a soft voice, "the appointment is at the John Radcliffe hospital in Oxford—that's sixty kilometres away from Cheltenham, so I could easily keep well out of the way until the Thursday—I'll just spend a few quiet nights there at a hotel in Oxford?"

Vallini sighed with relief. That sounded much safer. If she kept away from Cheltenham for the critical few days, then no harm could be done. "Well, OK," he conceded. "But there is one other practical difficulty. If I drop you within a hundred kilometres of Cheltenham, then Gemma would detect the translocation arrival on her equipment. That would be confusing and dangerous. So, I suggest I return you to the Sunday, but to somewhere well away from Cheltenham. Let's see, on the map... Oxford itself is not far enough away to avoid detection. But presumably you can use some transport system to get to Oxford? How about I translocate you to London?"

Betty's face lit up with relief. "Yes, That would be fine. I can get a train from London. But London is a busy place. I suppose we should aim for a park to translocate into without being seen. Maybe Hyde Park? In an area with trees?"

Vallini nodded, locating it on the map on his handheld device. "And we'd better make it after dark, so I'll aim for eight in the evening."

"Oh, not too late." Betty sounded concerned. "I'm thinking about train times," she added, by way of explanation.

"Ah, OK. Seven then?" Vallini suggested.

Betty nodded.

"Right." Vallini finished programming the place and time into his device. "Now, this is a long jump in terms of time, a couple of hundred years, so I'm going to take us back through the Way-Stations, the same as we did coming here, OK?"

"OK." The mention of the Way-Stations made Betty remember the fear she had felt on the journey out to this place and time. "So am I completely safe from Sentinel devices now, Vallini?" she asked.

"We flushed out and destroyed what we think were all the remaining Sentinels, and also destroyed their central knowledge facility. So, yes; you are as safe as we can possibly make you. Though to be honest, nothing in life is ever one hundred percent. But we are also maintaining alertness to any further Sentinel activity, however unlikely; and you can be sure we would urgently respond to any perceived threat to you. After all, it is in our own existential interest. So live your life without fear. Strive to achieve your ambitions..." He gestured to Betty to stand next to him. "Are you ready?"

Betty picked up the small bag containing her Rehab Station clothing and a couple of souvenirs. She had changed back into her own clothes— or actually the ones she had borrowed from Sveta and Gemma.

"Oh, I'm sorry Betty. You can't take those Station things back. You know why... But you have your memories—they're the most important

216

things to take home."

Betty looked beseechingly at him, but didn't push it when he shook his head. She had already extracted one big concession. She left the bag on his desk, went over to his side and put an arm around his waist.

"Good… Ready? Remember to flex your knees a little…"

There was the familiar puff of air. And they landed in what Betty now recognised as a Way-Station. She made as if to run a few paces forward.

"No, no. It's OK… We are not running from anything on this occasion. We can take our time." Vallini tapped on his controller and the Way-Station gave way to another, and then another. At least it was probably the same Way-Station, thought Betty, just that they were landing in different epochs and positions within it.

Then came the final jump to Hyde Park. Betty stumbled slightly, one foot landing on a stick on the uneven grass between the trees. She looked around and could see the Serpentine Lake some distance off to their left.

"Which direction do you want?" Vallini asked, pointing to their position on a map on his controller.

"OK. So, North West to Paddington train station," Betty deduced. She looked at Vallini, realising it would probably be the last time she would see him. "Thank you so much for all your help, Vallini."

"No. Not at all. I'm sorry you have had such a difficult time. But I think now you can relax. Enjoy your life." He put his arms around her and they hugged.

"Take care of Astrid." Betty turned and started walking away in the direction of the train station. When she looked back after a few seconds, he was gone.

*   *   *

Just before she reached the station, she found a tourist souvenir shop and went inside. She bought a large loose black hoodie, grimacing at the word 'London' printed on the back in large letters, but conceding that she would not find a plain one in a souvenir shop, and nor would other clothes shops be open at this hour of the evening. Glad that her credit card still worked after being exposed to the unknown effects of TC equipment, she exited the shop and pulled the hoodie on, covering the coat that Gemma had lent her. It gave extra warmth, but she mainly intended it as disguise, and to conceal her identity when pulling the hood around her head.

Inside the station, she headed for the ticket office. She hesitated, feeling a pang of guilt, before requesting a ticket to Cheltenham; not Oxford. She had not actually said anything untrue to Vallini, but she knew she had left him with the impression that she would go straight to Oxford and stay out of the way. Whereas, in reality, she needed to get back home first to pick up her medical documentation and samples before heading to Oxford.

"Sorry, love. The last train to Cheltenham has gone tonight." Damn, she thought, her plan was falling apart. She quickly considered the options. Rather than wait for the first train from London the next morning, she opted to train now to Bristol, the nearest city to Cheltenham, spend the night in a hotel near the station there, and then train the final few kilometres to Cheltenham first thing in the morning.

On the journey, she whiled away some time wondering what the consequences would have been if she had arrived back in Cheltenham that evening and had actually interfered with the course of events. Suppose she had got back to Cheltenham in time to pre-warn herself against the encounter with the Sentinel in the 'Red Lion'. Maybe the Sentinel would just have caught up with her on some subsequent occasion. But if it didn't, then that would mean two copies of Betty living in Cheltenham indefinitely?… She smiled at the strange prospect. But then if she had thereby avoided the abduction by the Sentinel, where had this second iteration of her come from? It was an enigmatic inconsistency. She wished she had asked Vallini about how it all worked, perhaps he would have known the answers. But, she would not have wanted to raise any anxiety in him about such mischief. Finally, she settled down to read a book she had bought at the station for the journey.

Monday morning, Cheltenham

Early the next morning her train was finally pulling into Cheltenham station. There was some nervousness rising in her as she pulled the hood around her face. There was no chance of running into herself, she knew, because her abduction lasted from the previous evening until late this evening. All she had to do was stay invisible to Gemma and Alex. Simple enough. Oh… And to Sveta and Joo-Won, if they were here yet—she wasn't sure. She realised Sveta's dress was showing below her hoodie, so she hitched the dress up a bit to conceal it, not wanting to exhibit anything that might be recognisable. She furtively looked round for a taxi to get her back home as quickly as possible. It was easy during the taxi ride to feel safely hidden, peering slyly out of the window at the streets, the traffic and the people. As they approached her house, however, the anxiety began to rise again. There was no reason why Gemma or Alex would venture near her house that morning—not that she could think of anyway. But she realised ruefully, that she had no idea of the details of their day. The taxi pulled up outside her home and she paid the driver, who seemed completely indifferent to her hooded identity. But then her heart missed a beat. Her car was not there. Scanning her memory back to the events of the weekend, it took her a few seconds to remember that she had left it outside the 'Red Lion', after coming back from the racecourse. So it wasn't going to be just a question of grabbing her things, getting in the car and disappearing; she was going to have to walk back to the 'Red Lion' to collect the Cabriolet... But was Gemma still in the hotel next door to the 'Red Lion'? She had no idea of Gemma's movements of that day. And Alex had mentioned something about them visiting the graveyard several times, which was on that same road. Betty now regretted this venture. She wished she had gone straight to Oxford. She probably could have managed without her medical documents; the health workers would have been disapproving but... Anyway, now she had no choice. The taxi had gone. And time was of the essence to get to the hospital in Oxford. Quickly she let herself in and rushed upstairs to find the medical documents, and the weekly tiny blood samples that she had conscientiously taken. She snatched a pair of sunglasses out of a drawer, for additional disguise, and grabbed her script for the 'Easter Play'. If she was going to lie low for a couple of days in an Oxford hotel room then she would at least use the time to learn her upcoming lines as 'Eleanora'. She quickly collected together some toiletries, remembering with a smile that she still had her 23rd Century toothbrush from the Rehab Station in her pocket. She had half-expected that Vallini would not let her bring back the bag of clothes, but had been determined to smuggle out some memento.

Then she started a brisk walk back to the 'Red Lion', wearing the new hoodie and sunglasses to maximum effect. On the way, she wondered if she also ought to be on the lookout to avoid Vallini. Along with TC, he had effectively ceased to exist from the moment she was abducted by the Sentinel, until the moment she was rescued. But she presumed that when his existence was re-established, he must have regained some continuity—some place where he had been to replace his absence. Would he have been in the 'Red Lion', or the hotel? Again she wished she had questioned him more closely about how these things worked.

Turning into Pumphrey's Road, she was relieved to see, in the distance, her midnight-blue Cabriolet, still sitting parked outside the hotel. She decided to just walk straight up to her car, get in it and go; assuming that her furtive glances around revealed no one she needed to avoid. The graveyard was deserted as she passed. Someone walked out of the hotel as she got close, but it was no one she recognised. She reached the car, threw her bits and pieces onto the passenger seat, started the engine, did a U-turn and headed across town to get to the main road for Oxford. Unfortunately, she had to pass fairly near the area where Alex lived and the lab was situated. But she kept her face hidden and concentrated on the driving. Finally, on the main road out of Cheltenham, she was able to relax.

*   *   *

Wednesday morning, Cheltenham

Two days later, her sojourn in Oxford duly completed, Betty arrived back at the lab, surprising Alex, who had been expecting to have to wait another anxious day for her to reappear.

"Well, am I glad to see you?" he greeted her. "Vallini had said it would probably be two days. Is he around as well?"

"No, it's just me," Betty replied as they hugged.

"And did you have an interesting time?"

"Oh, That's an understatement. I've so much to tell you Alex. It was amazing."

He smiled. "And I have actually had an awesome trip myself… But hey, I have one bit of bad news to tell you first, so that you can deal with it."

Betty tensed. "Oh no, what is it?"

"Well, your car has been stolen. You remember you left it outside the 'Red Lion' on Sunday evening before you had that unfortunate incident with Arbuckle and his Sentinel? Well, it was gone the next day. In fact, I think I saw it being driven the next morning, across the roundabout that leads to the A40, when I was walking up that road. I

220

couldn't see who was driving it though."

Betty's jaw dropped, a chill ran through her, and her heart skipped a beat. "Oh God, Alex... You saw it? That was so irresponsible of me."

Not understanding her shock, Alex sought to soothe her. "It's not that bad, Betty. It's just a car. Compared to your life being in danger..."

"No, no. You don't understand... Listen, after two or three days away, and after Vallini had done what he needed to do, I persuaded him to bring me back to last Sunday, so that I could attend my medical appointment in Oxford on the Monday. He was strongly against doing it at first because it would mean that I would be there in parallel with all that was happening here—the abduction and the rescue. But I persuaded him on the basis that it was very important, and that I would stay in Oxford, away from all the action; and therefore there was no risk. You see, he was concerned that if you or Gemma caught wind that I was back, then it would prejudice your motivation to rescue me, and the happy ending would all become unravelled. But I risked just sneaking back to Cheltenham to collect my medical documents and samples, to then drive up to Oxford. It was a stupid risk to take. I regret it now. God, that was so close..."

"What?... So you were around, post-rescue, all the time that we were still working to rescue you?... And that was you driving your own car?" Alex slowly wrapped his head around the parallel event-lines and the implications.

"But, if we ever meet Vallini again, you mustn't tell him what I did—he'd be furious," worried Betty.

"Nor Gemma," Alex informed her. "She was the one who noticed your car was missing."

"Right, well the official story is... that my car got towed away because it was in a no-parking zone, so I had to pay the fine and collect it? OK?" insisted Betty.

Alex nodded agreement. "Anyway, don't worry. It has all ended well... Shall we take an early lunch and have a long session telling each other our stories?"

"That's a good idea," agreed Betty, as Alex pulled on his coat. "So, Alex," she asked, as they strode out. "What do you know about Hadamard?"

"Well, he was a French mathematician who established innovations in matrix manipulation. I would have thought you know more about him than I do?"

"Yes, but I mean, if you had to name a piece of technology after him, what would it be? What would it involve?"

"Oh. Well, they have already named a circuit gate in quantum computing in his honour—the Hadamard Gate."

"What does that do?" queried Betty.

"It causes a qubit to enter a superposition of states. Why do you ask?"

"Oh, I'm just being unhealthily curious. Something I heard about in the future, but shouldn't have. Anyway, shall we get a takeaway and go and sit up on our hill?"

*　　　*　　　*

Earth-Standard StarDate 2243.219, TC HQ

Vallini was just completing his official report for the TC Seniors when he received a call from Command Dispatch.

"Vallini, we have detected some incongruous signals within your zone of responsibility. Thirty years to your future. The signals are not full-blown translocation traces, but probably indicate the preliminary development of equipment being tested, impinging on forbidden technology. We would like you to go and investigate. The coordinates and data are displayed on your screen now."

Vallini sighed, and looked at the data. "I apologise, but I would like to decline this mission, because I have urgent and important family matters to attend to. I would respectfully suggest that you send Silvana from here. She is now fully trained and eagerly anticipating a major mission."

There was a pause. "We acknowledge and accept your request and recommendation. Please pass the data to Silvana and ensure she is briefed with backup availability should she require it."

Vallini smiled. Not only would he get his personal time with Astrid, but Silvana would also get the thrill of her very own first mission. He remembered his own youthful enthusiasm, how it had given way somewhat to routine; though that routine had certainly been challenged by this latest mission, with the revelations around TC's non-pre-eminence and status. He needed time to digest it and think; as much as he needed family time. He called Silvana to come see him whilst he booked another ticket to Rehab Station-3.

*   *   *

Friday evening, Cheltenham

Betty was tossing a stir-fry in the wok when the doorbell chimed. She was not expecting anyone. She skittered down the stairs to the front door. The face in the video entry-screen was familiar, but different. She swung the door open.

"Gemma!"

"Betty!" They hugged.

"But you look so different, Gemma. Your hair is longer, and the purple is gone, and..."

Gemma laughed. "Yes. Remember I came to you from three years in my past. And so now I have had to wait three long years before I could come and visit you again. Because of course I knew what was going to happen, and I couldn't say anything to you for fear of changing the course of events. Strict instructions from Vallini. So I hope you don't mind me visiting now? I know you only saw me a few days ago from your point of view, but I've had to wait and wait, and I so wanted to see you again... I did check with Alex, as I had his phone number but not yours, and he said he thought your weekend was free..."

"Yes, of course. Come in," Betty reassured her. "Yes, Alex is right. I had a hectic time last night with the first full rehearsal for the play in which I have a main part. That was really hard work, so this weekend I am taking it easy. In fact, Alex and I were planning to do a little road trip down to Dorset where Arbuckle used to live. You see, apparently Arbuckle refused to let Joo-Won take him back to his own time unless Alex accompanied them." Gemma laughed, as Betty explained: "They spent a little time there and Alex has got rather attached to the idea of seeing the place again. I hope he won't be disappointed if it's all built up and modernised now. Would you like to come with us?"

"For sure. And I want to hear all about where Vallini took you to hide you away safely. Oh, and I've got a message for you from his cousin. It only came this morning—so that's my other excuse for bothering you so soon... But, a play rehearsal... I didn't know you were interested in theatre, Betty?"

"Yes. I love it. After this Strindberg play is over, I am hoping to

223

start work on writing my own play. I've compiled a set of viewpoints from discussions with my mother over the years—she's a psychoanalyst. And a video screenplay I saw whilst I was in Vallini's time, has helped to crystallise in my mind some further ideas on how I could frame and structure the contrasting perspectives. So I'm really keen to make a start soon. But it'll be a long job."

*   *   *

As it turned out, the village of Winterbourne Steepleton was still a rural idyll. Alex had delighted in wistfully pointing out the orchard, the gate, the lawn, the lane and the Rectory, now renamed the Old Rectory; and re-telling the story. Betty was touched—she had not seen Alex in such an enthusiastic nostalgia before, vowing that he would take much more interest in history going forward. And now they were wandering through the graves next to the famously-steepled church—which in this era served as architects' offices—looking for Arbuckle's memoriam.

"Naught but names etched on stone. Remembered, forgotten… unknown," chanted Betty softly, touching the headstones gently with her fingertips as she passed them. The yard was rather better tended than that back in Cheltenham, which had become so familiar to Alex and Gemma. It was Alex who finally stumbled upon the grave and excitedly called the others over. It was a fairly simple headstone, weathered, but the inscription still readable.

Here lies the Reverend Thomas Arbuckle (1803-1864), Rector of St. Ewold's. 'He hath awakened from the dream of life. And, departing, left behind footprints on the sands of time.'

They stood around the grave, silent for the moment…

"Well, I was expecting something a bit more pious," commented Alex, almost disappointed, since he had become fond of Arbuckle's charming religiosity. "But it's certainly obliquely pertinent—perhaps he wrote it himself?"

Betty shivered. "Are you alright?" asked Gemma, concerned.

Betty linked arms with them both. "Yes. It just made me realise that someone, like maybe Astrid, could visit *my* grave. Could be doing it right now; except of course that it's actually way in the future…"

Betty looked pensively toward the clouds over the hills in the distance. "It's as if all time is accessible in the moment. As if all the panoply of causally-linked events occur simultaneously as one chain…

And we now know there are other chains that could potentially replace this one. Maybe infinite chains of possible histories all exist simultaneously, with tiny ripples of change flipping the focus of actual *reality* from one chain to another... Or maybe they are *all* real... Maybe..."

ABOUT THE AUTHOR

Allan Brewer had a career in writing software before researching in computational biochemistry for a PhD. Some of his erstwhile colleagues may reflect he will be more suited to science *fiction* than science! He is now retired in Bristol, caring for his granddaughter and walking her dog.

If you have enjoyed reading this book please write a **review** on its Amazon page—even just a sentence will do—reviews are the lifeblood of an author.

If you would like to be notified of further novels by this author, or to contact the author, please email to **AllanBrewerBooks@gmail.com**

Or visit the author's website **AllanBrewer.Wordpress.com** for a blog on cherry-picked real science.

Other Books in the i-Vector Series

#1 <u>Schrödinger's Dog</u>   #2 <u>The Constanța Connection</u>

Printed in Great Britain
by Amazon

25862138R00129